THE SMOKIEST GRAVE

THE UNNATURAL SERIES

BY

TOSHA Y. MILLER

Dedication

--This book is dedicated to my beautiful younger sister, Erin. Even the darkest past can hold a bright future. I love you to infinity and beyond.

Prologue

D ay Zero

It was another typical summer day in 2018. The U.S. government hosted an international congregation of scientists in Washington D.C. to discuss a possible new weapon. In the process of the presentation, something went wrong, and the weapon activated.

BOOM!

A massive bomb explodes and sends everything in Washington D.C. up in flames, along with the Whitehouse. All that was left in its wake were dust and a giant crater.

With that dire mistake, everything society knew went up in smithereens.

As the rest of the government officials tried to rebuild after the devastation, they were caught unaware by the appearance of The Council of Supernatural Beings.

With vacuum of power in the government, a Supernatural named Sebastian, decided it was time for his kind to fill that void. As a result, a worldwide war broke out among the Humans and the Supernaturals.

It was a brutal, bloody war, with no end in sight. As the war progressed, the Humans nicknamed the Supernatural, the Unnaturals. In responds, the Unnaturals nicknamed the Humans, Naturals. Both names stuck which divided the world into two factions.

2086

The war is over, but the hostility between the factions is still very real. Due to the war, technology has not advanced and is in fact at a standstill. The left-over technologies are expensive. Modern gadgets such as light bulbs, microwaves, and televisions are luxuries reserved for the rich. However, stapled such as water, food, as well as magic amulets are available for all.

Technology is not the only thing that is segregated. Unnaturals remain separate from the Naturals. Although work has been done to bridge the hatred and create peace, one thing still hinders the work of peace; Dragonvires.

That one thing is the Dragonvires bloodline that still lives, which is a hybrid between dragons and vampires. Despite being a hybrid, their bloodline has been around for thousands of years; to protect the world from demons.

As a Dragonvire warrior, they have been given heightened abilities. With their dragon-beast side, they are stronger and can smell even the slightest scent. With their vampire-beast side, they are fast, have the ability to hear even the faintest sound, and their sense of touch is maximized.

The gods also gave their blood mystical abilities. The sweet crimson nectar can kill a demon with one drop, can help heal injuries, and can turn things into gold.

Alongside the beings called Sapphires, Dragonvires protected the gods in ancient times. It is said that Sapphire beings were exterminated in the Salem Witch Trials because they were so easy to hunt and kill. Their hair changed colors with their mood.

Even to this day, people don't know the degree of their massive powers. They only know that if a Sapphire is killed and its heart is cut out, it would turn into an amulet able to cast powerful spells. It is said, amulets only exist today because of their sacrifice.

A Sapphire hasn't been seen in a long time because of the Hunters. On the other hand, there were thousands of Dragonvires, and they lived in an angelic kingdom. Unfortunately, that kingdom was destroyed by the Unnaturals when they learned of the terminal effects of Dragonvires blood on the Unnaturals.

It was a shock when humans discovered Dragonvire blood didn't just kill demons; it also kills magical beings.

Back then, this made the Dragonvires the most in-demand thing out there. Whoever had information or could get hold of their blood was rewarded by the human government.

Today, they are still hunted by both factions for their blood. The society is convinced that once the Dragonvires are eliminated, peace will reign.

Individuals devote their lives to hunt Dragonvires. Those people are called 'the Hunters', and they have managed to win the fight so far.

However, the gods know better and plan to guide pure souls to help steer the world back to righteousness.

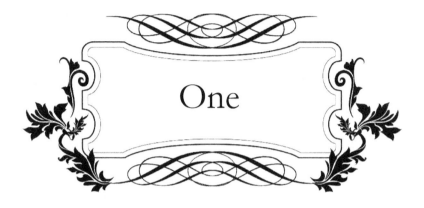

One

B*UM!! **BUM!! BUM!!!*** Cathleen "Cat" Spurlock
clenched her ears. The beat of the music hammered
deep inside her earlobes. Even her heartbeat played in
time to the fast music like a skilful musician. "Will they shut
up? I feel like my head is about to explode," Cat whispered.

Her plump lips were now numb from excessive biting.
She wanted to disregard the hair at attention on the back of her
neck, but that was impossible.

Why now, Goddess? Couldn't we talk later? This happened
every time the Goddess wanted to chat. It wouldn't be a big
deal if the conversations didn't make her go into a magical

coma. She was always tucked away somewhere safe when the coma started, not surrounded by unnatural hating people.

One moment she was on her date seated in an uncomfortable wooden booth, as she tapped her unpolished fingernails against her knees, irritated that the stupid bar couldn't get comfortable seats.

The next, her back was against the bumpy wall as she drifted down its rough surface. She didn't care how the little spiky mountains scratched her back in all the wrong places; she needed to hide in the shadows. If no one could see her, it'd be worth all the discomfort.

She scowled at the few people that glanced her way. *Nope, not hidden.*

She was sure she'd heard Bruce excuse himself to use the restroom, but it was better to find out than just assume.

Her squeaky voice called out to him, "Bruce?" She relaxed when he didn't respond. A deep sigh escaped her, maybe she had time.

It would be hard to explain her situation to a stranger, let alone a friend. *Yeah, it only looks and feels like I have one foot in the grave, but it'll all be over soon. Thanks for your concern.*

Her body wasn't unhinged yet, so she had time. She needed to get away and hide. The thin, fake tree next to her wouldn't help conceal anything.

She cleared her thoughts and concentrated on her surroundings. She was near the bar. Only five high gray tables with tons of black stools and low hanging lanterns were in her way. The brown booths along the wall would not be a problem.

At least she wasn't on the dance floor when the fever hit her. To get out of the bar was already going to be difficult enough and would arouse suspicions if she tried to manoeuvre around all the stools and tables to the exit with an unstable body. To move through sweaty bodies closely packed against each other would have been impossible.

Cat sucked in her breath. There was an employee-only exit sign close to their table when she sat down earlier. She turned to the right and used the fake tree to help herself up. The flimsy tree mocked her as the green trunk cracked and sent her back to the ground.

That was enough to make her chest heave and her pulse spike up.

"Hey, you okay?" A small, timid voice that was barely heard over the noise in her ears startled Cat.

Cat mumbled a response, but the woman did not seem to hear her and continued to move her lips, "What's wrong-" Cat cut her off, and gathered more of her face into her arms.

Her eyes never met the woman's as she spoke, "I'm fine, just had way too much to drink, and I'm a little embarrassed." She sighed to emphasize her embarrassment.

"Well, we've all been there. At least you are with Naturals, not some nasty Unnaturals. If you need help, just holler." Cat listened as the woman's footsteps receded. The sound made her shoulders relax. *That was close.* If they suspected magic on her, she'd be in trouble. *Dammit, why didn't I listen to mom?*

She sighed and leaned her sweaty head against the cold wall. Her hands trembled, and goosebumps rippled across her pale skin. Her vision was fuzzy around the edges. She hoped a good rub would clear them.

"Ugh, of course not." Her fist hit the ground as her vision darkened even more. It was too late to depend on her eyesight; her body was about to go into a trance.

If she tried to get up now, she'd have to feel her way around which would draw too much unwanted attention. Her eyes would shine brighter than mercury silver with magic.

She wanted to talk to her mom. Maybe luck would be on her side and her mom would have some transport amulets around. She searched her pockets. They were shaky and frantic. If she could call her mom, her mother would come down to help her. But unfortunately, after frantically searching through the nooks and crannies of her pockets, she found nothing.

She should have listened to her mother's caution, but her friend Rebecca had set up this blind date months ago after she learned that Bruce was interested in her. There was no way she could back out. As much as she hated blind dates, she wanted to get over her fear of dating and be normal for once.

Cat squared her shoulders. *All right, enough of the pity party, I need to get out of here.*

She took a few deep breaths as she got to her feet. To stabilize herself, her hand went on the rough wall. When her feet were steady on the floor, she took a deep breath and smiled. *Good.*

She took a few steps toward what she hoped was the exit but ended up staring up at the ceiling, flat on her back. Basically, her body decided that wasn't going to happen, that lying down was the better plan. *Body 1, Cat 0.*

She wasn't one to give up. There MUST be a way. She was not a fan of the upside-down turtle Cat.

Why me? Why this gift? Couldn't I teleport or fly instead? Now that would help me out of here. She lay there, sprawled out on the hardwood floor like a drunk.

Fresh adrenaline flowed into Cat's body as people hovered over her. She could tell it was two men by the smell of their musky scent mix with whiskey. She hated people hovering over her like she was a caged animal. Maybe if she ignored them they'd go away. *Fat chance, Cat.*

When they didn't, she opened her eyes. Everything was even fuzzier, but she could make out the two figures as they stared down at her. "Leave me alone," she rolled to her side and put her head in her hands.

One of the guys bent over, "Looks like the little lady is smashed."

Cat could feel the heat of his body get closer to her. Her eyes are letting her down now. His face is an indistinct mess. She pushed against the hard floor as she tried to keep a distance between them, but the ground wouldn't budge. "Get away, both of you," she snarled.

The other guy knelt and touched his partner's shoulder and they both laughed, "Let's have fun with her. She's drunk, no one will know. They'll think we want to help her get home."

Someone from far away shouted, "Hey, what are you two doing to my date?" A wave of wooziness hit her, when she moved in the direction of the singsong voice. It was Bruce.

In a fluid motion, the two men stood up. *Great, no normal person can move so smoothly. They are Unnaturals.* She held her breath and waited.

She could interfere, say one word and throw them off their feet. Or she could freeze them with another word. Yet, doing so would be a death sentence for her. She needed to stay hidden.

There had to be a few Hunters in here who wanted a new magical being to kill. Because of them, she had to hide what she really was to keep her family safe and to gain respect.

She worked as an investigator for the CIU; a company called Criminal Investigation for Unnaturals who choose a group of top ranked fighters to protect the Naturals, aka non-magic folk, from the Unnaturals who are supernatural beings like shapeshifters and witches. The ironic part was, the CIU started out with the aim to protect the Unnaturals from Hunters.

Now, her job was to bring in the Unnaturals the police couldn't take down. Anyone unlucky enough to get on their complaint radar will be brought in. Most of them were harmless.

Since high school, Cat had devoted her life to help those who are too weak to fight for themselves. She knew all too well the feeling of helplessness, what it did to people, and if she had it her way, no one, and that includes her would ever feel that way again.

If her clients saw her like this, she'd be out of a job. Cat needed to get home, to where she was safe with all her wards and weapons. If anyone tried to come in unannounced who meant her harm, they'd be fried from the inside out.

She was glad no one knew about her abilities. Charms, like killing defence charms, are a must-have for most homes and businesses and had been on sale at any local witch's brew since the war.

She must have passed out. Someone was lifting her up. She stiffened, "Don't worry babe, it's just Bruce."

She knew it was him by his aftershave and cheap soap smell. He struggled to hold her in his arms until he used his knee to get a better grip.

Cat tried to help him; she knew she was a little on the heavy side. Her efforts didn't do much, only turned her stomach. "Oh no," she pulled away from him, as she stared at the ground, and let go of her stomach contents.

Just for tonight, she wanted to be a normal girl on a normal date. She had ignored her instincts—and her mom's—and now she prayed for it.

Stupid gift. That seemed to be her favorite words these days.

***

Bruce was halfway to the exit, as he struggled to hold her in his arms when her power exploded. Gold, sparkly flecks shot in all directions and gray smoke emanated from her body.

Cat put her head back and opened her mouth to let the steamy heat out from her blazing hot body. Bruce's muscles quiver under the stress and nearly drops her. *For the love of the gods*... his mouth fell open. *She's an Unnatural.*

"Oh my God, is she-" a woman poked her nose into Cat's face. Bruce pulled her closer like a lover in need and shielded her from onlookers.

"No, she's smoking, it's the only thing that calms her after shots." Bruce said and kept his pace, as he shoved people aside to keep the curious eyes from gawking at Cat. He wasn't a fan of Unnaturals, but he was not about to leave her in a lion's den, either.

***

The smoke snaked from her body, signalling to the Goddess that Cat was ready. When the Goddess had something to say, she couldn't force Cat to see or speak to her, but she would make it damn near impossible to ignore her call.

Cat could only imagine what the smoke smelt like for Bruce. That acid smell of her vomit breath would assault any nose with a vengeance, regardless of whom or what they were.

Her long russet colored hair floated at the tips. Now Bruce knew for sure and without a doubt Cat was an Unnatural.

She didn't want that. If he knew, he could want to kill her, and in a few minutes, there was nothing she could do about it.

Who could blame the Naturals for hating Unnaturals? The war had been long and brutal. The battles had left the ground a sticky crimson that consists of Naturals' blood.

The story she heard was that the Unnaturals would have won the war easily because of their superior strength and power if the world did not find out what Dragonvire's blood could do to magical beings.

Dragonvire's blood was used for centuries to heal wounds and to turn things into gold. It was never known that the blood can also be used as a weapon to kill Unnaturals.

Only one drop of their blood could kill even the most robust Unnatural, so both sides wanted the weapon. The Naturals to use it, the Unnaturals to prevent the Naturals to use it.

Of course, when the Naturals got hold of that blood, the odds during the war tilted in their favor. The rest of the war intensified around the world with this discovery.

Dragonvires were strong, but they were no match for the world. And the world wanted them for their blood, no matter the cost.

When every bullet, spear, and sword was decorated with the poison of the Dragonvire's blood, the Unnaturals lost the war. The Naturals victory wasn't enough to wipe everyone of them out. Just enough to make a truce between the factions. Now, they must live together, and hope the difference between them can be settled someday.

Cat woke up when the frigid air slapped her in the face. Her green eyes fluttered, and the power flashed in her eyes. Those green depths were shone like bright sapphire.

The last time she was alone with a man, a vision changed her life. So much that even to this day, that horrific event dictated her life.

Now it was happening again. Here she was, helplessly waiting for the Goddess to speak to her. As she laid in this man's arms, paralyzed, as a tear escaped her. There was no way she would go through that again. *By the Gods, this better not be how I die...*

The Goddess needed to upgrade and get a cell phone.

Two

CAT HAD AN unnerving feeling crawl up her spine as if spiders were gathered all over her skin. To top it all off, she couldn't move her arms and legs anymore, so she couldn't brush herself off.

Lub-dub, lub-dub filled her ears, and she could taste copper in her dry mouth.

Her heartbeat was so fast and loud it couldn't be hers, could it? It sounded like it was close to explosion. She heard muffled male voices, but with the sound in her ears, she could not hear what was being said.

The vision was taking over, numbing and paralyzing her. The voices spat at each other. The vibrations of sound from the other masculine voice poured over her body like warm water. It gave her goosebumps.

Cat sniffed the chilly air. *What if they were the two guys from the bar, and had come back?* She inwardly cursed when her nose got nothing. The Goddess' pull blocked all her senses. She stuck out her tongue and tried to taste the air instead.

She tasted Bruce, but the tangy sensation on her tongue seemed different somehow. She knew from the scent that it was him because his aftershave was lingering in the air. Although, now it tasted like aftershave and rotten fruit mixed. She got no information on the other guy, only a slight char taste like the top of a matchstick.

The other male spoke again. She still couldn't make out his words, but whatever he said, he made Bruce's voice squeaky.

Bruce was pressed against Cat's body, as he kept her upright, up until something made him step back. Awkwardly, Cat's legs buckled under her weight, and she went straight to the floor as soon as he stepped away.

Ouch, her knees took the full impact of her weight when she flopped to the ground. *Crack*, her head hit the hard cement next, making beautiful black roses bloom in her mind's eye. The petals opened, and an intense pain shot through the side of her head.

The slam against the hard ground made her body hurt twice as much. The pain was enough to pull her away from the vision's depth, but as soon as the roses faded, the magic viciously snapped back into place.

A cold sweat chilled her overheated body. She could only guess what was going on around her. Their movements sounded like a fight. Swords clashed and the stomping of two people was like music to her ears. At least, they were old school and not throwing amulets around.

An amulet that activated as she lay on the ground paralyzed was not what she needed. As much as she tried to focus on the battle noises, the pull of the magic was too troublesome to ignore. Too distracting. The impudent magic was like a fly buzzing up her nose and ears. That kind of annoyance was difficult to ignore.

The irritating spider feeling died away slowly, so did the danger too. She tried to relax as much as she could, but it was hard. She knew by experience that eerie feeling meant evil was close.

In third grade, her teacher had the bright idea to take her and her class to a prison for a field trip. Cat remembered his old, weak voice saying, "If you don't listen and behave, you could end up here." Most of her classmates were terrified, so the teacher's scare tactic worked. Unfortunately for him, all the horrible and murderous vibes at the prison were like poison ivy to Cat, and she ended up in the hospital. He lost his job, and her mother was furious.

She remembered her mom's small hands wrapped around her teacher's thick neck. The memory made her laugh. She never again mistook the feeling of little legs that crawled inside her skin when she got near an evil person.

The few times she touched Bruce, all she could sense was his dishonest nature. There was no evil there. Something about him had changed.

The Goddess's form shimmered into focus, but her curvy body changed at the last moment. She heard male groans right before the vision took over. *Dammit.*

A handsome male face inserted itself into her path. She didn't know who he was. But even so, she recognized his chiselled features and blue eyes. He was like a Viking God, except for his blue eyes, those were like an angel, beautiful, and kind.

As the rest of him appeared, she forgot how to breathe. The man was striking. His silky black hair, sharp nose, and full lips were mesmerizing. He made every hot guy she had ever seen look like an ogre.

"The future of my people depends on you. I need your help." His long black hair danced around his broad shoulders as the wind blew.

The wind, with a mind of its own, moved at a higher speed until a thick gust of air pushed him over. There were people behind him.

Cat laughed at the sizeable blue-eyed man being thrown to the floor. Whoever said the Goddess didn't have a sense of humour had never met her.

Four people stood completely immobile in a cave, heads tilted, and stared at nothing. They looked like mannequins. In unison, they snapped their heads in Cat's direction and said, "We will perish without you. Please choose us, Cathleen." One of them stepped forward; a guy, who looked like a younger version of the sexy man.

"My life is in peril. My brother will not be able to save me, but with your assistance, he might have a chance. Please!" Cat's heart broke at the look in his blue eyes. They were terrified and pleaded for her help.

Damn Goddess, couldn't you have just talked to me? You are killing me with the reenactments. Cat knew this wasn't them talking. This was her way to reveal their faces and make her feel obligated to help them.

He opened his mouth to say something else, but it was hard to focus on him with two of his friends flinging their bodies at each other. Their long arms tried to choke one another while he spoke. As soon as he finished, their bodies faded into a cloud of smoke.

The woman of the hour appeared wearing a white gown. The gown was long, the hem reached her small feet. The dress was a perfect contrast to her long, midnight-black hair that gently floated off her shoulders. Her yellow cat eyes and light brown skin were a perfect contrast. She was, by far, the most beautiful woman Cat had ever seen. She brushed away smoke, the only thing that remained of the people that had been speaking to Cat.

Those beautiful eyes, familiar to Cat since childhood, had even been in her dreams. The Goddess was finally showing herself, "Hello my lovely Cat. It is time to choose. When you wake up, two things can happen. One, you run away and go back to your normal life, be successful and have many children." Her sweet voice paused for a second and she tilted her head to the side. Cat love to watch her hands gracefully glide around as she spoke. It reminded her that there was still grace and beauty in the world.

"Or?" Cat rolled her eyes as she stepped toward the Goddess. She felt like a little mouse next to her.

The Goddess's eyebrows went up in surprise. Cat was always compliant. She never gave her sass. "You can pursue the man who saved you tonight." Her hand drifted toward the smoke and indicated that she meant the blue-eyed man.

"That is why I had to speak to you right away." Her eyes filled with sorrow. She never said it, but that was her way to epress her remorse. "Oh, my sweet Cathleen, it appears that the wretched monster that ruined your life has struck again."

Cat's heart dropped at the Goddess's words. *What the hell does that mean?* "I would like him to try it again. He wouldn't be the one-" The Goddess's put up her hand to stop Cat.

"I don't have much time. You'll see what I mean when you wake up. I need you to listen if you choose the second choice. This way will lead to many battles and tough times, but if you choose this path, you will save many lives. But know this, nothing in the second choice is set in stone. Lives could be lost, even yours."

"The choice is yours, my lovely child, I cannot force you to do this," the Goddess said. "It's too ugly for that. I'll be here if you need me, just look at the smoke." She put her hands together and said, "Bless it be."

"Wait," Cat shouted, as she made for the disappearing smoke. "You can't just throw a bomb on me like that and then leave!" She threw her hands up. "I have so many questions. You can't leave me here, dammit. Does this communication thing go both ways?"

There was nothing left. Her heart ached at the empty shadow. "Fine." Cat dropped her arm and let them swing at her sides.

Cat's hands twitched to the beat of her heart. Her body was awake from its coma state. Cat inhaled a few deep breaths and expanded her lungs to the max.

There was nothing she could do to stop the black smoke from taking her back to reality. It didn't matter that she wasn't ready to decide. It didn't matter that she didn't want to give up her normal life.

She bit the inside of her cheek and wanted to be selfish. All she had to do was say no. Her way would be easier, and she could still help people. *But you could never live with yourself if you let the people the Goddess showed you die.* A deep voice inside her demanded.

She stomped her foot and hated it because she knew that she was going to accept the Goddess's offer. Cat shrugged, defeated, the Goddess did say she would save lives if she helped the man.

And if she was honest with herself, according to the Goddess, she owed a debt to the beautiful-eyed Viking man. She wasn't sure what for, yet, but the Goddess never lied. She claimed he saved her life, so now she needed to find out how.

Cat put her hands on her hips, *okay dammit, I'll do it. But you owe me. Maybe let me win the technology lottery and we will call it even.*

Before she could smile, a sharp pain twisted her upper arm skin, "Ow," Cat jerked her arm back and wrapped her hand around the sore area. "Did you just pinch me?" She looked at her hand to make sure she wasn't bleeding. She wasn't. "Well, that was rude."

Cat made up her mind even though she wasn't pleased with it. Good thing, because she fell through the rabbit hole into the darkness. Its cloudy texture kept pushing her down until Cat crashed back into her body.

Three

BRUCE EXITED THE bathroom and saw Cat lying on the floor. He couldn't see well in the dim candlelight. *Maybe I should have taken her to a fancy restaurant.* Only the expensive places had extravagances like light bulbs.

He walked closer and noticed Cat in an awkward position, like a bird on its back. She maneuvered around, trying to get up, but failed. His eyes grew wide when he saw two men walking to her. Both were in army jackets and dark boots. They stood there and hovered over her. When they got closer to her, he put his feet in gear. His footsteps were fast and loud.

Bruce was not well acquainted with Cat and her friends, but it was clear she did not want those men to bother her. The gentleman inside him screamed for justice.

With minimal effort, he shooed the men off.

He scooped Cat into his arms like a brave knight who was there to rescue his damsel in distress. Hope built up inside of him that he'd be the hero of the night and finally get the girl.

Well, that dream did not come to pass and went crashing to Hades when reality set in. Bruce looked far from being a knight in radiant armor. He looked more like a clumsy sidekick in training. He had a tough time as he tried to lift her, and when he did, he had to use his knee to support her. The woman was not light. He loved the extra curves on her body, but his muscles shook with the stress of trying to carry her.

What the hell is going on? Why was she on the floor? Did she take tons of shots when I was in the bathroom, or what?

His heart sped up at the look in her green eyes as if her eyesight was gone. Her eyes looked around but did not see anything. He didn't want anyone else to see her like this, so he pulled her to his body. Or at least he tried. Cat pulled away and threw up all over the floor and on his new shoes. *No, not my shoes.* Cat curled in his arms and the thought of his ruined shoes was gone.

He was surprised when the grief for his shoes left so quickly. Something about her made him forget everything else. In fact, everything else in his life was a fuzzy mess.

As he sped through the bar, hitting her head on the tables by accident, he walked by a few random people who asked if they could help. Bruce would have loved some help, but he denied them. He didn't know what was wrong with Cat and why she was like that, but it didn't look like something natural was going on.

If luck were on his side, some fresh air would help.

Halfway through the bar, all hope of that being the issue shattered. Her eyes shined with an Unnatural light and yellow sparks flew out from her in all directions.

He slumped over and pulled Cat closer to cover her weirdness from everyone in the bar. This time, his attempts to shield her worked and no one asked any more questions.

They would want her dead the moment she was found out, unconscious or not. The Men's Bar is strictly Naturals only bar. The pitchforks would come out like in the Salem witch trials.

The cold night air bit at his wet lips. *Where is her jacket, and where the hell is mine?*

"It is way too cold out here for this, Cat." He looked down at the soft mix of her gold and pale complexion and changed his mind. *Okay, for you I'll freeze my balls off.* There was no one around, just the creepy darkness tucked into every corner.

He leaned Cat against the wall to free one of his hands while he grabbed a lighter out of his pocket. There had to be a light trail alongside the building. Places without electricity kept a line of triggered candles on a shelf.

He managed to hold her and flick the flame at the candle. Once one was lit, they all flickered to life. He wasn't a fan of Unnaturals, but he loved their magic.

Now he could see, and the shadows didn't bother him as much, but he was aware of the air's icy bite on his exposed arms. He wanted to go back to the bar if only to get his jacket, but Cat couldn't stand up by herself. She looked like a wet noodle in his arms.

She would get frostbite on the ground if he put her down.

It wasn't snowing yet, but a white, crystal ice coated the ground. Bruce groaned, he left his phone on the table.

"Do you have a phone, doll?" Bruce leaned her against the wall and made her stand with difficulty. After some seconds of doubt, he looked through the pockets of her jeans for a phone, his hands shook from the cold weather. Nothing there, only one other place it would be, her bra.

Women put them in there, don't they? His great-grandfather told him stories about ladies doing that before the war. Of course, the phones were bigger and more advanced than, but women could still do it. *Right?*

His hands fumbled with her lumps. They were so soft and squishy.

Guilt welled up inside of him as he searched. They fit perfectly under his fingers. *Calm down; this is wrong. It'd be a lot more enjoyable if she craved for my touch.* He let go, but that didn't stop the thoughts and images that developed in his head of all the things he could do with those fun bags.

As his eyes lingered on her soft mounds, a dark green cloud of smoke drifted from Cat's body. The smoke was thick and wildly intelligent. Before he could even blink, the cloud reached out to him.

"What the hell?" He flinched at the force of the fog against his skin.

He was so shocked that his body was scared stiff. No, no, no, the green cloud sank into his sweaty skin. Its thick green depth slithered itself into his pores like worms eating their way through dirt.

The smell of rotten flesh in the depths of the cloud stole Bruce's breath and made him want to move away.

It was too late. He tried to pull away, as he wanted to breathe.

His flight or fight took over and made his muscles flex. The green smoke cemented itself to Bruce's limbs sinking into his ears, mouth, nose, and eyes.

It was devouring him inside out.

"Noooo!" He could feel teeth consuming his soul. The intense pain was too much for him to stand. He pushed away from the pain and wandered deeper inside himself. The feeling felt so far away now.

Maybe too far for him to come back.

An evil roar ripped from his mouth. Bruce tried to fight it, but the all-consuming darkness that was making his soul disappear was too powerful. The sinister shadow played dirty and attacked all his organs until Bruce was only a memory in his own flesh.

"Ha! It feels good to be back," he inspected his hands, "I thought you would never get laid again. You insignificant little prude." It was Bruce's body, but Bruce was gone. In his body stood a demon. He stopped to check Cat out. He loved plump women.

"Oh, I'm going to have fun with you, prude." He pressed his stolen body tighter against her. She wasn't asleep, but her eyes were closed. He lifted his finger to poke one of her eyes but his reflection on a self-help poster on the wall stopped him.

The long, white poster paper had one of those fake mirrors in the middle. Next to it in black ink read:

Do you feel like an Unnatural now? Well, there's a cure for that.

He leaned in closer to his reflection, as he laughed. "You've looked better." He was too large for this human body, so the skin was stretched and anomalous. He wouldn't be able to use this disguise for long.

The worst thing was that his eye sockets were long and pulled tight as if he wore a costume. And that was the case.

He moved her chin around and noticed that she was awake, but her body was asleep. "The curse your ex-lover put on you should have made you completely unconscious." He shrugged. "Oh well, I'll work with it. The important part is…" He moved his body around, showing off, and wiggled his fingers, "I got your new boy toy's body. You don't know my name, so you can't send me back." He wiggled his hips against hers, but there was no reaction.

The invasion curse, he was trapped in was like being in a box inside of this woman. If he hadn't used binding black magic to do the curse, he would have vacated her body sooner. So, he wasn't sure if this happened to her a lot…

Maybe that's why it took her so long to have someone touch her sexually? Could she be in a coma?

He leaned in to whisper, "I'll give you a hint, Lusion." Lusion flung his head back and laughed. The sound was a sadistic shout of victory.

Lusion bent to sniff her neck, as he enjoyed her honey scent. His hands drifted over her body and grabbed a breast. "For the love of Hades, you will be fun."

He lifted her eyelids and saw the powerful shine of teal. They were so bright that he could barely make out the rest of her luscious face. He touched the tip of her hair and ran his fingers through her loose locks. *Whoa, it looks like I got a live one.*

The demon unzipped his pants. He lifted her shirt and reached for the buttons of her jeans, loving her soft skin. He was going to enjoy cutting her milky flesh. Distracted by her body, he didn't hear someone walk into the alley.

"I'm not sure she's as excited as you are lad." A man stood at the opening of the alley looking at his hand like it was a prized possession.

"Mind your own business, mate. She is my cursed object, now bug off." Lusion didn't turn to him, but his shoulders straightened.

"Sorry... mate, I don't think I can do that. You see, I'm not a fan of rape, and it's in my blood to stop such occurrences." The man leaned against the alley wall like it was his regular hangout, as he grinned at the demon.

"Well then, why don't I suck all the blood out of you. Then, you wouldn't feel so obligated," Lusion stepped away from Cat's body and turned to him. Cat tumbled to the ground.

A wave of excitement danced up Lusion's spine like an expert masseuse's touch at the sound of Cat's head cracking against the ground as it hit. He looked the man up and down.

He's big; might be fun to take down. What captivated him the most about the man was his icy blue eyes. Hatred swam in those shiny depths.

He tried to stretch to his full height, but the human body wouldn't let him. Lusion grunted and put all his attention on the man. He needed to kill him; he'd deal with reaching his full height later.

First, kill the man. Entertain myself with the girl who kept me trapped for so long in that curse later. Then work on this wretched body.

"Valgostine!" Lusion put out his hand, and the butt of his weapon appeared in a cloud of green smoke. The long, curved sword shone in the moonlight. He loved to hear that breathtaking snap of his birth weapon when it arrived.

The beautiful silver sword was part of him. No matter where he went, he could call the attractive thing to himself. If only he could use his magic to kill the intruder, but most of his actual magic wouldn't come back for a few hours.

Lusion grinned and traced his finger along the sharp edges. Chills crept over his body, one swipe of his blade and that man's soul would be his.

He wished a long, painful process was possible, but he needed to hurry. The sexy matter on the ground needed his attention. If she died too quick, he wouldn't have any fun.

Lusion stepped forward to attack his opponent. He hesitated when he saw the long sword the man pulled from a sheath on his back. *Who is this guy? Unnatural, or Hunter?* Lusion couldn't sense magic in his aura.

"Tricky, Tricky." Lusion brazenly rubbed his fingers along his chin. "I think I'm starting to like you, mate. Are you sure you are not half demon?" He wiggled his eyebrows, loving how the man recoiled at his words.

"I'm sure." He stepped away from the wall, as he glared at Lusion.

The man grabbed the bottom of his blade and slashed his exposed palm. The thick liquid drizzled out as if with a mind of its own. Hendrick raked the thick blood over his sword. Lusion didn't see blood drip, so he assumed it was already healed. *Unnatural, it is then. No matter, he'll still die by my sword.*

"What the bloody hell? You are a weird one, mate. If you wanted to be hurt, you should have just asked." Lusion lifted his sword, and let it swing around his body to show off his sword training before he charged forward.

Four

HEDRICK FEET WERE swift and soundless. He **needed to hurry**. His next task was urgent. *I need to move bloody quicker.*

Rrroooaarr! Hendrick almost smacked into a pole as he stopped. His body tensed, and his teeth elongated.

Only one thing could make that kind of scream; *a male demon in our dimension?* He wrinkled his nose in disgust. Demons were vile creatures with no compassion whatsoever.

Something deep inside called him. The thickness weighed down his heart, as it dared him to do his job and kill the demon. He still had the mentality of a protector, but now, he used those skills as a Bounty Hunter, or assassin if the bloke deserved it.

Even though he wasn't living with the gods and the rest of his kind, the ancestral blood flowed through his body. That blood called to him.

The fact that he was once a king, taking care of the weak was his duty. No doubt in his mind that the demon had an innocent with him. That's kind of how they roll.

After the war, he ruled in secret over the few people that were left in his kingdom. All the others were killed in an attack by Unnaturals. His soul clenched at bitter memories. These days, he was a nobody, hunted by everybody for his blood power.

With a groan, he turned his massive body in the direction of the demon's scream. He absently knocked the dirt from his last chase off his black shirt and leather pants.

Leather is the best thing to wear with a life like his. It was durable and moved well in a fight. He would go crazy if he had to wear jeans.

The smell of rotten demon stink hung heavy in the air. The foul sour smell drifted into his lungs and made him choke.

Bloody hell, it's a ripe one. A punch of adrenaline slammed through him. *It's been too long. I forgot how inspired I feel when I anticipate a demon fight.*

He stopped short of the alley entrance and got a whiff of heaven. *Whoa, what is that?* He could tell the smell was from a woman. The beautiful honey aroma was not like anything he had ever smelt before, although it was vaguely familiar.

He strode to the alley. Saving the woman was the right thing to do, and it seemed like fun. Hendrick looked down into

the dark length with only a few lit candles to keep the alley
from looking pitch black. This was the type of alley that no one
walks down because they worry monsters lurk in the shadows.

In the middle, two people stood pressed against the
wall closest to a door that he assumed was some restaurant.

The man had the woman pushed up against the wall in
a way that, if someone wasn't focused on them, they would see
two lovers enjoying themselves. With squinty eyes, Hendrick
looked closer and noticed the man was stood over an
unconscious woman.

The man had her in a position that looked like she was
standing up on her own. One foot on the floor the other lifted
to his waist, and her head leaned against the wall.

A smirk crept across Hendrick's face; he was ready for a
demon attack. "I'm not sure she's as excited as you are lad," he
said antagonizing the demon to get his attention. *I wonder how
long this conversation is going to last before he attacks me. The wanker.*

He watched the demon lift his sword. His ugly green
face was a little too big for the human's face. Hendrick could
see the demonic being under the human's skin which was
cracked and stretched. Not an attractive look.

With some of his own blood on the sword, Hendrick
knew the demon didn't have a chance. He still needed to be
careful, though. One swipe of the demon's sword and he'd be
trapped there for all eternity.

With a loud crash, their blades collided, making massive
sparks fall to the ground. Lusion clenched his teeth together
and swung again, lower. Hendrick blocked the sword and went

for a jab to his arm. Although he missed, the demon stepped back and moved his sword to the right which gave Hendrick an open opportunity.

When a person fights as much as Hendrick does, the movement becomes like a rehearsed dance. He knew what the demon's body would do by watching his body language.

Hendrick jumped to the side as Lusion attacked, slashing his sword at the demon's exposed chest. He essentially killed the demon with that one blow. All he had to do was wait for his blood to take effect.

***

"Dirty scoundrel," Lusion tried to block Hendrick's next blow, but the sharp edge of the silver raked at the exposed area on his chest again. He cried out in pain and rumbled on the ground.

His hand clung to his chest as he let his sword drop to the ground, "Why in Hades does this burn so much?"

The edges of his vision darkened and shrunk inward.

The demon had heard stories of the ancient Dragonvires and had even killed a few—but that was a long time ago. So, he knew the effects of a Dragonvire's poison. *But how? The bloody things have been dead for years.* Or so he thought. He thought the blood on the sword thing was weird, but Dragonvire's shouldn't exist anymore.

In a fit of rage, Lusion attacked. He let his claws shoot out of the human skin. His arms swung furiously at Hendrick. Those razor-sharp nails blurred from the speed that tore into

Hendrick. They were too fast to stop them all. A few more minutes of this and Hendrick would be a goner, as well.

***

Hendrick looked at the cuts on the demon's skin, and at his wide, bugged out eyes. He had never met a demon strong enough to resist his blood poison for this long. *Time to bring my beast into this.*

Hendrick called on his strength. The power he pulled forward wasn't enough to draw his dragon beast out, but it was enough to make the demon's movements slower.

Hendrick and the demon fought, each tried to get the upper hand as they slashed and punched each other. Thankfully, Lusion didn't have his sword in his hand. So, Hendrick didn't have to worry about getting trapped in the sword.

Hendrick only had to hold him off until the poison drifted into his nervous system. Without a fight or flight instinct, people don't fight as well.

And then he noticed a change in him. Lusion got sloppy, and he left gaps in his defenses. Hendrick took advantage of this and gained the upper hand until he had enough time to transform completely. His square teeth extended into long points and his body morphed into a more prominent, stronger being. Hendrick's bronzed skin turned glossy as his body transformed into his gray dragon form. He needed to make this quick, so no one saw him.

It has been a long time since he'd transformed into his dragon beast. The last time he did, a Hunter found him and his family. Hunters were Naturals that use heat tracker amulets to find Dragonvires, which worked well when they shifted into their dragons.

Lusion gained his composure and struck out with his knee. The blow hit Hendrick between the legs making him howl in pain. He almost tumbled to the ground, as his breath quickened, but stopped himself. Once the black spots stopped dancing around, he could fight again. An evil growl vibrated through Hendrick's throat.

***

As Hendrick reacted to his assault, Lusion slid for his sword. It glided effortlessly along the cement because the blood and wintry weather made everything slippery. Hope flared to life in his black heart; he was only inches away from his weapon.

"No, you don't." Dirt and garbage went up in the air as Hendrick flapped his large dragon wings and pushed off the ground. His scales stood on end like a cat ready to attack. With ease, his dragon body slammed into Lusion and stopped him from grabbing his sword. In defense, Lusion lifted his hand to block Hendrick's teeth from ripping into his flesh, which wasn't useful. Hendrick ripped off his arm and threw it aside like garbage.

"Aaa!" Lusion clenched his teeth at the blast of hot pain. He was too weak and slow to try to call on his powers. All he could do was scurry away.

***

A loud plea echoed in the shadows of the alley. Lusion laid there, winded, and tried to stop the bleeding by wrapping his shirt around the stump.

Hendrick watched how pathetic his last minutes were and let him wallow in his misery for a bit. Hades knows, he had done the same to others. Hendrick changed back into his human form, as his bones cracked and snapped back into place. The pain was like hot fire on his skin.

He rolled his shoulders as his soft human skin stretched along his form. With bitter hatred in his bright orange eyes, he grabbed his sword and drove the point into Lusion's heart.

The demon went utterly still.

If Lusion moved, Hendrick's sword would damage his heart, making him weaker. Both stared at each other knowing what was going to happen next. In a blur, Hendrick twisted the blade.

Doing so wouldn't kill a demon, but the injury brings them excruciating pain and weakens them, so when he swung his sword with all his might at the demon's neck, it was a mercy kill. Hendrick hated demons, and he wasn't one of them.

With a nasty crunch, he hit his target. The sound of the blade slashing through flesh and breaking a bone was like biting into an ice cube. All he needed was one good crunch with teeth and the ice breaks. The sound was something Hendrick could never get used to.

He took a deep breath as he watched the bloodied head roll away as it made wallow sounds. If he didn't have

Dragonvire blood on his side, he probably would not have won the fight.

How the hell did this woman get caught up with a demon like that?

He stepped closer to the woman that laid on the ground. His heartbeat increased when he saw the blood streaming from her head. *She's hurt. She must have hit her head when she fell.*

She was lucky. The cold ground had slowed the blood seeping from the wound, but she wouldn't last much longer.

Hendrick's head went around in a circle as he commanded his vampire beast to show itself. An ice-cold wave lassoed his humanity and pulled it to his core until the vampire was settled in his skin.

His mouth tingled, and a slight growing pain lengthened his teeth. Now that he could pierce his thick skin, he bit his wrist. The popping sound caused a shiver to go down his spine. It had been a long time since he had fed with his fangs. *Calm yourself.*

Thanks to his dragon blood, he didn't need to feed like a regular vampire. To feed with his fangs wasn't necessary, but he still craved biting and feeding on beautiful women as he once had. Human blood made him more powerful.

Hendrick pushed her onto her back, a little bit of his blood would do the trick. He would have to be careful no one saw him doing this. By Dragonvire law, he was not supposed to heal a stranger, unless they give their consent. But he couldn't just let her die.

Hendrick put his wrist to her mouth, "Heal," he commanded his blood power. The best part about Dragonvire blood is that the Dragonvire has control over what their blood does unless they get murdered. Then, their blood is tainted with hate, and it releases the poison into their bloodstream. Otherwise, the blood wouldn't be harmful.

Her eyes still shone like bright sapphire and smoke snaked out of her mouth as he forced the Crimson into it. The woman's dark, blood-streaked hair hovered over the ground. Despite all that, Hendrick still thought she was gorgeous. Her thick body and pouty lips were attractive.

Hendrick was surprised when the woman's power soaked into his skin, as well, and made his slashes knit back together. Her energy was like electricity that danced along his skin. He looked at his chest with his mouth opened wide.

Wow.

"Oh, I like you. I thought my kind were the only ones that could do that." He lifted his wrist from her mouth and stood up. The last thing he needed was this woman to wake up with a man standing over her and a dead body next to her. With power like that, who knew what she can do.

To his right, he saw the edge of a wallet that stuck out of her pocket and grabbed it. As he touched her, she stirred and stretched her legs. Her power decreased, and the smoke retreated into her mouth.

Hendrick hid in the shadows of the alley. This wouldn't be his first person he thought needed help but instead, they wanted to use him, or trap him. Last time he'd lost his best friend.

He thought he could trust a woman that needed his help, but she was the mastermind. She had a binding curse, and Mike paid the price for his stupidity. She drained him dry, and if his other friend wasn't close by, he would have died as well.

When he saw this woman's reaction to the dead body, he would know her intentions. He couldn't afford for this to be another trap.

If that's the case, she will meet the same fate.

Five

C AT'S FINGERS SLID into a warm thick liquid that was heavy on her skin. A gut reaction made her jerk her hand away and when she looked down at her trembling hand, saw the crimson layers on her fingers. Blood. "What the…" her voice squeaked. She scooted away from the puddle and looked around.

If she hadn't been an investigator that had to look at blood and dead bodies all the time, she'd probably have freaked out. Thankfully, this wasn't her first rodeo.

She looked around to decipher where the blood had come from because the battle she had seen hadn't happened this close to her.

Oh, that's right. The image of her falling followed by the pain splitting her head, and the man healing her replayed in her mind.

It's my blood. She looked around, as she noticed the splashes of blood everywhere. *Well, this puddle is mine.*

She didn't know whether she should relax or be worried. Cat gulped and stared at the ground. Now, the puddle didn't seem as much in comparison.

The blood was from Bruce. As her mind slowly relayed the events that happened while she was in her vision, she saw Bruce. His disheveled headless body sprawled on the ground, the slashes in his chest steaming.

Cat tilted her head and wrinkled her forehead. Curiosity got the best of her. She walked over to the body and knelt to inspect him better. *What the hell had the mystery guy used, acid?*

All thoughts of the unknown weapon disappeared as grief settled in. This was her fault. *Bruce is dead because of me.* A flash of the vision of what happened while she laid on the floor bleeding popped into her head. Lusion said her ex-boyfriend put a curse on her.

It helped a little to know most of the blame was on him. He had used an unforgivable curse to get her back because she left him.

Cat shook her head at the stupidity of his actions. She had seen curses like that only a few times. They always came with a horrible cost. Usually, the person that cast the curse had to give up their soul.

"How the hell did a demon get into you, Bruce? Don't you know better? You run away from demon smoke," Cat's watery eyes sprung a leak and soaked her face.

"I never lose people; I'm supposed to save them. I can't, no, why, please." Her voice stumbled around so quiet, but she could barely hear herself. She shook her head as a horrible raw pain squeezed at her heart. It was a cold sensation that crawled inside of her.

She turned her head to the right and noticed Bruce's head. It just laid on its side, mouth open and hair still perfect. Cat went to the head. She wasn't sure if she walked or crawled, her brain was a fuzzy mess.

His cloudy, staring eyes made her face heat in anger.

She knew she shouldn't touch evidence, but it didn't matter. She would burn the body. If she didn't, someone could sew the head back on and turn him into a ghoul.

"I'm so sorry Bruce. All I wanted was one normal date. I didn't mean for it to kill you," she said softly at a level beyond the hearing range of normal people.

***

As quiet as a roach, Hendrick approached Cat. He moved slow to not scare her. He watched her shoulders stiffen, and in a fast-jerky movement, she turned towards him. His heart sped as her green eyes darted up to his face.

Hendrick cautiously put his hands out to comfort her. He wouldn't hurt her, and it broke his heart to see her cry.

He didn't say anything for a long moment. His eyes absorbed her tears and pain. He remembered what his mother used to tell him when he lost people in battle. "I know this will sound cheesy, but my mother used to tell me the same thing after I lost someone in battle. You gain strength, courage, and confidence by every experience in which you really stop to look fear in the face and then say to yourself, I lived through this horror. I can take the next thing that comes along."

Hendrick gave Cat a half smile. It always worked for him to know that things happen for a reason.

***

Hendrick's exquisite voice vibrated in Cat's being. His voice restored confidence to her, like a best friend holding her in his arms. She closed her eyes and let the sensation drown out her sorrow.

Her emotions were all over the place. She wanted to be angry, sad, afraid, and grateful all at once. She didn't know what to say to the pity in his blue eyes. It was enough to make her forget how to breathe.

She didn't want to feel sorry for herself. She wanted justice. She shook herself mentally; this was not the dominant Cat she knew. This was the weak Cathleen coming to the surface. She focused on what he said, not just the sound of his voice.

She looked at him as the weight that made her heart heavy with understanding. No one can help a person cursed by a demon.

Her mom used to say, we *all dance with death every day, but a person that danced with a demon is already at death's side.* There was no way Cat could have saved him. She didn't know a demon lurked inside of her. As soon as the demonic being had him, he was already dead.

That thought helped her have a clear mind. So, she was able to concentrate on the man in front of her. She knew the moment she laid eyes on those bulky muscles and sculpted body, he was her Viking hero the Goddess had mentioned. There was no way she would let him leave alone. She was too curious.

He looked a little scruffier than her vision, but his kind eyes were the same.

She wasn't sure what to say. Often, she was the one who dealt with other people crying. "Nice, your mother was a smart woman. Eleanor Roosevelt said some important things." She had to admit it was a good quote. One of her favorites, in fact.

He stepped forward, as he came out of the darkness completely, "I'm impressed," he said, as he took another step closer.

She was a great fighter with excellent skills with her weapons and amulets, but she wasn't sure how she could help a massive man such as him. He looked like he could fight his way out of anything.

Cat sighed. She'd seen the look in his eyes many times. It was the look a man can only get if he has been through a war.

"What's your name?" Cat asked while still on the ground.

"Why? Are you going to arrest me, detective, because I killed a demon?" Hendrick crossed his arms and smirked at her. She noticed her wallet in his left hand.

He knew well that she couldn't take him in for that. Demons don't have rights. She had never been to hell, but she was sure they had their own rules and laws there. But they didn't cross over here.

She smirked back at him, "Why? Do you need to be arrested?"

"Not likely," he mumbled absently and leaned back to put some distance between them.

"Well, then put away that guilty look. Or I might have to put some cuffs on you." Her face got warm. She couldn't remember the last time she had flirted like this.

His daring stare made goosebumps ripple along her skin. His eyes said he might put handcuffs on her if she kept that up.

The silence was too much for Cat, so she blabbered on, "My name is Cathleen, but people call me Cat." She stopped, pointing at the wallet in his hands, "But I guess you already knew that, didn't you? Stealing is something I could take you in for," she said, only half-serious.

"Oh yeah." He held up her wallet and tossed it over to her. "I only borrowed it. I have a lot of enemies, and I wanted to make sure you didn't work for any of them."

She lifted her eyebrow at him, as she waited for his name. The way a mother does to her troublemaker child.

"Hendrick," he said, those blue eyes showed how uncomfortable he was to talk about himself.

"Alright Hendrick," she paused and softened her eyes to say, *thank you for trusting me.* "I need to repay you for your help, so let me give you a place to rest for the night," she said without thinking.

Should I take this man to my home? I don't even know him. But he did save my life… That would be the best way to offer up my assistance when he needed it and be safe with my weapons. She mentally drummed her fingers, *Okay, my house it is.*

"Why would you invite a stranger to your home? And what makes you think I want to go home with a woman that had demons at her side?" The last part hurt Cat a little, but that was him just fishing for answers.

"First of all, my invitation to you is a kind gesture for the guy that saved me from a horrible experience with a demon," Cat said, as she raised her voice to nearly a yell.

"And second, my ex-boyfriend from high school, the dirtbag he is, put a curse on me. So, if I ever had another sexual partner, the demon could possess his body and make me his slave." Cat's arms flung around in frustration and fury.

She was livid at her ex, Lance. It was one thing to ruin her life emotionally. Now, the bastard wanted to destroy her actual life by getting her enslaved by a demon.

She passed Hendrick with a scoff. She was madder at Lance than him, but he was an outlet for her.

Right now, all men were the enemy.

"Come with me or don't come with me. I could give a-" that's all she got out before he interrupted her.

One moment he was ten feet behind her deep in the alley and the next, she was pressed against the wall, his face inches from hers.

"Sweet kitty, do you always trust strangers? For all you know, I'm as bad as that dirty Blaigeard." He got closer to her. Close enough that Cat could feel the heat of his body on hers.

For some reason, she wasn't afraid. The weird feeling in her stomach spoke of something else entirely. Her lower belly threatened to flutter like in the romance novels her friends made her read. Cat didn't like it at all. Anything that could affect someone's body like that was dangerous.

***

Hendrick thought the same thing, but the lack of fear on her face made him smirk inwardly. He kept his face in the crease of her neck as he breathed in her scent. That sweet honey scent of hers was intoxicating. His beast threatened to come out and play.

It has been so long since a worthy fighter had tangled with him in his bed. They had all been broken from the war. There was a snake-like sensation up his spine that warned him his vampire beast wanted to take control.

***

Even though she wasn't afraid of him, he was too close for her liking. Without thinking, Cat put her hands on his

shoulders, and she kicked the back of his knee. They buckled underneath him. She heard him make a startled sound, which only fueled her excitement.

She quickly put her right foot on the wall and pushed as he lost his footing. The momentum made them roll to the ground. Cat used this move all the time, so she knew exactly how long it would take for their bodies to hit the ground. It was just enough time for her to grab a dagger from her hair.

Cat pressed her dagger to Hendrick's throat as he hit the ground. She landed with one foot on the ground and one knee on Hendrick's chest to pin him down. She hovered over him like a warrior princess. The way her hair fell on either side of her face meant she probably looked like one, too.

She bent her head lower for a dramatic effect, "I don't like people in my personal space. Next time you do that, I won't hesitate to use my blade." Cat loved the look of surprise in his eyes. She prided herself on being the best, and when people doubted her, her soul hums with excitement when she proved them wrong. Yep, good old Chinese hair daggers were the best. She only had half her hair up, so the blades were smaller than her other ones. Yet still very effective.

She got up fast and hauled him up with her like a sparing buddy. Her eyes drifted down, so she didn't have to look at him. *Holy Goddess,* Cat sucked in a breath as she gave her bloodied clothes a disparaging look. *My white blouse has seen better days.*

"You didn't answer my question," Hendrick folded his arms against his chest like she didn't have a knife pressed against his throat. She liked that. Most men stomped away, angry that they had lost to a woman. But she didn't like him asking questions.

The tables have turned, and it was her turn to look at him suspiciously. Cat knew two things, she was an Unnatural and she had the power to prove it. But what she didn't know was if this guy could be trusted with her secret. Not too many people could do what she could. The more powerful the Unnatural, the more hunted they become.

If people found out, she was an Unnatural all her hard work would be for nothing. She'd lose her job, friends and put her mom in danger. They might even make her move out of her neighborhood.

The Goddess wouldn't have put him in my life if he was a bad person. The thought made her shoulders feel relaxed and words coming out. "I can sense evil in people." She shrugged, "For the most part."

Cat scanned his body. If he squirmed under her gaze, she would know he felt like he was evil. Only insecure and guilty people move. She was disappointed when he didn't. "You are not evil, just cocky and annoying."

That stern persona of his melted away and he stifled a laugh as he brushed off his clothes, "No wonder Izzy warned me about you. You are quite a firecracker."

She straightened, and a nervousness made her body quiver. As if she had passed a test of his or something. "You know Izzy Flake?"

"Aye, I saved his life a while back. He has been a troublesome but faithful friend since. But he told me not to tell anyone you are an Unnatural," he looked up at her as he took his gaze off his pants.

"That's not something people in this town know." She gave him a pointed look and dared him to say something stupid, so she could use her daggers on him.

He shrugged at her and smiled.

Cat was taken aback by how different his body language was. He looked like he was talking to a friend. Whereas ten seconds ago, he looked like he was talking to an accused felon.

That sounded like her Izzy though. So, she tried to follow his lead and relax. Izzy had always been clingy when it came to influential people he could add to his collection. Although, what can one expect from the town gossip. He knew everything and was eager to tell his secrets to anybody he considered an ally.

The funny part was, he was attractive. When she first heard of him, Cat had pictured big glasses and zits, not the sculpted frame with perfect blonde hair he turned out to be. His friend, Rebecca, wanted her to date Izzy, but Cat was never interested in the blabbermouth.

Rebecca wanted Cat to hook up with everybody, though. So, that's not saying much about him.

"Sounds like him." Cat turned and walked away from Hendrick. "So, let's just go get some rest. By the look of it, you need it."

She could feel his eyes on her back. He sarcastically spat at her, "Lead the way, then."

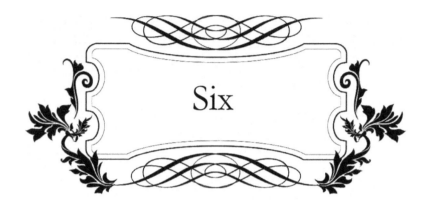

Six

AS SHE STEPPED OUT of the dark alley onto the street, she saw the local street lighter bring the lanterns to life. His dark clothes put a shadow around him that gave her the creeps. *This is the last time I come to this neighborhood on a date.*

There is nothing bad about the lower income neighborhoods that can't afford light bulbs; she used to live in one. But every time she agreed to meet in a place like this, dreadful things happened.

The first time, the guy was a nose picker that carried around a doll. Then, of course, the incest twin that liked to talk nonstop about how his sister broke his heart. And now, I have a vision that almost blows my cover and my date was murdered. Nope, her poor heart could only take so much.

Cat smiled when she saw her faithful black sidekick still parked out front, in good health, with nothing wrong with it. She grabbed the magnetic protection amulet under the front of the car. "Alright Yari, what's the big idea leaving me alone tonight?" Cat cocked her hip and faked disappointment.

If Cat could have her car as a partner, she would. Living partners didn't last long with her, which is why she didn't want one. Although, the one she had now wasn't too bad.

She pressed the button as she smiled at her car and made it beep to life. For as long as she could remember, her family had Toyota cars. This one though, was the first with a clicker. The sweet beep made her chest swell with pride. Most cars didn't have that anymore. But there weren't too many cars around anymore either.

During the war car bombs were popular, the fuel disappeared, and now, not a lot of people have cars. Also trying to fix them is ridiculous. No one knows how to work on cars anymore.

With another click, she opened the trunk to grab the gasoline and matches. This wouldn't be the first time she'd had to burn a body to prevent it from becoming a ghoul. Against the laws of nature, ghouls can survive almost anything. Although, it was hard to come back from being turned into ash, no matter what the person had been.

She looked at her shaky hands with disappointment. *Get on with the program, body.* As always, her mind and body didn't see eye to eye. She looked at the alley as if it was a horror house. This was the first time she had to burn someone she knew. It was apparent that she had an issue with it, but her body wasn't as good at hiding the truth. *Traitor.*

Hendrick noticed her unease but kept silent. He knew all too well the horrible torture involved to burn a friend. Before either of them could think of how it happened, the dead body was already on fire in the blazing flame.

Cat stood dumbfounded, the gasoline container and matchbook weren't in her hands anymore. She licked her lips and looked behind her to where Hendrick now stood, "You must be a vampire. I didn't even see you move." She straightened, as she tried not to admit how grateful she was. "Good for you. Not many can startle me," she gulped, distinctly uneasy. She was glad the Goddess had spoken to her before that information revealed itself. She didn't know too many vampires. The ones she did know can't be trusted.

Her eyebrows narrowed at his 'I told you so' look. "Still want me to accompany you home?" Hendrick said and did not try to hide the taunting tone.

"Yes, you saved my life. As long as I'm not on the menu, I don't care what your diet is." She couldn't help herself and taunted him right back, "But if you are scared, I understand. I did just kill the master vampire of this area for being loose-fanged," Cat pushed past him and went inside the bar to grab her purse. With luck, her properties would still be there.

The sweaty bodies and beer smell pushed her face back. *Ewe, not one of my favorite smells.* At least, the table where she sat was close to the back exit, so she could leave out that way.

Her eyes roamed her booth, "Awe, come on." She grabbed her black shiny purse with a loud angry sigh. "They took my lip gloss too. Assholes." Her purse was still at the brown table, but the contents were scattered on the seat. Anything of value was gone. She silently thanked her mom who taught her to keep her wallet and keys with her, always. *If only she would have included her cell phone.*

She turned to the bartender and pointed her finger like a pistol ready to put a hole in his head, "Send your surveillance amulet to the CIU immediately. Tell them to give it to David." She stormed out when he nodded. Cricket chirps could have sounded in the background if not for the dominating bass in the next room.

When she got back to her car again, she pressed the button to unlock her door. She hopped in and turned on the engine, as she totally forgot about Hendrick.

When Cat remembered, she looked around. Her anger was ready to peak. She spotted him in the shadows of the alley with his arms crossed like he spent most nights there hanging out. When he still didn't move towards the car, she gestured to the passenger seat.

Why the hell is he just staring at me?

"Fine," Cat said as her anger got the better of her. She pushed the pedal as if her life depended on getting away. Her car never went mind-bogglingly fast. She was sure it had

something to do with the crappy gasoline, but the way Yari picked up speed and zoomed away, Cat wondered if she had held back for so long.

She could help him another day. If he wants to be a jerk, that's what he'll be treated like.

Cat was miles away when Hendrick's blurry body stopped in front of her car. She knew the dark imprint of a man in the middle of the street was him because of his eyes. They always seem to be staring into her soul.

Cat slammed on her brakes, "Are you crazy?" she yelled out the window. "I could have hit you." He tilted his head and looked at her with a bit of craziness in his eyes. But they turned back to their usual sarcastic orbs.

"I thought you wanted to take me to your home?" He smiled at her like he knew all her secrets.

He was pushing her buttons. "You overgrown donkey," she whispered in a callous tone as she gestured for him to get into the car. When he opened the door, the cold breeze ruffled her hair. "I think something went wrong in your development."

Her sour mood didn't last long after he got into the car, though. Her lips puckered, and her eyes grew large with humor. He looked so confined in her car. Those long-trimmed legs and massive muscular arms didn't quite fit well.

"Are you okay?" Cat stifled a laugh but did not make an attempt to hide her amusement though.

"Peachy," he looked at her way through narrowed eyes. "You okay?" he was breathless, and pebbles of sweat rose from his skin. "I'm fine; I don't like small vehicles; I'd rather fly." He stiffened, "You look good in this vehicle, though."

She looked at him, puzzled. *Why had he just deflected?* Men only do that if they want to distract a woman. She inwardly scoffed at herself when her cheeks warmed.

Apparently, it worked like a charm. *Really body, don't act like a schoolgirl.* They rode in silence for the next fifteen minutes.

Cat pulled into her apartment's parking lot, as her eyes looked around critically. She began to regret why she invited him to her home. Things she didn't care about yesterday became something of embarrassment to her now.

Her building had cracks and holes in it that were still there from the war. She thought it could use a new coat of paint, too, but her neighborhood was in the middle-class area, which meant it was unlikely to happen. If Hendrick was ugly, or at least looked casual, she wouldn't mind as much. But the man beside her held too much temptation. She felt like she was inviting him for a one-night stand.

Cat was glad she made enough money as an investigator, so her place wasn't a complete disaster like her first apartment. That building looked like it was going to collapse if someone walked too hard.

Cat opened her door and held back a curse through clenched teeth. It was freezing outside. She used that to her advantage and practically ran to her door.

She preferred it even if she looked a little crazy, the run did not allow him a good view of the damages to her apartment, and it kept him hidden from her nosy neighbors.

Click. Cat opened the door some seconds later after several struggles with the knob.

She paused when she noticed shapes in the pitch-black area in her apartment. She had forgotten to leave the night-light amulet on in her living room. A few years ago, an Unnatural had broken in and almost killed her. Lights, spells, and weapons were compulsory for her now.

She flicked on the lights, as she exposed her apartment with its mismatched furniture. She looked around at the warm colors that didn't quite match, burgundy, rich brown, tans, and gold. They calmed the storm inside her, which in her book was the only thing that mattered.

Cat walked in and settled her keys down on the table next to the love seat on the right. The second one stood adjacent to the other that separated the room at an angle, so she could see anyone that comes through the door.

Cat was sure that the fact that it needed a good cleaning had not escaped Hendrick's eyes. Granted, she never let the mess get too bad, but the place was never spotless except for holidays when the family came over. Now that her grandma, father, and little sister has died, the family consisted of only her mom. She did have a cousin and a few other scattered relatives, but she hadn't seen them in years.

I should have cleaned up before I left. The place is a disaster. She must have tried on every top and bottom before leaving and they were still scattered everywhere. *Oh no, is that my underwear? Could this get any more embarrassing?*

Meow.

Cat's heart warmed when she saw her Bombay black cat strolling her way, "Hello my Xena warrior," she said, as she opened her arms. The over excited cat jumped on the rich brown couch and leaped into her arms. The weight of the cat made her stumble back.

Hendrick's hand steadied her. She gulped, and her chest got warm from his touch, "Oh, my God, you are too much. I'm okay, sweetie. It was a bumpy night," Cat told Xena, as the little thing shook in her arms. As Cat's familiar, she would have felt the whole night.

Cathleen is fearless and powerful, popped into her mind. She smiled down at her smart familiar as a warm bolt of power radiated through her body.

"Thank you, sweetie." Cat's body relaxed under Xena's touch. Xena had a cooling power she loved.

It was safe to say she was thankful for her familiar. Every Unnatural has a familiar; wolves have their pups, vampires have their human blood, witches have their mice, ghouls have the decapitated head from their first kill, and demons have their enchanted weapon. She wasn't quite sure what beings used cats, but her ancestors did.

Xena rubbed against her neck purring. Cat could tell the moment Xena realized they had an audience. Xena's eyes got big because she noticed Hendrick behind Cat. She was sure they'd pop out of her head if they opened anymore. Xena crawled over Cat's shoulder to look at him. Her temper showed itself and made the fur along her back stand up at attention.

"It's okay baby girl; he's a friend. He helped me tonight," Cat whispered, as she petted Xena's soft black fur.

***

Xena's yellow eyes glared at Hendrick. He stepped back a little to make sure he wasn't challenging her. One thing he had learned about familiars—especially smart ones like a cat— was their fantastic will to defend their human. He had seen familiars attack the worst kind of beast to give their humans a chance to escape.

Hendrick didn't move. He let Xena scan his aura to show he meant Cat no harm. When she finished, her back relaxed. She continued rubbing her body on Cat's neck and gave Hendrick a silent, *you're okay to come in* with her eyes.

He closed the door, having to slam the door into place.

***

"Sorry," Cat's shoulders went up high and she ducked her head like a turtle that wanted to retreat into its shell. "I had to get a new door, and I'm not sure I put it on right."

She sighed at herself, "So, are you hungry, or thirsty? I don't have tons, but the food will be hot, and the drinks will be cold." Cat shifted her weight on her feet *I'll take awkward for two hundred. Should I bake cookies?* They always baked cookies and made coffee in old movies.

She focused on the mess instead. Her eyes kept darting back to Hendrick as she grabbed all her clothes off the love seats and the floor. Hendrick's well-defined nose was up as if he wanted to get something in the air while he surveyed the area.

"I know it's not much, but I like it. There's not a lot of places in here where people can hide when the lights are on." Cat looked at him and wanted to know what he thought about her home.

"I like it. Very homey." Hendrick picked up one of Cat's panties sprawled on the floor.

She yelped slightly, going beet red. "Give me that." She could feel herself smiling, but she didn't know why. Maybe she had an emotional malfunction issue.

Hendrick forked over the goods and drifted his attention elsewhere. He scanned the walls looking at all the positive quotes and pictures everywhere. This was Cat's happy place, so she filled it with good things.

Cat saw him looking at her bookshelves covered with books and pictures. His eyes rested on one image. Now, he stood and stared at it which made her heart beat faster.

He turned towards her. "I enjoy this picture the most," Hendrick pointed to the second shelf where she had pictures from her childhood.

She laughed when she saw which picture he referred to. She was fourteen and at a beach party. The event was the first time she wore a bikini in front of several people. She was heavier, so the bikini didn't cover much. "I was a freshman in high school, pervert." She gave him a light shove.

"Your body wasn't what caught my eye; it was your smile." His face cleared of worry lines and became youthful.

But something slammed shut in his eyes and they hardened again, "You were truly happy. I don't remember the last time I smiled like that." He glided his finger across the picture.

"You and me both. So, do you want to eat?" She tried to change the subject.

"No Lass, that won't be necessary. I need my rest, remember." Hendrick wanted to ask why she didn't smile like that anymore but knew she didn't want to talk about it by the way her shoulders and jaw tightened. He didn't need that much rest. A good four hours would be perfect for him, but she needed space.

Cat walked to her bedroom throwing the clothes in the closet. *I'll deal with that later.* "Okay, take the bed, there are clean sheets on the night stand. Put your own sheets on though. This isn't a motel." Cat narrowed her eyes at him, as she dared him to disagree. She'd throw something at him if he did.

"Nay, it's your bed," he pointed at her queen-sized bed that was high off the floor. The black comforter and gray pillows were uncharacteristically neat and inviting.

She turned back to him when she wanted to get the blankets out of the hallway closet and put them on the couch. Her eyebrows went up. *When did he acquire an accent?*

"How about we flip for it? That way I still have a chance, and you won't feel bad about it if you win." She grabbed a quarter off the side table and he nodded his head, as he agreed with her terms.

She called out heads as she flipped the thumb size silver piece in the air. Her eyes studied the silver circle swirling around in the air. She gave a pull of her powers to urge the quarter to land on tails, she caught the cold metal. There was no way he would fit comfortably on her love seats. He was too tall.

Hendrick's shoulders went down, and he let go of the breath he held in, "You could always join me," he leaned on the wall and made a few loose strands of his shoulder-length black hair fall around his face. *No one should be allowed to look that good.* Everything from his strong jaw to his large inviting hands were sculpted to perfection. The whole thing wasn't fair and the fact that her body responded to him like a love-struck puppy made Cat mad. She was supposed to have better control over herself than this. "Not happening." Her eyes narrowed.

She turned away, as she dismissed him. Xena already laid spread out on the love-seat, "Good night, lass." She could feel his eyes burn a hole in her neck.

Cat smiled.

Seven

KNOCK, KNOCK, KNOCK, , the sound of someone pounding on the door startled Cat. If her heart could jump out of her chest, tonight would be the night her heart would make a break for freedom.

Hendrick peeked out the bedroom, his chest bare, "Expecting company, lass?" Cat gave him a funny look, but let it go with the thought that it could be her imagination. *There's that accent again.*

"No. It's probably my friend Rebecca though. I'll get rid of her." Cat kept her gaze on his creamy smooth skin like she was hungry. She blinked a few times and put her finger to her eye as she pretended to have something caught in the crease of her eyelids.

When Hendrick looked like he was about to accompany her to the door, Cat put a hand on his chest. She looked at her hand and was taken aback by how hot his chest was against her fingers. She mentally shook her thoughts clear, "No, you don't. I'll never get rid of her if she thinks I'm in here with a man. I can barely get her to leave me alone at work, let alone at home. All she wants is for me to get a guy and have a naughty time with him."

If only she knew what that meant for the guy.

"Sounds smart. I'd be glad to put her at ease." He stepped forward, which made Cat's hand press harder into his chest. The way her fingers widened put too much pressure on her wrist. The weight against her was beginning to hurt.

"I can handle it," Cat's face narrowed into a scowl and pushed him back slightly. The way he gazed into her eyes was as if he was intrigued with them.

Knock, knock.

***

Hendrick walked away, defeated. *Why should I want to meet her friend, anyway? Get a grip old chap, before you find a grip around your neck.* He sighed. This was another reminder that he could never have a normal life.

"Goodnight again," Hendrick walked back to the room, his shoulders lower than before. He closed the door and retired for the night.

***

Cat waited until he shut the bedroom door before she walked to the front door. She did not want to deal with Rebecca tonight. But the woman would keep banging until she finally answered. With a big, soothing breath, she turned the knob. "Hey, Rebecca." Cat opened the door wide to let her in.

If she didn't, Rebecca would push her way in through the door. The first few times her little frame invaded her space had annoyed Cat, but now she liked her thoroughness. As if Rebecca was checking up on her as a sister would.

Rebecca's long bleach blonde hair swung around as she walked into Cat's apartment, "So, how did it go tonight? Is he the one you are going to open your legs for?" She pointed at Cat's legs, "You need to have cobwebs down there by now. It's been how many years?"

Her small stature and delicate curves sometimes reminded Cat of a child, but her mouth never did. "Hello to you, too, Cat," Cat faked an insulting gesture as if not saying hello hurt her feelings.

"Yeah, yeah, Hello." Rebecca looked at her with her hip cocked. That's the way she stood every time she wanted answers and Cat wanted to dodge them.

Cat looked at Rebecca's fingers pressed against her thigh hard enough to make the blood vessels near the surface bulge. She always had a weird twitch with her fingers like she wanted to drum them in impatience.

"It went well. We had dinner and danced the night away," Cat lied. What was she supposed to say?

No, it went horrible. My ex-boyfriend decided to further ruin my life and put a curse on me. So, whoever touched me sexually would die and horde around a demon. So, Bruce is dead because he was attracted to me. And thanks to Hendrick, the demon is dead as well. By the way, he is half-naked in my room, want to see?

Rebecca would never leave the house until Cat told her every detail. Then, she would still want to know if Cat would have slept with him. Rebecca's world revolved around sex. She opened her legs to anybody she thought was cute. Cat's mom called her a kitchen door, *there was always someone coming in or going out.* At least Rebecca didn't really know Bruce, so she didn't feel obligated to let her know. She'll find out later in the radio news.

"And?" Rebecca encouraged, she got closer to Cat. She could see Rebecca's sparkling eye makeup close and personal.

"He's definitely a possibility."

Something fell in her bedroom which made Cat's shoulders rise to her ears. Her heart began to thump louder. She didn't remember ever being this nervous when she was trying to hide a guy from her mom as a teenager. Why should she be nervous about what her friend would do?

What if she takes him from me? That was the truth she didn't want to admit to herself. Guys respond to women who open their legs easily. Because she didn't do that, and Rebecca did, there was a possibility. *No, she would never do anything like that to hurt me. We have been best friends for years now, get a grip Cat. Besides, he is not yours.*

Rebecca ignored the sound until she noticed the sleeping Xena on top of a stack of blankets on the love seat.

She looked at Cat and her mouth stretched into such a broad smile Cat was afraid she'd rip her lips. "You whore, you brought him home," Rebecca smacked Cat's shoulder in a playful mood and wiggled her hips. "I knew he'd be the one. So, what are you waiting for, go get some."

Rebecca walked quickly to the door with a pep in her step that Cat had never seen before. "How do you know we haven't already?" Cat put her hands on her hips as she toyed with Rebecca.

"Oh, I would know. You would be glowing with sunshine, and you would be more relaxed. Later girl, be safe," Rebecca slammed the door as she practically ran out of the house.

Before Cat could lock the bolt, Rebecca pushed open the door again. "Sorry, I almost forgot. Your mom called me so many times. She wanted to talk to you," Rebecca handed Cat her small shiny phone.

"Oh great, sorry I lost mine tonight." She took the phone and clicked redial.

"Rebecca, have you heard from her?" Cat's mom's worried voice panted from the other end of the phone.

"Ma, it's me." Cat didn't have a chance to say anything else because her mom screamed and shouted in Cat's ear.

"What the hell is the matter with you? Why are you ignoring my calls? I told you something bad was going to happen tonight dammit," Cat's mom must have hit something because she heard glass breaking over the phone.

"Now Linda, I-"

"Don't call me by my name; I am mom to you!" Her mom interrupted. Her voice made her bottom hurt sympathetically. That was the voice her mom used when Cat deserved a spanking as a child.

"I'm sorry mom. I lost my phone, and I was on a date," her lips went down at the edges as she gave an upside down oops smile. Sometimes, her mom could feel when Cat was hiding something.

"I told you something bad was going to happen, and you still went out?" She waited for Cat to answer. Linda could sense terrible things happening in the future, like Cat could in people.

She never could see into the future, but most of the time they could stop the dreadful things from happening by following her directions. In high school, Cat had her suspicions about her mom lying a few times to keep her from going to parties.

"Yes."

"Why? Do you want to end up like your sister?" With those few words, her mom might as well have smacked her in the face. Her sister Christina had died a few years ago. She hadn't listened to mom's warning. Now, if Cat ever didn't listen to her, she expected the worst.

Her mom would be on the phone with her all night, telling her how stupid she was for not listening and Rebecca was already pointing at her invisible watch telling her to hurry up. So, she went for the only weapon she had. "Because I wanted to get some, mom. It's been such a long time-"

Her mom cut her off with a shriek, "Oh my Goddess, shut up, shut up. I do not need to hear my daughter talk about sex," she sighed. "Just call me tomorrow," her voice was gentle and loving.

"I will, but it'll be with my emergency work phone, okay?" Cat gave a little sigh of her own. Her mom agreed, and they both shared a good night with one another.

Her face was sympathetic when she handed the phone back to Rebecca. She had probably wasted all her minutes.

Great, I saved enough money to get her a phone for her birthday and I use all it up. "Sorry."

"No worries girl, now go in there and get some. Hopefully, he's big," she said as she thrust her hips forward, laughing.

Cat laughed as she closed the door. You'd think it was her room a man was in. Cat knew she had weird friends, but the little she did have, she loved. She reached for the locks, clicking them into place which made her feel safe.

As she walked back to the love seat, a displeased moan escaped Cat's mouth. If she hadn't thought Hendrick would leave in the middle of the night because he couldn't sleep on such a small couch, she'd be in her room drifting off to sleep.

This better be worth it, Goddess.

Eight

SKRRREEEK, SKRRREEEK. **CAT** awoke to ugly scratching noises. The high-pitched noise reminded her of nails on a chalkboard. She covered her ears and pulled her knees into her chest.

"Stop!"

As if listening to her, the screech stopped. Cat sat in the darkness of her living room with the bitter taste of blood in her mouth and a vein throbbing in her throat. *What the hell is going on?* The steady frantic beat of her heart drummed in her ears as loud as the screech.

Her eyes dashed around the room. All her pictures and quotes didn't make her feel the warm, happy feeling they

usually did. So, she reached for Xena, but the blasted cat wasn't
at her side. "Xena?" Her voice echoed in the distance. A cold
chill went through her soul when she couldn't find her Xena.

Instead of the usual, safe feeling she got when she was
home, a nasty itch told her that the house wasn't safe. And the
way the shadows crept closer to her didn't help. If she kept this
up, she'd go insane.

She folded her arms across her chest and squeezed
them tight. She laid back down, but as soon as her head hit the
pillow the shadows zoomed in close, hovering.

No! Cat sat up fast enough to make her dizzy.

And the headache drifted to her arms like gold chunks
going through her veins, pushing on her skin and her insides.
She rubbed at her arms, *I don't like this.*

With clenched teeth, she stood up. *Maybe a walk around
outside will clear my mind.* The chilly air might do her some good.

Skrrreeek, Cat fell to the floor holding her ears again.
Thankfully, the noise only lasted a few seconds. *I don't know if a
walk is going to fix the kind of crazy I'm experiencing, but it's worth a
try.*

She stormed to the door, flinging it open with only a
few tugs. The moment her hand let go of the door knob the
oxygen was gone, and she couldn't breathe. It was like her body
had forgotten how to inhale and exhale.

She ran out the door. Instead of the apartment's white
hallway walls, small rocks dug into her feet. She was outside in
the middle of the road. *What the heck just happened?* If this was

one of her enemies luring her into a trap, she was going to spend an extra twenty minutes beating their skulls.

The outside stung her eyes. It was not the dark coldness she was expecting. Cat looked around causing her mouth to drop open. There was a strange tint to everything.

Everywhere she looked it was as if someone had put a tan filter over her eyes. Cat tried rubbing her eyes.

She turned to her neighbors, remembering how beautiful her garden was the last time she saw it. The colorful gardens were no longer that gorgeous pink and red she loved, and everything was an ugly, light tan. She rubbed her eyes frantically, desperate for things to be normal again.

When she took her hands from her eyes this time, all the neighbors stood in the street. "Hey, do you know what's going on?" A guy in a button up suit stood in front of her holding a bag in his hand.

Cat didn't get a chance to answer; angry shouts erupted all at once, from everyone. They all wanted to know the same thing. Tension rose until the air was thick and tasted musty.

She was about to run back to her apartment to get Hendrick when something changed in the air. The wind made her mouth dry, like she had sand in the walls of her mouth. She pushed her tongue against them.

Her eyes searched for answers. She could feel the anger and fear on her skin. The intense feeling stung and prickled her skin at the same time. Cat could feel that something big was coming. She could sense the evil. She didn't know what it was.

All she knew was if she didn't do something to stop the buildup, people were going to start attacking each other.

Cat groaned, trying to shout louder than the noise, "Please everyone, let's all calm down, I'm an investigator. Let the CIU handle this. Will everyone go back to their homes? This will be taken care of," Cat felt awkward, but she lifted her chest in confidence. She put her hands up in front of her, hopefully, to say calm down.

With a sharp snap, the screeching stopped.

They all turned to the houses on either side of the street as a unit. Their robotic twitches freaked Cat out. Her feet absently stepped away from the group. She could feel her hands shake as another wave of adrenaline poured through her veins. When they all stopped, and in slow motion turned around, she almost took off running.

"What's wrong?" Cat squared her shoulders standing up straighter. The way everybody's eyes were on her like she was dinner made it hard to think.

"Where do I live?" a few people yelled. Some of them added a lot more curse words, but the question was, all the same, no one knew where they lived.

How is that possible? Their plain tan expressions got aggressive. And their aggressiveness was directed at each other.

"This is all your fault! You did something to me," a woman from down the street yelled at another woman who looked identical to her. She lifted her foot and slammed her small foot in the other woman's gut.

"I don't even know you, whore!" The other woman held her stomach and fell to the floor. Cat looked at the encounter like they were aliens wiggling their tentacles at each other. *They are sisters for crying out loud, how do they not know each other?*

Similar beatings were happening all around until both women and men were shouting. *Okay Cat, stop being stupid and standing around. You should do something.* A voice deep inside shook her awake and she moved.

She walked to the person closest to her and said, "You don't know where you live?" Cat knew that was a stupid question, but she didn't know what else to say. The woman was looking out over the sea of people like Cat was. Thankfully, she wasn't one of the aggressive ones.

Cat didn't recognize her at first, but then her face registered in Cat's mind. *Holy son of a Bastard,* it was her neighbor Della. The rich dark chocolate skin and curly locks were gone. In their place was a light tan skin and straight tan hair that made her look sickly.

She looked like everyone else. Literally. Cat's wide, pained eyes slowly looked around, absorbing the realization that everyone had the same dark tan bottoms and light tan shirt. Cat could feel herself start to hyperventilate. A tsunami of adrenaline crashed into Cat making her anxious.

She barely registered Della shaking her head *no*. Della grabbed her throat, indicating she could not speak. *That's enough, I need help.* She turned around with every intention of

going back to her house and pulling Hendrick's lazy butt out of bed.

The problem was, Cat had forgotten where her home was exactly. *Dammit, me too? So much for thinking Unnaturals were immune to this craziness.*

Cat was hot and sweaty. Grabbing at her clothes, straightening her I love sleep pajama top to make sure everything was in place. So, her clothes hadn't changed like everyone else's yet, *good.*

Cat looked around and ruffed her forehead. *How long was I talking to myself?* The sun was lower in the sky now. She licked her lips turning to the crowd, when the noise stopped. And that eerie cold quietness prickled at her skin again.

All the bugged-out eyes were directed at her, looking her up and down. In the corner of her vision, she watched Della stepping closer to her. But, her body language was different. A lot more aggressive; with her long, plump arms tight at her side, her fist curled into balls, and her shoulders raised high. Cat could see her shoulder muscles pulse, "Why don't you look like everyone else?" Della yelled as her eyes turned dark.

Della had been the first person to show her kindness when she moved in the neighborhood. Cat didn't want to hurt her. So, she broke free, as gently as she could when Della's tight grip squeezed her wrist. Della was a lot stronger than Cat thought she could get and she wasn't letting go.

Crack, something in her arm snapped. "OW!" Cat pushed Della away gripping her arm. *I think she broke my arm!*

She looked around for help but saw only hate in the sea of tan, blank eyes. In unison, all their faces narrowed, and their pupils dilated to the max.

There were way too many for her to fight off. If they all had the same strength as Della, she was in trouble. "Everyone, let's work together and figure this out," Cat was slowly backing away from the crowd advancing on her. As if she was a mouse in a snake pit.

She tried to reason with them, but their faces contorted into something not entirely human. The skin over their faces stretched tight and ripped. Their dislocated jaws snapped open and closed.

There was nothing human left about them. Within seconds, they transformed into something she has never seen before. Her heart threatened to burst from her chest.

She groped for her sidearm, tensing when her fingers touch smooth cloth. She rolled her eyes at her stupidity. Of course, she was not armed this time. She ran out of the house in her pajamas.

Skrrreeek the noise sounded once again making everyone cringe and hold their ears. The pain didn't last long though.

What it did do was push the mass of people over the edge. "Oh, hell no," Cat bent her knees steadying herself as bodies launched themselves at her. Frantic and rushed movement surrounded her scratching and biting at her flesh.

"Aaah!" Cat was on the ground before she could strike back. Her arms were flaying about trying to keep the tons of pawing hands off her.

Dull square teeth bit into her cheek and pulled a chunk of her muscle away. She could hear the muscles rip off as if they were paper. That was the only one she registered. The rest was nothing but a burning agony like lava splashing on her. She knew if she didn't do something right now, they'd kill her.

Cat tapped into her powers, letting the electricity of her gift spike through her. Not caring if all the Naturals in the world knew what she was. She was not going to lay here and get eaten.

Her battle cry was piercing as she punched and kicked anything moving. "Volant," she yelled with all her might. In one quick, throw of her arm, she flung them off her until she could stand up.

Smoke from her mouth poured on to the ground hovering around her feet. The sly cloud intertwined with her feet to make her powers grow.

They kept coming, kept chomping. She didn't want to kill them, but if she didn't, they would kill her. She used one final whopper of a push spell to make them all get off her.

To Hades with this. I'm not dying here.

Her hand got warm and burst into flames. She only hesitated for a split second, when she saw them pause to look at her hand with fascination. Before they could attack, a massive whirling hole opened creating a rainbow of blues to dance around everyone. Cat wasn't sure if the portal stopped the chompers or if they were mesmerized by its swirling sensual heat, like a moth to light.

Running away sounded like a great idea. She tried, but her body froze in place. It would not move.

Stupid body. She struggled until the ground shook under her. The sound of thunder, loud thunder, rippled the ground. She bent her knees, ready for more attacks. But it didn't happen. Instead, everyone, including her, got sucked in.

The jelly walls of the portal spit her out on a pile of wet leaves. When her mind slowed to a normal speed, Cat looked around, she was no longer on the street. A tan forest with long trees and fog gently ravishing the ground was in front of her. *I'm never going to like tan again.*

Above the trees a wall of clouds was shielding the ground dwellers from a blazing storm on the other side. The lighting flashing and thunder roaring pushed against the clouds trying to bring their hell to the other side. *I need to get out of here.*

Cat took two hesitant, slow steps, making sure none of the chompers woke up out of their trance from the portal. She jerked slightly when one next to her groaned. *Please don't look at me. I am a tree, you will not bite me.* Cat thoughts turned into a song she repeated over and over.

In the distance, through the woods, a small sparkle of turquoise shined brightly, like a beacon. Everything inside her said to run to the color. The fact that turquoise was her favorite color didn't matter. She wanted to get the hell out of this nightmare.

Her eyes darted left and right. There was a slight clearing ahead. If she could quietly sneak past the chompers all around her, she could run to the color.

Only a few steps away from being in the woods.

Cat hoped her body could handle the run, she was afraid to look down. She was pretty sure the image would hurt her eyes.

Faster than Cat had ever run, she pushed off the land making her bare feet move as quickly as the ground would let her. She wasn't expecting the dirt to fight back. Her feet sunk into the mud like quicksand. Cat's pace slowed.

She passed four chompers before they noticed her movements. Their mouths clicked and twitched as if they weren't sure they wanted to chase after her. Cat hoped they decided to go on break. After what seemed like forever, she finally cleared the sticky mud. She let out a loud, frustrated groan as she pushed her already weak muscles from exhaustion to move forward.

Click, click.

The teeth that snapped behind her made her franticness increase. Cat knew if they caught her this time, she wouldn't have the strength to fight them off. The thought gave her the will to move faster. Despite her legs screaming at her to stop.

Oh no! The chompers were too close for comfort. She could smell their ragged breath and hear their teeth chattering. Flying arms and legs tried to cling to her.

She was tired, and the light was still far away. She could hear a little voice in her head to stop fighting. If she stopped now, it would be a quick death.

"Here Kitty, Kitty," a deep beautiful voice purred in her ears. She snapped her head to the left, following the voice.

"Hendrick!" Cat pushed herself to move faster, a few more steps. Hendrick's glorious face smiled at her, waving her to him. *He is my beacon?*

Hendrick stood there in a bright turquoise shirt that shined with mystical energy. She yelled for him over and over, yet he never took a step toward her. All he did was open his arms to her.

Dammit to hell Hendrick. Help a girl out here.

Despite her efforts, sharp claws dug into her shoulders, as a chomper jumped on her back and knocked her forward. "Aaahh!"

This is where her fighting skills paid off. She grabbed a chunk of the chompers hair and threw the body over her shoulders like a big bag of dog food.

The only problem was, gravity was working against her. She hated that what is in motion stays in motion. So, Cat went down with the chomper. Being a talented little minx, she already expected to tumble forward. She used the chompers momentum to roll herself forward until her feet hit the ground and she was up and running again.

"Hell, yeah," Cat punched the air as she took the last step into Hendrick's arms.

She had never wanted to be in someone's arms as much as she did his. As expected from his glowing body, he was in possession of a jumper amulet. Once their bodies made contact, an invisible force slurped their bodies away as if they were noodles.

Nine

IN ONE QUICK swirl, Hendrick was gone. Cat's disheveled form stood alone in the animate darkness. "Hello," Cat cringed at her voice echoing. "Ooo, ouch," the adrenaline that was keeping her moving and the pain away, slowly seeped out.

Gggrrrrrr.

A low menacing growl had Cat swinging to the right. All she saw was pitch black. No shadows, no movement, just never-ending darkness. *Did I die and not realize it? That's something I'd remember, right?*

Another hit of adrenaline quenching her need like a junky with a needle. She sighed in relief. Fighting whatever growled sounded better than standing here in pain.

Without warning, the Goddess's shining aura stepped out of the darkness. There was no hesitation or second-guessing, she ran to her, gripping her soft silk flesh that reminded her of five-star motel sheets.

She felt terrible. The blood running down her chewed body was soaking into her. In Cat's grip, a loud gut-wrenching crack came from the Goddess, so she loosened her grip. The sound hurt Cat's ears, like two serrated knives clashing together.

Did I just break a bone?

A sympathetic pain spiked in Cat's back for the Goddess, "I'm sorry, did I hurt you?" she let go of her warm and secure body out of respect. Cat was sure the Goddess could heal herself, and it would take a lot more to hurt her than that, but how rude would continuously breaking her bones be because she didn't want to let go of her.

Her white gown, mystically floating at her ankles, was splattered crimson. "I'm well," her glorious voice sounded like a song to Cat and gave her the reassurance she needed.

Cat wiped her nose, too ashamed to admit she was crying, "Where are we? No, scratch that. What in Hades did I just go through?" she smiled hysterically, "If that was a harrowing vision, I'm going to be mad. You need to just start telling me things."

She straightened her shoulders, she was nowhere near plucky, but she did feel better. The Goddess caressed her face, wincing at the bite marks, "That, my dear, was the future. As I said before, nothing is set in stone, and unfortunately, things have altered. This future you witnessed is the result of an extraordinarily powerful curse amplified by Dragonvire blood."

"So, you're telling me that hell hole I was just in was the future? Not a vision? I could have died!" Cat swung her arms around punching an invisible foe while a massive amount of questions rambled in her head. "Why in the hell didn't you just tell me 'Hey Cat, I need you to save the world?' Not throw me unprepared into the future like that. Look at me!" Cat's eyes drifted down to her body as her hand made an up and down motion.

"Oh, God, I'm going to be sick." Her stomach threatened to spill out, and her vision spun at the nightmare of her body.

How the heck am I still alive?

Gaping holes with claws or bite marks covered her legs, stomach, and arms. The only thing not chewed on was her breast which was exposed and dangling out for the world to see. Someone must have ripped off her clothes because the only thing she was wearing was her pink panties.

"You would not have been as inspired to keep it from happening. I needed you to see what hell on earth felt like. I did not send you into the future. I brought the future to you." The Goddess tried to touch Cat, but she sidestepped her, not ready to forgive her yet.

So, she took a big breath through her nose and continued, "As you already know, our seer was attacked by demons, so her visions are not as good as they once were. Although, she is sure of this future."

"Can't you do something? Why do I have to be the one to take this on?" Cat move side to side as a wave of anxiety rose up inside of her, "I'm finally getting my life where I wanted it. Or have you forgotten the hell, I've already lived through?" Her stupid eyes teared up again. Which made her even madder.

"I can't, I'm sorry. You were given free will for a reason. If I interfere, I will be taking away that freedom. Everyone's idiotic lives will be in my hands. Believe me; it's not something either party wants, however, I will assist and guide you as much as I can."

Cat could feel her face heat up, "Are you asking me to give up my life?"

"I'm asking you to help stop this from happening," the Goddess clenched her jaw, not expecting Cat to give her attitude.

Cat scoffed, "Wait, what? I thought I was helping Hendrick." She looked at her half-eaten arm, "You are asking a lot of one silly girl? I couldn't even make it out of the test round. Look at my body!" A little acid lifted in her throat. She did look disgusting. "Am I going to turn into one of those things?" Cat knew she was hyperventilating but couldn't stop herself. She looked like an old chew toy.

This is all too much dammit.

The Goddess walked over to Cat when she saw her hand resting on her heaving chest. "Let's get you fixed up. You have been here for a while, so the pain is gone, but you look like Hades's wife." The Goddess's words made Cat step back. Goddess magic differs from Unnatural magic. Powerful as it is. It was also unpredictable sometimes, like wild, untamed magic.

"I've been slowing your blood, but if one drop falls you will never be able to leave here, Cat." She leaned in, and Cat let her. As much as the Goddess was not her favorite person right now, she trusted her.

Cat expected to feel the bitter slap of her wild magic but what she got freaked her out more. The Goddess's soft wet lips pressed against Cat's forehead, essentially kissing her. The contact made her skin go numb.

Why are her lips wet?

At the flick of her tongue Cat stiffened, straining her shoulder muscles. *This is weird.* Her tongue traveled to her scalp, Cat couldn't take the tingling sensation anymore.

Her whole body tingled and went numb. As if her body was asleep. A mental image of her banging her forehead on a wall like she beats her feet on the floor popped into her thoughts, "Okay, okay, that's enough."

"Aaah!" Cat's knees buckled under her from a shock of pain pulsating in her legs. She would have gone crashing to the floor if the Goddess hadn't raised a hand to stop her. So, now, she was dangling off the ground while still being attached to the Goddess' tongue.

She could feel her skin knitting itself back together. *Oh my God, oh my God.*

Cat moaned at the warmth washing over her limbs and stomach. If she wasn't listening to the Goddess slurping something up on her skin, she might have fallen asleep. All her discomfort was gone.

"Are you drinking my blood?" Cat tried to push away from her, but there was an invisible force holding her still. "Stop." The Goddess complied by stopping and stepping back.

"My sincerest apologies, it had to be done. You might have some memory loss later," the Goddess said, her voice a little more hoarse than usual.

"And why, may I ask?" Cat looked down at her once chewed body. Her pale skin was now flawless, maybe even better than before. "You couldn't have made me darker?"

The Goddess ignored the last part, "There are many answers to be had, but very little time. We have now done a blood exchange, by rights tethering us together," her voice was horse.

The Goddess smiled with so much warmth it distracted Cat. The smile was a motherly glow. Cat had seen that look before on her mom.

"Why are we always in a hurry? We seriously need to sit and chat about things. I have so many questions, Goddess. The biggest one being, when did you give me your blood?" Cat folded her arms, trying to make sure the Goddess understood how upset she was.

"As a baby, I knew you would be special. I gave you my blood to protect you," her tone was mild and carefree as if she had given Cat a stuffed animal, not her blood.

"You gave me your blood when I was a baby. So, I couldn't say no?" Cat put her hands on her hips.

"Yes, I know how that looks, but as a Sapphire, you would not have lasted long without it. That, and cutting your hair." She mumbled the last part.

"Wait, what?" Cat scoffed in confusion.

"When Sapphires cut their hair, their powers decrease. Thus, your hair doesn't change colors with your mood. I only wanted to keep you safe. Hair coloring is the biggest way to find a Sapphire. I have seen many of my children slaughtered because their hair betrayed them."

"You told me if I didn't cut my hair I'd get lice and why do you keep calling me a Sapphire? You said I was part witch." Cat was pacing again, "Sapphires are legends, they are not real." Cat shook her head like she expected some of the hurt she was feeling to fall on the floor.

"Why all the lying?" Cat said breathlessly.

This is just not my day. To find out she had been manipulated her entire life was a bullet to the heart. She could have told her the truth. The Goddess had always been a second parent to Cat.

"This is not the time for this." The Goddess was eager to move on; Cat could tell by her hand's stiff movement. They were usually smooth and flowed through the air as if they were soaring through the wind.

A huge roar erupted somewhere to the right of her. If Cat could have jumped out of her skin, she would have. "What was that?" Her nerves were shot. "What is that thing? I heard it growling earlier."

"That is why our meeting has to be cut short. It's a hell-hound trying to break free from its cage, and he will." The Goddess's voice became high-pitched.

Cat wished she could see where the beast was, the fact that it was in the darkness somewhere was the worst feeling. Her attack could come from any angle. Cat's heart dropped to her feet.

"There is no time. You need to use your ability to help Hendrick or his brother will die by the next full moon. Our seer said everything is too unstable to know anything more. With Chris's royal blood, the curse will affect the whole world in a years' time." The Goddess hurled a glowing transportation orb behind her, burning the edges of her long sleeves.

A crash sounded where the roars came from earlier. The Goddess's body turned into air as she floated to Cat's side. Cat, not knowing what to do, naturally went for her gun, but the coarse feeling of her weapon wasn't there. She mentally smacked herself again.

Damn.

"Oh, for all the love of the light, it is time for you to leave," she looked behind her. "Be well my beauty, the fate of the world depends on it."

"That's a lot of pressure," Cat stumbled as the Goddess shoved her to the yellow glowing portal, landing her back into her living room.

Xena slumped over the couch was the first thing Cat seen. Xena was probably as exhausted from the night's strange activities. Cat gave her a few long, loving swipes on her back. She let herself enjoy Xena's calming pheromones.

Right now, she had happiness, and that's all that mattered. She'd worry about the world ending tomorrow.

Ten

THE SUN SHINING in the window woke Cat from a deep slumber. She grunted with annoyance and hugged her favorite gray fluffy pillow tighter. *I don't want to get up.* She took two long, deep breaths through her nose and let them out slowly to relax. Her body got heavy again, and she sank deeper into her pillow.

With the buzz of her fan, the hum of the amulet making that fan run, and the firm wall behind her she was at peace. She pushed harder against the wall and closed her eyes.

Before she could drift back to sleep, Cat's eyes shot open when an animalistic growl sounded behind her, "If you keep doing that, I'm going to push back."

Cat leaped up feeling her heart send an alarm to the rest of her body. *Danger.* Somehow, she ended up standing on the bed with a heavy flashlight from the nightstand in her hands. She gripped the firm long handle harder to make sure it did not slip.

***

Hendrick lifted his lips to his nose to hold in a laugh. He thought she really did look like a kitty cat at that moment. *Yep, like a little kitty. If the lass had claws she might have gotten stuck on the ceiling.* Hendrick's heart warmed at her lovely face.

Hendrick checked his emotions, putting his guard up again. She was too tempting for him; he needed to shut this attraction down before it got out of hand. Staying on guard is what had kept him alive this long. She is no different from any other woman. As soon as she finds out he is a Dragonvire, things would change, as they always do.

"What the hell?" Cat swung the flashlight's head at Hendrick. With practiced ease, Hendrick dodged the blow by ducking under her swing, "Why am I in bed with you?"

"Don't ask me. You came in here in the middle of the night talking about chompers and sleep." He nodded to her gray pillow which had a thick puddle of drool soaked into its middle, "You flung that on the bed and conked out within seconds. I dinna have the heart to put you back on the couch. But now, I wish I had. You've been rubbing against me all morning." She looked at him with a contorted side look. He was lying there in only his boxer briefs looking up at her like she was crazy.

She still stood on the bed, flashlight at the ready. "So, nothing happened?" She didn't remember anything sexual happening. Her dreams had been filled with chompers and hellhounds because of the Goddess. With her mind shot and body sore, Cat, didn't know what to think.

Although, I guess that happens when chompers eat most of your body and a god has to put you back together by licking your forehead. Yep, my life isn't weird at all.

Cat's eyes drifted between her hands and the flashlight, "Also, where is my gun?" She wasn't ready to relax yet.

Hendrick's raspy, morning voice chuckled, "I wouldn't have done anything until you begged me to and if anything did happen, you most certainly would have remembered." His body relaxed as he laid back into the softness of the bed. With a sigh, he crossed his legs and put his hands behind his head, "Oh, your gun is still on the couch."

Cat lowered herself to a sitting position on the bed giving up her fighting stance. "Someone's cocky," she said, and with a loud thud, dropped her swinging weapon back on the mahogany nightstand. She crossed her legs and pushed her long t-shirt down to make sure she was covered. She silently thanked the Goddess that she had put on clothes before going to bed last night. If she woke up naked, this situation would have been remarkably different.

"Not cocky, just telling the truth," he moved in closer to her. Close enough that she could feel his warm breath on her shoulder, "When I do show you, I'll expect a full report." He smiled, baring all his pearly whites at her massive blush.

Cat's body betrayed her once again. Her core inflamed so intensely, and she was sure she was going to burst into flames. The worst part was the scent of arousal her body emitted. The sweet smell was strong enough for him to fooled.

She licked her lips, "It's doubtful that would ever happen," even Cat's voice betrayed her. The sweet purr was sultry and breathy, like she was on a sex chat line.

Hendrick let out a hearty laugh. She wouldn't have been so affected if not for his smile. Those happy lines curving his eyes and the way his face relaxed suited him. "I like your smile," Cat said without thinking. Her mouth fell open, and her eyes bulged out. "I mean, I like that you smile," she shook her head trying to focus her thoughts, "Nothing."

"What?" Hendrick barely pushed out between laughs.

If her cheeks weren't red before, they were definitely a deep cherry now, "Nothing. You know what I mean," she repeated, waving her hands around as if a fly buzzed around her head.

"No lass, I donna think I do. Why donna ye tell me," Hendrick was holding his stomach from the burn of laughter. He was laughing so hard even his accent slipped through his inner shields.

She did an epic scoff, letting the sound turn into a groan. She got up, ignoring him when he protested. Hendrick

was having the time of his life watching Cat stomp around as she grabbed clean clothes to change into. By the time she finished, her locks were almost red.

Hendrick sat up, letting his chin lead the way. *Did her hair really change colors?* He must have imagined the fuzzy curls rimmed with crimson.

She scampered into the bathroom before he could take a second look. The only people he ever knew that could do that were his sister species, the Sapphires. They were one of the God protectors that amplified Dragonvire's power by the smoke they produced. And they could transform into cat guardians. That was all he knew about them.

He shook himself. That is silly, all the Sapphires were killed. When she walked back into the room, her hair was back to its rich brown color. *There's no way she's a Sapphire. I'd be able to feel her aura, right?*

"What?" Cat stopped in her tracks after throwing her clothes in the dirty laundry basket next to the closet. She put her hands on her hips daring him to say something stupid.

"I didn't mean to embarrass you." He moved to the edge of the bed and pulled the black comforter off the floor.

***

Cat was so taken aback by his sudden change. There was no hint of amusement, not even in his eyes. She was noticing that was his tell. The rest of him would be saying one thing, and his eyes said another.

She wasn't quite sure what to say, so when her stomach rumbled, the pleading noise decided for her. "I'm going to make breakfast." Her stiff body turned away from Hendrick as she walked to the kitchen. Once she was in the kitchen though, she was better. It was good to be cooking for someone other than herself. Other than her cat, of course.

As if Xena heard her thoughts, she came into the kitchen. She went to her perch on the kitchens window seal purring loudly.

Cat pushed the button on her old radio, relaxing. She didn't have enough for television, but the radio worked wonders. They played music, read books, and announced the news which was all she needed.

She sighed a peaceful happy sigh and dove into her cooking. *Bacon, eggs, toast? Potatoes…?* She put her hand on her chin as she leaned against the counter *beer? No, no, I better not.* She was in her own little world. So much so that she didn't hear Hendrick come into the kitchen.

Cat's hips swished from side to side in time to the music pushing out of the speakers. She hit every beat with an expert flow, rolling her body as she chopped up potatoes and dropped them into the skillet.

She smiled at the warm, joyful feeling her insides made from her movements. She used to dance a lot at parties when she was in high school. But Lance ruined that for her. She met him dancing at a club. After him, there were no more dancing.

The sweet, happy girl was gone and, in her place, was a troublemaker. She did everything from breaking into houses to trashing cars. And even hurting herself in attempts to forget that wretched night. She learned dancing helped her remember the pure happiness she once had.

Before she got her life together, she considered herself Cathleen, a weak and vulnerable little girl. Only when she took every defense class she could and made the choice to stand up for people who were weak did she become Cat and land the job as an investigator. Shooting things helped, too.

***

Hendrick crept in the kitchen like a mouse trying not to get caught; a skill he'd acquired over the years, so he didn't disturb Cat's cheerful movements. He couldn't remember a time he let go and danced in such a way.

He noticed the white walls and cabinets covered in positive quotes before settling his eyes on her. It was a small kitchen, but well put together.

He opened his mouth. *The lass has a microwave? Her job must pay well.* Since the war, things like that cost an arm and leg.

Cat caught his full attention when she pushed out her butt in a circle. It moved around in slow motion to the music, making Hendrick forget how to breathe.

When she did it again, adding some more swaying, his eyebrows went up. Her salty movements were calling to him. He wouldn't mind those curves swaying his way.

The oil popped next to him, stopping her movement, which had his lungs grateful, because he sucked in a big gulp of air. Cat turned around and let out a surprised squeak when she saw him.

She put a hand on her chest, "You scared me half to death! Warn a woman when coming in."

He put his hands up to defend himself with tenacity, and said, "Just wanted to see if you needed any help."

His lip twitched when she responded. "No, not unless you want to chop the onions and spinach. I like them with my scrambled eggs."

"I'd be delighted." He walked to her chopping board, "I see you live in luxury?" He left the question open for her to explain. He liked how she looked surprised.

"Oh, the microwave?" She waved a careless hand towards him, "Don't be silly. Most of my real work ends up in favors or gifts. But, that was my grandma's microwave."

"She was able to keep it hidden from the science keepers?" He asked with wide eyes. The science keepers were a small group in the human government that attacked everybody's homes, stealing big devices to gain power over the masses. They figured if they could control something the people wanted, they could dominate the public.

"Yeah, my family had a lot of secrets. So, they were pros by the time the war came their way. Do you remember it?" Cat glanced his way, her eyes shining with curiosity.

"Aye, I lived through it and before it."

"How old are you? If you don't mind me asking," Cat said, prying into his secrets.

"Well, over a hundred," he retorted, lifting an eyebrow as he waited for her response.

"Wow. That's why you seem so Natural. You must be pretty powerful." Vampires become more human-like the more power they obtain. They can eat and drink things, breathe more, and hide their energy level. So, it wasn't abnormal to ask a question like that.

The rest of the morning was a blissful dream. Cat made a delicious meal that Hendrick scarfed down as if the food would go to waste if he didn't eat the yummy goodness right away. Those were his words, not Cat's. They even got to listen to half a scary story on the radio. Hendrick mocked the whole thing, but he made the story that more enjoyable.

Cat knew, because of the Goddess's warning, that he was going to find out about his brother soon, so she was going to enjoy the peace as much as she could. And watching Hendrick smile like a school boy wasn't half bad. He looked like a normal person sitting on her loveseat with his feet up. Those deep lines on his face when he was serious were nonexistent.

As if the Goddess wanted to smack her in the face to remind her that she was not allowed joyous afternoons without saving the world first, Hendrick's phone rang, extinguishing their good moods. He excused himself from their conversation about tasty foods and walked into the kitchen, "Yvonne, what is it?" He whispered into the phone.

Cat could hear a female voice reply to him, "Oh, Hendrick it's horrible! They took him," she was crying, so Cat could barely understand her.

"Yvonne, now stop that and take a deep breath. What's going on, and where is Chris?" Cat stepped into the kitchen,6 deciding to stop pretending she wasn't listening. As she walked in she noticed a vein on Hendrick's arm which was clenched around the head of her sink.

"That's what I'm trying to tell you. He was taken! Both of us were on our way home together, and boom, this big white van pulls in front of us. There were at least seven guys, Hendrick. I was going to help him, but one of the men punched me in the face. I tried Hendrick." Yvonne's words were frantic and fast like saying them again would hurt Chris even more.

"Yvonne this isn't your fault," Hendrick moved his hand to the edge of the kitchen counter to make sure he didn't break the sink, but he ended up breaking the counter. *Bugger.*

"Chris said he was worried that Hunters were following him. Ethan was supposed to be there to help." Hendrick was cleaning up his mess by aggressively throwing the chunks of plaster dust in the wide sink. "Now, you need to tell me everything you remember about the people that grabbed him. Don't leave out any details."

She sobbed a few more times before answering, "Okay."

"Was there anything, in particular you remember about them?" Hendrick asked, using his most alluring, deep voice to calm her. He knew the effect his voice had on women. It was a gift he picked up from his dad.

As planned, she perked up, "The only thing I remember is the python tattoo on their left forearm. They smelled like a campfire and one of them was named Lance."

Cat didn't say anything, but the name struck a chord with her. That name haunted her darkest nightmares. She didn't think it was the same guy, but she still recoiled from the word just the same.

She kept listening though, if anything, the name made her want to help even more. She'd be happy to kick the ass of any unknown men that were unfortunate enough to be named Lance. Even more happy if she knew where the bastard Lance was, so she could kick his.

After ten minutes, Hendrick said goodbye, telling her to get in contact with his team. He and his people did not get to spend much time together for pleasure, but they were always there for each other in times of crisis.

His soul cracked as he thought about his little brother in the hands of murderers. He was going to get him back even if it was the last thing he did.

Eleven

HENDRICK OPENED AND closed his fist as he stormed out of the room. How could he have let this happen? He was supposed to be there today. The plan had been to meet with a man for his bounty money and go to Yvonne's. He chose to go to Cat's house instead.

Chris was afraid someone was following him, but that's what he always thought. The one time he decided not to rush over there was the time Chris was right.

His flight was in two hours, he needed to leave soon. Hendrick's mind raced, planning how to get his brother back.

***

"Hendrick, I'm going with you," Cat said following him into her bedroom.

"Nay."

"You're going to need me. I'm really good at finding people."

She tried not to sound desperate, but she was sure that's the way her words were coming out. If he didn't let her go the world was going to end. How was she not supposed to be desperate?

***

"Nay. Ye have done enough, lass," Hendrick scooped up his ripped dirty shirt off the floor. "Mac na galla." Hendrick's body stiffened, his eyes got wide, and his mouth fell open enough to let a fly in if he kept it open. His subconscious mind must trust her.

He had never let himself speak his father's language in front of a stranger. It just spilled out as if he was in the company of his people. Hendrick made a point to sound like a Natural and, around here, Naturals only use English.

Cat's head went back in surprise, "What?" He saw more than surprise in her eyes. Her pupils dilated, and a sweet nectar aroma scented the room.

He tried to ignore her reaction and moved on, "Nothing, I was cursing out my shirt for looking so hideous." His smile was long and straight like she caught him with his hand in the forbidden cookie jar.

"What language was that?" her cheeks heated.

"Why, lass? Does it tickle yer fancy?" He asked in a full Scottish accent with a provocative stare at her. If he wasn't careful, his vampire side could come out. His fangs extending might make her defensive, "Gaelic."

***

She should have recognized a Scottish saying since her best friend while growing up was Scottish.

Cat made a half scoff, half motorboat noise. "No, it just sounded cool." As she spoke, her left shoulder drifted towards her chin.

If that was not a sign of her lying, her voice also went an octave higher and her forehead scrunched. She looked away from his accusing glare to walk to the closet, wanting with all her might to change the subject.

"Here, I think this might fit."

She handed him a large, black, men's t-shirt. Hendrick looked at the shirt like the black cotton was diseased. He made no attempt to reach for it.

"Is this what it has come to? Wearing the old boyfriend's clothes?" He shook his head as his hand reached for the hanger.

"This is actually my shirt. I like sleeping in large men's clothes."

His eyebrows went up, "Tis," he cleared his throat, "Thanks. Shall I remove my breeks and be done with it?" He laughed. Toying with her made him happy.

The room was perfumed with her arousal which had his sparking to life. Hendrick remembered how the women used to do the same thing before the war. Now, if he so much as said, "Ye," they would accuse him of being a demon.

Could I use it to my advantage?

His wicked mind raced to find a feasible way to play this out. The main one he couldn't do, throwing her on the bed and having his way with her might make things worse. So, he went with his second choice, push her away.

He hoped if he could keep her distracted and uncomfortable, she wouldn't want to come with him. What he was doing was too dangerous. Most people don't survive teaming up with Dragonvires.

***

"I don't have trousers to fit a doaber such as yours," she watched him freeze in mid-shirt change. Her mouth fell open and her eyes got large. Why the heck did she say that to him?

Cat turned away from him again. Her face burned with embarrassment. *Damn!*

Hendrick burst into laughter and almost fell over. The rich chuckle decorated the room. The sound made her turn back around with an annoyed look on her face.

"I've never met someone with as much wit as you. I like it," he squeezed into the shirt. "So, who was the Scottish man in your life? I just asked you should I take off my pants and you responded," he said the last word slowly and paused afterwards watching her face go beet red, "in the same way. It's something only a man could teach you."

Cat was grateful he didn't say what 'it' was out loud. Her best friend Duke used to make the same joke. She would respond, 'I don't have trousers to fit a doaber such as yours.' Which was the equivalent of, your penis is too big to fit in my pants. They would laugh so hard they'd end up on the floor holding their stomach.

When she said that to Hendrick, though, the meaning was different. Doaber was all sexual. The only one laughing was him. She was mortified.

***

"One of my best friends. He was gay, though, and he actually wanted to wear my pants." She smiled, but the creases didn't quite reach her eyes. Hendrick could tell that fake smile was covering up sadness.

As much as Hendrick did not want to be rude, he saw his opportunity. He knew this was a sensitive subject for her. If he pushed hard enough she would crumble.

That would be stepping over so many lines… Ye have to ye sobbing pixy. Stop acting like a fragile pixy and put yer foot down. She can't go with us. His dragon beast popped in his mind.

His beasts were a part of him, but they were also like inner voices telling him what to do sometimes. Especially his dragon, he thought he knew everything. Whereas his vampire just wanted to bite and hump everything. He mentally sighed, he had to do it, so she would stay home and be safe.

What are you doing Hendrick, you could use the help. Izzy said she was bad ass at fighting, his vampire beast chimed in. He smacked both back down. He didn't need their input; his mind

was made up. There was no way she was going, he didn't need another person's blood on his hands.

"How long was it until you two shagged? I bet the lad was kind and perfect in every way. Scottish men usually are," The fresh scent of lavender stung his nose from the shirt like it was trying to hurt him for being rude to its owner.

Cat looked at him dumbfounded, "How do you," her voice trailed off as she shook her head at his question and wagged her finger from side to side in his face, "That's none of your business, prick."

***

"Well lass, that's only something a man says to someone he wants to shag, so I'm assuming he wasn't gay and that he just wanted to get in those knickers. By the look on yer face, he succeeded." Hendrick's bitter voice hit home.

Cat's insides burned, making a sour and salty taste of hatred boiled over. She wished she had a sharp object in her hands. Throwing one of her daggers at him sounded good right now.

"Whatever, go to hell asshole," Cat walked towards the bathroom before she found something sharp to use on him.

Cat slammed her palm onto the counter. *How dare he bring up my past like that? Who does he think he is?*

She had been an investigator for a while now, so she could tell when someone was trying to evade her. Yet, she played right into his trick, which made her even angrier.

Damn him.

The tears kept falling despite her anger. She thought about Duke and the way they had laughed together. The whispers of laughs in her mind filled her with joy, but a stronger, bitter feeling of betrayal overwhelmed the joyous feeling.

What pissed her off most was that Hendrick was right. Duke was a lowlife jerk at the end. He took her virginity and left without so much as a goodbye.

Remembering how she had trusted him made a bitter, unpleasant taste rise in her mouth and she clenched her stomach. Even now, the thought was like a massive kick to the gut. She hated this feeling.

Click.

The sound of the door as it shut was like an alarm going off in her head. *Asshole, left me crying in the bathroom, son of a bastard.* A piece of her fused back together again at the realization. Her eyes narrowed as her head slowly rose from her hands.

A bitter rumble coming from her throat shocked even her. *Not going to happen. She took on this mission, she was seeing it through.*

In a frantic hair flying dash, Cat rushed around her apartment filling a small go bag covered in elephants. She expected to be gone maybe a few days, so she didn't need much.

She was grateful that stuffing a toothbrush, undies, and two sets of clothes only took a few minutes before she was

ready to leave. Grabbing the spare cell phone her work gave her in the hallway.

She searched her blue backup bag. It was full of sleeper amulets, daggers and an extra cell phone.

The black small phone looked like heaven to her. *You beautiful thing.* She dialed David's number and tapped her toe as she waited for him to pick up.

Cat and David were partners in the CIU. Well, they were supposed to be partners, but she liked to do things on her own most of the time. Eventually, David was okay with that because he still got to put his name next to hers when she tagged a new Unnatural.

Their relationship worked out perfectly, she got to stick to her loaner roots, and he still always had her back when she needed him.

As she waited, she caught sight of her thick, yet muscular reflection in the mirror, *Goodness, I need to stop eating tacos.* She sucked in her stomach.

She had never been a small, skinny person and the way she ate she was glad her job kept her active. Snickering at herself, she waved a hand at the as if to push it away.

"What's up, small fry? Did you kick some Unnatural ass and need a cleanup man?" he sounded angry. She must have pissed him off somehow. "Or were you just calling to say sorry for standing me up last night. Then you treat me like a nobody secretary." She could imagine his big, dark arms crossing.

"Oh dammit, I'm sorry Dee. A lot of stuff happened last night, I forgot." She was supposed to meet him for a beer after her date with Bruce. Last night was their year partnership anniversary, considering most people never got past a few months, the year mark was a big deal.

She paused, waiting for his outrage. She tried to be patient, not wanting to get even more chewed out. Her anxiousness took over and her leg bounced up and down.

She walked to the car.

When he stayed silent she continued, "I need your help though." Cat's long oops smile had her neighbors giving her wrinkled foreheads outside of her apartment.

"I should drop you on your ass and leave you there," he said. He must be really distraught with her this time, O*h well, what's new.*

"But you won't." Her smile grew to an expected one, and he could hear the change over the phone. She was pushing him. Hopefully, he took the bait. She could hear his hand brushing through his beard. The sound reminded her of running through the dried yellow grass. As Cat's partner, he was the cleanup her mess person, and he wasn't a fan of the job.

"Damn straight. You are going to owe me a good birthday present." She pictured him scratching his chin as he thought about something evil or costly, "I'm picturing a wonderful birthday suit waking me up with breakfast in bed."

"Only in your dreams, douche," she said, only partly irritated with him. The man flirted with any woman within ten feet. He was attractive, so she didn't blame him. David used what he had to make others feel good. With his warm dark skin, hazel eyes and a body built like a rock; most women loved the attention and men wanted to be his friend.

"Black people can't be douches, Cat. Because when we go up in that, we get stuck." He laughed at his own joke, "I know that made you weak at the knees."

Cat rolled her eyes, "Don't make me shoot you," she paused before continuing. David was a good partner, and a faithful one too, but he was also a stickler for the rules which meant he might not help her.

"Anyway, I need your help tracking someone named Hendrick. He's a bounty hunter. But it's just between you and me, Dee." She waited for him to respond as she pushed the clicker on her car. She heard the woman on the phone ask Hendrick if he caught his bounty, so Cat hoped she was right.

She did a little dance right before stepping into her car as the *ti, ti, ti* sounded telling her he was tapping his fingers. Cat had found out a few months ago that David was half Unnatural, so he had a unique ability to find Unnaturals. Nobody knew, or if they did, they were in denial.

"I have four bounty hunters in town." His voice was rough, like he had to force himself to say the words.

Her shoulders relaxed, "Any of them leaving town?"

"Only one, he has a flight an hour minutes from now at the local airport."

Why did it have to be an airplane? Her heart beat with wild anticipation. She knew she could catch up with him, but now she didn't know if she wanted to. "Okay, that's him. What flight?" *He wants to get out of town as fast as he can, and he probably has some type of connections that can get him a quick flight.*

David was drumming his fingers on his desk, "I need you to do something for me before you go."

Cat sighed, "This is not the time."

"Cat, you know me," David hissed his words. She smiled, slightly glad her influence had taught him to not be a pushover like he used to be.

"Alright, what?"

"Booster is in town," David said, knowing Cat wanted to tag him. He was the only target to ever outsmart the system by following the law. Or so he wanted people to think. But she knew better. He was a drug dealer trying to evolve into a murderer. Cat hadn't been able to find the proof.

"You know we can't bag and tag him unless he breaks the law."

"Which he did this morning by missing his court date." David sounded happier than a chubby kid eating cake. "The chief says we have to go in with a partner, no alone stuff. Those were his words."

"I bet they were." Cat gripped the steering wheel until her knuckles were white. "Alright, text me the address." Her phone didn't have cool things like a GPS, but she had a map. She turned on the ignition with her face tight. She had wanted this bastard for a while now, and today might be her day. "Oh, bring my CIU weapons. The boss made me leave them-"

David cut her off, "You got it." She could hear him scrambling around for his things, "By the way, if I get my ass chewed out for helping you without authorization, I'm chewing yours."

She skidded out of the parking lot bursting into laughter, "You'll lose all your teeth, Dee," she said with a smile.

"Now that's a hard ass-" Cat interrupted him this time.

"Besides, who the hell is going to find out you used some special gift to find a guy for me? We got this," Cat brushed her fingers along her eyebrow, wishing he knew about her being an Unnatural, as well. He would probably be the one person that wouldn't discard her for her gifts, but she couldn't risk it.

"I'll meet you there in ten," his joyous laugh warmed Cat's heart. David had become a good friend this past year.

Adrenaline crashed its way into her like water slamming her body. She was finally going to bring this guy down. If she was lucky, she would beat Booster's sorry ass and make it in time to beat Hendrick's jerk ass.

That sounded like a good day in her book.

Twelve

DAVID WAS WAITING for Cat at the corner of Booster's block wearing his standard jeans and long sleeves black shirt. Even if she hadn't known David for a year she could tell the intense, brooding man was him by the short buzz cut.

Not a lot of men wore their hair like that anymore because, in the winter, hair was the only way to keep warm if they didn't have enough money to buy a heater. In the year she had worked with him he had never changed his hairstyle. Cat could spot him a mile away.

***

David watched her pull into a parking spot a few feet away from the cars near him. He kept leaning against the fence in case Booster had scouts watching.

I'm just a typical guy leaning against the fence enjoying the sunny day, Booster.

The only thing about him that stuck out was the lime green CIU police badge around his neck, but he did his best to conceal the symbol. Protocol said the identification had to be easily seen by people.

He wasn't a big fan of them, but he had rules to follow.

***

"Took your time, didn't you?" He was mad at her again. She could tell by the way his eyebrows were all squished together like two stiff caterpillars. Those brows always gave away his mood.

She got a kick out of their dance every time though, "Don't caterpillar me. I was driving from my house," Cat walked past him pointing at her eyebrows.

She smiled when he touched his eyebrows. "Suck it," David put his hands at his sides mumbling angry words at her.

"Really? Suck it?" Cat was now bunching her eyebrows in distaste, "Have you been out for drinks with that guy again?"

"So, what if I have?" David said, watching Cat's smile grow. That famous saying: you are who you hang out with, described David. Whenever he spent any length of time with people who thought they were hot stuff, he cussed more and said things like 'suck it.'

Cat dropped the matter. She didn't want to fight.

She clenched her jaw. David didn't have anything in his hands. "Where are my daggers?" She smacked his shoulder, "And where is your car?"

"It's parked closer to the house." He looked at her and lowered his eyebrows, bending over. "About that, you don't really need them, right?"

"Seriously?" She stopped walking. "I can't use my street daggers on duty David-"

He laughed, pulling six gold daggers with CIU carved on the blade from his large pants pocket. "It doesn't feel good to get toyed with, huh?"

"Suck it," she said to ease the tension between them. Her attempts worked; they both laughed.

Cat stuffed some of the daggers in her hair and two in her boots. With her leather pants, she didn't worry about them cutting into her leg. She rubbed her gun on the leather holster wrapped around her leg.

They turned into Booster's junkyard, still smiling widely. The house wasn't an actual junkyard, but the lawn smelled like one and garbage was piled everywhere. Cat thought with the dead yellow grass and the deep potholes everywhere the place was looking like a junkyard as well.

The house wasn't the worst place to live, though. Its unpainted walls and chipped wood still told a story about the war, but the area wasn't the worst house in town. At least the roof still held firm.

David knocked on the door, yelling his standard CIU greeting. His yelling and heavy breathing reminded Cat of a story her great-grandma used to tell her called, 'The Three Little Pigs.'

We'll huff and puff Booster.

A skinny woman in a tight blue dress with dark circles under her bulging eyes and matted blonde hair opened the door. David introduced them, showing her his wallet picture as if the badge around his neck wasn't enough. But the girl looked like she didn't understand him, so Cat tried.

"Where's Booster?" The woman pursed her lips and turned her head away from Cat. When the woman didn't respond, Cat went to work. "I was hoping you'd do that." Cat pushed through the door, slamming the woman against the dirty yellow wall behind her.

Cat grabbed a dagger from her hair and put the sharp golden point to the woman's throat. "Wait, wait, wait." The woman put her hands up. Her eyes opened even wider.

"Oh, now you understand English?" David said from behind Cat, irritation in his voice. He followed them both in through the door. "If you tell us what we need to know, she won't hurt you," his thumb flicked at Cat.

Okay good cop, bad cop it is.

Cat gave the woman an evil, sadistic smile. Her eyes were pleading for her to say no, so she could make her. "He's in the room. Don't hurt me," the woman yelled unnecessarily.

"She tipped him off," Cat heard a shuffling in the back room of the house.

"Seriously," David grunted storming off toward the sound.

Cat punched the woman right in the middle of both eyes. Her limp body crumbled to the floor, "If he gets away I'm going to make your life hell," Cat said to her unconscious body as David slammed his shoulder into the back door, forcing the rickety thing open.

Cat joined David in the room when she heard him groan. The room was full of used needles with sharp broken edges dripping with crimson liquid. Some of that fluid was splattered on the walls.

When she saw the three half-naked people tied to chairs, bruised and poked full of holes the room looked like a haunted house. The two women and one guy looked like they had been through a dryer with a bunch of rocks and needles.

What kind of monster could do this?

The guy slowly lifted his head. His long brown hair was a rat's nest covering his face. "Help," was the only thing the man seemed to have the strength to say. His groggy voice faded as his head drooped back down.

David yelled her name which pulled Cat out of her shock, "Cat!" She shook her head to focus and saw David at the window next to the bed in the corner.

He was holding Booster's leg halfway through the window as he dodged Booster's fireballs. The orange balls exploded when they hit the walls, barely missing him. David wouldn't be able to hold him much longer.

She still had a dagger in her hand. With her head tilted down and a sadistic grin she thought wickedly, *This is going to be*

fun. David knew that look, so he scooted his hands lower and grabbed Booster's feet.

That was all the go ahead she needed. She flung her golden blade through the air at Booster's ankle, efficiently cutting through his myelin sheath, rendering him unable to run away. Cat loved the sweet sound of pain as she hit her mark.

***

Booster yelled in pain from outside the window, "You stupid Natural!" He knew who cut him. Only Cat had enough balls to do that kind of thing to him. The last time a CIU agent tried to hurt him, they had mysteriously disappeared. So, they were usually cautious around him.

***

"Nice to see you, too," Cat retorted, smiling when David let go so he'd crash onto the gravel outside.

"All hell! Why did they send you two?" Booster cried out, landing hard on the yellow grass outside and threatening to have her badge for throwing a dagger at him.

Cat left David to bag and tag Booster, so she could get the witness she hit. She heard David calling their situation in, "Dispatch…" Cat didn't stay to listen to everything.

As she turned the corner to grab the woman, a sick feeling in her belly made her stop. Her skin crawled as if someone was watching her. She unclipped her gun holster, letting her hand hover over the cold metal just in case. With a sharp twist, she pulled out her gun and swung the point to the floor where she left the woman.

What the hell? The woman had escaped? Cat had hit her hard enough to blacken both her eyes she should have been knocked out for a good twenty minutes at least.

"Dang," Cat hit the wall denting the surface, "That can't be good," Cat whispered, a disturbing feeling hitting the pit of her stomach.

I have a feeling I'll be seeing her again.

Thirteen

THE PEOPLE THAT were bound were on the growing list of missing people. It was enough to get the whole department out to Booster's house. Cat knew they looked familiar.

"Told you so Dee." They had bet on whether the people were druggies that double-crossed Booster, which was David's assumption. Cat's guess was they were victims that happened to be in the wrong place at the wrong time.

"Looks like the witch has done the deed again," a gray and green suited police officer pretended to whisper to his colleagues to spike a reaction in Cat. Unnaturals were hated, so he might as well have called her a dirty whore or ugly worm. They all meant the same thing to a Natural.

Cat knew he didn't really know she was an Unnatural but hearing him say those things made her blood boil. *Ignorant Naturals at their best.*

She tried not to react, but her breathing increased as she pushed the thick breath out of her nose, "So that must be why I get to go home to electricity." She put her finger to her chin for a more dramatic effect, "Oh, wait. No, that's because I get things done and get paid the big bucks. Isn't that right, David?" Her finger ran along the muscle of his shoulders. *It's time for us to be petty.*

David turned around from a conversation with someone else, intrigued like a long-lost lover rekindling their passion, he devoured her with his eyes, "Sure is. The electricity works well too. We use a heating lamp and a massage chair and watch porn as she rides me." David grabbed her by the waist with a smug look directed at the cop. Cat only smiled, loving the angry look on the cop's face.

The room erupted in, *oohhs.* What David had said was the ultimate trifecta. Because electricity was scarce, people had come up with sex goals to accomplish when they got 'rich.' Which usually never happened. People might do one of those in their lifetime, but not all three.

Cat leaned into David, going against her usual brother type relationship, but this particular officer had been giving her hell ever since she turned him down. Now, whenever they were

in the same room together, he tried to make her feel like dirt. This is when having a trustworthy partner came in handy.

Cat's mouth quirked up at the edges, she would never forget the way the cop's mouth dropped open and his forehead turned red. No one had ever said no to Brad Fetcher. His father had a lot of connections in the police force considering he was the chief.

If she were a shallow creep like him, she would have gladly said yes. It just so happened she was not. He got everything handed to him in a silver spoon, so he definitely wasn't her type. She wanted a man that was strong as she was and had to fight for what he wanted in life.

Cat didn't say anything, and she let David grab her by the waist and slyly rubbed against him to make Brad angry. The spoiled look on Brad's face was enough for her. She gracefully moved away from David letting her hand graze along his chest.

And the Oscar goes to Cat, a fake audience in her head applauded. She had to stop herself from waving like an idiot.

The Chief's ears must have been ringing because he walked in and stormed around like always. His blonde hair was greased back, and his stern, sharp features demanded attention. He was semi-attractive, like his son, but his brown eyes had specks of gold that gave away a softer nature than his son's.

"Spurlock! Outside, now!" he ordered. His small potbelly, which he hid well with expensive suits, swung towards the door.

Oooh, he used my last name, he must be mad. "Yes sir," she said, following him. She heard Brad snicker to his partner. *I*

swear I'm going to beat the hell out of him and record him screaming like a girl. Then, show it to all his friends.

Stepping outside felt great on Cat's skin. She loved the way the sun soaked into her pores making her feel better. "Chief if this is about Booster, I-"

"I don't care about that worm, this is about you leaving. David put in for time off for you," he said with a cold, distant look. Cat couldn't recollect if he had ever smiled. So, the look didn't bother her.

"I have business out of town, sir. I'll only be gone for a week at most." Cat tried to explain, but the chief had the same blank look and distant brown eyes he wore when he wasn't listening.

"No. Not going to happen. We won't survive without you. Cat you are the only Natural I know that can keep up with strong Unnaturals." He put a hand on her shoulder. "You wouldn't want to see the town go to the crapper, would you?"

"Sir, it's a week, not forever. If that bit is true, why don't you hire Unnaturals to catch other Unnaturals? Then I could-" He interrupted Cat again. Taking his hand off her like her words were actual flames burning him.

"You can't be serious. I wouldn't hire a filthy Unnatural. They belong in cages, not at my side in a fight." His tone was bitter and husky. She could tell he meant every word, and it was like rapid punches to her gut.

Seriously, you're an ungrateful slug.

"I'm sorry you feel that way sir, but I'm going. If you don't like it, fire me." She put her hands on her hips and let her tone reek of loathing. He grunted at her.

Just then, David walked up beside her, "Cat, can I speak with you?"

She was in a staring contest with the chief, waiting for him to back down. And he did. He took a step back and addressed David, "She's excused." He turned to her, "I'll expect you back in a week." With that he walked away, his plump body extremely rigid. She wouldn't be surprised if smoke came from his ears.

"Do you have a death wish? You looked like you were about to fight the chief," David exclaimed, putting his hand on her shoulder and shaking her lightly.

"That's because I was," she said finally, looking away from the chief and into David's eyes. Those hazel orbs had been her steady rock. She marveled how they were able to calm her. She smiled at her friend.

"You can't go around beating up the law. He is the only reason you get away with half the stuff you do. If you get fired-" Cat interrupted him.

"Then, I would start my own investigation unit," she said, flaring her nostrils in anger. *Damn stupid blindsided Natural.* David was going to say something when a massive amount of red and green leaves fell from the tree above them.

Hurry Cat, your window is closing. The Goddess's voice chimed in her ears. The Goddess has told her that talking telepathically with her was forbidden, so her voice startled Cat.

I know… I'm trying back off, Cat grunted at the Goddess. She didn't mean for her to hear the last part, but when she saw a vision of tons of sunken, angry eyes eating her alive, Cat knew she had heard. "Aaah!" Cat screamed, not expecting that. "Alright, I get it."

David, thinking she was talking to him continued, "Okay. As long as you control that temper, you will be fine. He wasn't kidding when he said the town needed you."

Cat blinked at him, trying to catch up. A Natural wouldn't be talking to the Gods. "I'll try, Dee."

He smiled at her, letting his eyebrows soften. "That's all a partner can ask for. Are you leaving for the airport?"

"Yeah, not sure I'm going to make it, though," she said, disappointment making her shoulders droop a little. She took a few steps toward her car down the road.

"Yeah, you will. I got my cousin to set the alarm off if you ended up staying here too long. That should buy you time. They'll figure it is fake soon, though," David said, hitting her with his shoulder as he walked beside her.

She perked up and gave him a big smile, "When?"

He looked at his watch, "He should be doing it any minute now. That gives you an extra thirty minutes. Give or take a few minutes. And before you ask, I already booked you on the flight," he handed her the blue flight ticket.

"You are the best partner." She punched him in the chest and ran to her Yari. The dirt road created a dust build up behind her.

She kept bending her ankles to the side with all the potholes, "Ouch."

It's a good thing I am strong and can make magical amulets or I'd be out of a job.

"You're welcome. And you owe me one!" David called after her. She really did owe him one. As she ran with the warm wind in her hair Cat's heart fluttered with joy, she was so happy to have a friend like him.

She laughed as she pictured herself smacking some sense into Hendrick. All she had to do was make it in time.

Ready or not, here I come.

Fourteen

*H*OW HAD IT *ever come to this? In all my years, I never thought this would happen to me.* Hendrick stood there dumbfounded. His feet stuck to the floor in shock.

He was cornered in the men's room, backed against the wall. *I've killed numerous demons from childhood on. Why is this woman so different for me? Da would laugh his silver tale off if he was here.*

Cat stood in front of him with her arms stretched out at her sides holding gold daggers and blocking the exit. Her menacing stare and lethal body were ready for action.

The way she changed her tactic by slipping the knives back into her hair and putting her hands on her hips made

Hendrick's blood travel lower in his body. She was going to fight with her body, not with weapons, like a true warrior.

Stop that, she is not even naked for crying out loud. If you start to rise, I'm going to put a bucket of ice in my pants. That did the trick. He lifted his head higher, proud of himself.

He could plow through Cat, of course. Yet, he doubted she would give up even then. "You are not going," he straightened his shoulders, making her blazing eyes twitch slightly at the corner. Ordering people around worked when he was king, and he hoped it did today.

"I was hoping you'd say that," Cat looked at him with a long, toothy grin, eyes tilted menacingly at him. He couldn't lie; she was kind of freaky when her hair floated.

Without warning, she dashed toward the wall throwing him off guard. He was expecting her to hotfoot his way. Cat's long legs bounced off the wall launching her up in the air. Her fist slammed into Hendrick's face making a loud, satisfying crunch. As soon as her foot touched the ground she side-kicked him in the chest.

A wicked smile accompanied her taunt, "I owed you payback for being a bastard."

***

He wasn't expecting her to attack as fiercely as she did, so he pathetically took the hits full force. *She hits stronger than most men.*

"I deserved that," he held his jaw trying to move the firm bone around to make sure nothing was broken.

He knew if he didn't fight back, she wouldn't respect him. No true warrior would. And they both knew if she didn't best him right now, she wasn't going. He didn't need another person to take care of, he needed another warrior.

Let's see what you got.

"Ya think?" she lifted on her tiptoes, her fist was still pointed at him with her arms bent, ready for action. He could see the excitement shining in her green eyes. They were even a shade lighter.

Hendrick smiled enough to make her chest a little red, "Ye still not going." This time he expected her attack, so he stopped the skillful fist flying towards him. His fist collided with her ribs.

She still managed to kick him in the gut, though. So, they both toppled over, holding their sore areas. "Are ye trying to kill me?" As a dragon not shifted yet, his stomach was a soft spot for him. Even with his vampire side, his core stayed tender.

"No, but maybe hurt you a little," she said breathlessly.

She advanced again, trying to kick him in the face. But his broad hand grabbed her muscular leg, stopping the leather boot inches from his face.

***

Cat didn't let that stop her; she used her other leg to kick him. She pushed her foot off the floor, and when her foot connected with his head, he let go of her leg. She didn't waste any time. She jumped on him and wrapped her long skillful leg around the back of his knees.

Once she felt the soft curve of his leg, she kicked his knees out making them buckle, and she pulled him to the ground on top of her. She threw him over her shoulder with a big push of her legs using the momentum of their fall. With all her weight on her shoulder and her head to the side, she rolled backward until she was on top of him.

This time she didn't grab anything sharp to keep him down. Her smug smile and her knee on his chest was enough. "I win." She sat all the way up when he blinked at her a few times.

"How the bloody hell did I let ye do that to me twice in one lifetime?" Hendrick shook his head in shock. As a last resort, he tried a different tactic, "Ye know lass, if ye wanted to be on top, all ye had to do was ask."

She snorted, "If I wanted you, Hendrick, you would already be mine." She crossed her arms over her chest.

"Is that so, lass? Now, who is the cocky one?" He lifted one brow in question. Knowing if she didn't get off him soon he would be hard with excitement.

Cat rolled her eyes and took her legs off his chest. Hendrick took cunning advantage of her move by grabbing her leg. Using his strength to show her he could fight back if he wanted to. He brought her leg down to straddle around him and pulled her closer, "Why do ye want to help me?" he was inches away from her face making his breath caressed her skin and causing her sweet honey scent to sink into his clothing.

With wide eyes, she gulped, "I believe it's my destiny." She was telling the truth, whether he believed her words or not was his problem.

***

He laughed at that, letting her go after a few mumbles of disapproval. "Okay," was all he said as he got up, brushing off his clothes.

She did do well in the fight. So, she could be handy. As much as he didn't want her in his world, she could help bring his brother home.

***

She thought he was going to say something else, but he licked at his two front teeth and sucked at them like pulling food off his pearly whites. The sound made her step back. She had only seen people do that when they were agitated.

He walked toward her with slow, powerful strides and reached for her duffel bag. Cat frowned and pulled the bag away from him, smacking his hand, "What are doing?"

"If ye coming lassie, I'll be holdin' yer bag," he let his accent deepen, knowing the sound ruffled her feathers.

When he saw goosebumps decorate her milky skin, he knew she was frazzled. Deep inside, he wondered if her reaction was to him or the memory of the other lad. He was betting it was the latter. The thought had a dark green pin of jealousy lacing its way into his heart.

Stop that.

"Why?" Her face crinkled at him. She tightened her grip on the duffel bag. She was afraid he was going to throw it out the window and make a run for the plane.

He crossed his arms, not wanting to forcefully take her items away from her. He wanted her to give them to him, "Ye a lassie, right?"

"Yes," she dropped her bag and copied his movement locking her head to the side. She was not fond of his games, but he certainly like to play them.

"Well lass, where I'm from men hold a beautiful lassie's bag. So, hand it over." His large hard went in the space between them, waiting. He even wiggled his thick fingers when she didn't do it right away.

Cat debated attacking him again but didn't want the hassle of fighting. She gave over the bag, shooting hate lasers at him with her eyes.

The damn man has to win at something. Even if he loses the battle, he'll conjure up another battle to win. *It's annoying.*

They both left the bathroom together. She had locked the door, so a line of snickering men was waiting to go in. This must be the only men's bathroom. *If he high-fives these twerps, I'm going to smack him.*

She smiled when he left the men's hands hanging in the air. *Yeah, take that, twerps.* She stayed close to him just in case. Since he possessed vampire traits, he could outrun her. She wouldn't be able to keep up even if she tried. However, she could still jump on his back for the ride.

They both stayed dead silent the rest of the way to the security check even though she kept sneaking glances at him trying to read his face. Cat hoped with all her being that he had an amulet to help him get through the Unnatural x-rays or this was about to get nasty.

***

Hendrick wished he could use his dragon and fly, but that would get him killed by a Hunter.

They both were too tense. If his amulet didn't hide his Dragonvire beast, they were both in deep trouble. In other words, dead. Now was time for a prayer.

Fifteen

HENDRICK HEARD A small beep as he walked past the Unnatural detector. *Great.*

He bit his tongue, so he wouldn't stiffen. He needed to act normal. A small man gravitated to him, his scrawny hand on his belt.

The dreaded, "Sir, can you step over here please," came next. The phrase was blistering to his ears. If only they were in a dark alley and not in this crowded airport, he would punch the scowl off the security guard's face.

Two kids ran past him flashing light amulets to temporarily blind each other. The stomping of their feet made his heart speed up. Their pink hair and short stature gave them away as pixies. Their laughter calmed him.

He looked around, *there are no other guards coming, so the amulet might have worked.*

"Is there something wrong?" Hendrick smiled as nice and innocent as he could. He also made sure his accents weren't detectable and tried to make himself look shorter. *I'm a normal American, just like you lad.*

The security guard murmured something under his breath, "One-way or round-trip?" he pointed his black stick at Hendrick and looked at him like he had feces all over him. The guard looked fragile and wimpy, but Hendrick knew with one yell from the guard, twenty guns would be pointing at his heart.

He knew that, but his royalty instincts kicked in making him straighten up. Which wasn't a bright idea, he already was taller than the small lad, and now he towered over him.

Hendrick could see the guard's hand twitch as his fingers hovered over a button on his thick black belt. The rest of his uniform was a dirt brown, so the shiny belt stuck out.

Both vampires and dragons are proud beings. When both lineages mix in one person, the pride and predatory instincts are much stronger, harder to control. So, if someone tries to talk down to them, it is hard not to react. Both beasts chocked their way out to prove their worth.

Bampot, you are supposed to look harmless. Hendrick tried to regain control of himself. The guard didn't know any better. At least he didn't say bampot out loud. Using his father's language to call himself an idiot was a sure way to get into trouble.

"Sir, I think you should come with me." The guard rested a hand on his belt near his amulet bag. They were probably sleeping amulets.

Hendrick was about to say something and probably make matters worse when Cat ran up, her glorious honey scent coated the air, swirling around him. The smell alone was enough to calm his beasts, which was funny, because his body's reaction was to stiffen, thinking she was going to attack again. But as her soft full lips dove for his, he relaxed.

Clever lass. Show them I am a loving Unnatural. If she uses her badge, she's smart and willing to soil her reputation to help me… A pinch of guilt fluttered inside of him. This was why he didn't want her with him. *Once you're in my world, you usually can never go back to your old life or die.*

She kissed him with so much passion he forgot where he was. He grabbed her lower back pushing her soft body to his. That's how the ladies in the court used to kiss him. Like he was the only man they had ever seen and ever wanted to see.

Those memories made him freeze up. If his dad could see him now Hendrick would never live it down. *Ye let a wee little lassie, show ye up?*

When she pulled away slightly to say something against his lips, he wasn't ready. "You ready baby?" Cat's voice was a sweet lover's whisper. She tried not to laugh at the 'wow' look paralyzing his face.

***

Cat was breathless. That was the best fake kiss she'd ever had. So much electricity, she could probably make a lightbulb shine in her mouth if she tried. She was surprised he hadn't shocked her into silence too. She considered devouring his lips again as she gazed into his blue eyes waiting for a response, *maybe I shocked him too much?*

It was a good thing she played this role of a flirty girlfriend for a living or he might have ruined their cover by taking too long to answer. She had to cover for him, so she ran her tongue over his lips with one quick swipe, "I love the way you taste, lover." That definitely got a reaction, he pressed himself against her like he wanted to mesh their bodies together.

That's when the airport security guy coughed into his hand.

Thank the Goddess, what was Hendrick waiting for? She turned to the guard, feigning embarrassment. "Oh, I'm sorry I didn't see you there. I'm CIU investigator Cat-"

"Spurlock. I know," The guard shuffled his feet and turned a shade redder.

She gave him a quizzical head tilt, "Do I know you, officer?" Cat was trying to be polite, after all, so she called him an officer. Buttering him up would work to her advantage. The last thing she wanted was to piss him off.

"Yes, kind of. You saved my little sister from a nasty vampire attack last year." He gripped his black stick letting the uncomfortable glare in his brown eyes get the best of him. The ends of his eyebrows were so long his eyes looked strained under their weight. He clenched his jaw tightly, finally meeting her eyes.

Good for you boy. Cat couldn't help but smile. She remembered when he spoke to her to ask her out, he wouldn't make eye contact.

Their vampire radar must have gone off. *That's what I was hoping.* "Oh yeah," she put on her famous shining smile. Maybe she could use that to her advantage. "You are Bilma's older brother, Josh. I remember because afterward, you asked me out for drinks to thank me," her voice drifted off. The look of horror in her green eyes. *Dang it, there you go letting your mouth ruin things again. The Gods seriously messed up in my development.*

"That you refused." He stepped back, white-knuckling his stick. Josh turned as red as if she slapped him a few times, hiding his freckles.

Cat looked at Hendrick when his hand at her hip pushed her toward him, *now you want to join in? I could smack you.* "Yeah, it's policy not to mix business with pleasure," she said, quickly changing the subject. "So how is Bilma doing? She still calls me sometimes for help."

"That's good." With the mention of her helping his baby sister, his posture softened, and he let go of his death grip on his weapon.

A large woman chose that moment to yell at the guard from the X-ray Unnatural detector across the room. "Move it along Newbie. There are other people to question. If you can't keep up we will find someone else who can," her angry voice bit out, too. Josh literally flinched as if she raised a fist to him.

His brown eyes darkened with hatred towards the woman. *Poor guy probably gets pushed around a lot.* With his too-large, blocky teeth, equally large nose and skinny form he was probably the go-to target for everyone.

Maybe I should give him a few lessons when I get back. She had done it for his sister, and she might as well extend her help to other family members.

"You can leave," he waved them on. In a slouch, he went back to his post. The sympathy rolling off her was too much. She'd have to deal with that when she got home. He looked like life had beaten him down good.

"That was a close one, and you're welcome," Cat took a deep breath. When she noticed Hendrick was still holding her hip, she blushed, "You can let go now."

Hendrick let go as if she had spontaneously contracted a contagious disease. He grumbled a thank you and strode towards the moving table to grab his belongings. If Cat hadn't noticed the tension in his shoulders, she might have been offended.

No reason to get your ass kicked, Cat, just ignore him. At least, he said thank you. So, she followed him in silence, grumbling back. He acted like she was wrong for helping him out. *If anyone else questions him, I'm keeping my mouth to myself, ungrateful jerk.*

She grabbed her shoes from the airport bucket and put them on, dreading what she was about to do. Why had she fought so hard to go along with him again? After all this is over she needed to check her sanity.

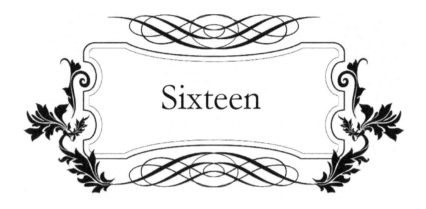

Sixteen

THEY BOARDED THE plane and found their seats. The room stunk of mold and feet, so she pinched her nose to try and escape the odor. Cat frowned as she studied her surroundings. She imagined how the planes used to be from the stories her grandma told her. If they were still like that then maybe her palms wouldn't be sweaty.

Ever since the war, airplanes had lost all their class and technology advances because there was no one around that knew what they were doing to keep things like that up.

There were no more televisions or phones on board and the closest thing they had to an air mask was a brown paper bag. Most beings that chose to ride in a plane nowadays were scoundrels and master Unnaturals. That's why they screen for them, to identify the Unnaturals and weigh the possibility of an attack.

The planes tacky gray walls and tightly bunched up seats made Cat feel sick. *This is going to be the longest ride of my life. I'm going to need a few shots to get through this.*

As soon as they sat down, a sneeze erupted right behind Cat's head. Cat imagined the germs spraying the back of her headrest and wafting around the edges to fill her nose. The thought sounded an alarm in Cat's mind making her heart slam against her chest. The walls were closing in around her and the oxygen was leaving the plane as her anxiety took over.

Her hands trembled uncontrollably, "I hate flying. Why couldn't we have driven there?" Cat said with a death grip on the chair. She clutched the arms rests and they cracked in her cold, clammy grip. Hendrick watched the veins bulge in her arms and hands that were in a tight pale ball. If she weren't careful, she would puncture her skin, and the vampires on the plane would not be happy.

"I told you we don't have time for that. You said you wanted to come along and help." Hendrick wanted to grab her hand and let her know there was nothing to be afraid of, but he held back.

The person behind Cat blew his nose again. *Stupid Naturals and their illnesses.* She was lucky that her immune system was not like a Natural, so she didn't need to worry about most illnesses.

She turned around and gave the heavy man a death stare. She might have even let her green eyes shine sapphire a little. *Get a hold of yourself.* She tried but was failing miserably.

As a child growing up, Cat had seen basic illnesses take the strongest person down. She lost her childhood best friend to the flu. That's why she hated sick people that knowingly spread their germs around, like this man.

This big, bald guy with an ugly, too-long gray goatee and expensive suit looked like he could afford medicine, but maybe others on the plane wouldn't be able to.

Cat debated smacking him around or knocking him unconscious. *I should wait at least until we take off, so they can't throw me out... Would they throw me off in midair?* The thought chilled her to the bone. Maybe she should wait until the plane landed.

She turned back around and told him to cover his mouth. As she did, the engine rumbled shaking the plane. The sound made her heart pound harder, so she braced herself for takeoff and let her body relax.

As expected, she did not enjoy the pressure crushing her head in as if two strong hands had her head in their grasp. But once the massive machine steadied, her pain and nausea subsided. Cat was able to relax for a while until the turbulence rattling the airplane made the panic in her flare up again. The flight attendant came to help after Hendrick pushed the assistance button above his head.

Her plump body was barely holding her pink uniform together. She wiggled over to Hendrick, "How may I help you?" She was looking at Cat's tense posture, her chestnut brown eyes opened wide. Her rosy cheeks turned a shade lighter. "Oh, I see," her small plump hand went to her mouth showing off the scribble tattoos on her wrist.

"Let's have your strongest drink and soda." Hendrick inclined his head to the woman silently telling her he had the situation under control.

The plump woman rubbed her hands on her pink uniform and pulled at her sleeves, shaking her head. "Peanuts help too," she snapped to attention, walking to the front of the plane.

"She was against us in the war," Cat's voice was breathless and panicked. Cat felt silly for making such a fuss, but she couldn't stop her body's reaction. She could always bottle up her fear.

Not this time. The situation was too much for her. Cat's younger sister had died in a plane crash a few years ago. Christina hadn't listened to mom's warning. Cat wasn't sure what happened to the plane, the massive thing just fell out of the sky.

Since then, anything that involved heights terrified Cat to the point of paralysis. The fear had even affected her job once. A few years ago, she had to go after a crazed Unnatural. Bad luck for her he chose a fifteen-floor building to run into.

Instead of trying to get out of the building, the stupid guy ran to the roof. He caused havoc in his wake, blowing things up which led four people to their death. When Cat finally reached the top of the building to trap him, she almost

had a heart attack. Nevertheless, she managed to overcome her fears and get the psycho.

Unfortunately, there was no way to get over the fear today because she was trapped inside, in a woozy hell she created in her mind. The ground was too far away. And it didn't help that the plane smelled like rotten eggs because of the emotions seeping from her pores. The sickly scent was not making other Unnaturals around her happy. The unpleasant odor repulsed even her.

"She is not our enemy any longer. You are safe," Hendrick grabbed her hand finally, giving in to the urge. She needed help and he could provide the security she needed at the moment. Cat nodded over and over.

"Can you get her under control? Her odor is giving me a horrible headache," a man from the back of the airplane grumbled to a flight attendant passing out drinks.

Hendrick was even rubbing his nose from the assaulting smell. Seeing that made her want to leave that much more. Jumping out of the plane with a parachute sounded better every second, "I need to get out of here. I shouldn't be here," Cat said, looking like a scared, cornered animal. Her green eyes were wild. They darted around looking for an exit.

Hendrick let go of her hands and grabbed her face rubbing her cheek with his thumb. Cat's gaze settled on his mesmerizing blue eyes after a few seconds, but she wasn't looking at him. She was trying to hide in herself to get away from her fear. "Actually, look at me, Kitty." When he was satisfied that her beautiful orbs focused on him, he continued,

"Ye are safe. I'll never let ye fall." He took a big gulp before continuing, "I can fly higher than this plane can soar, love. If I'm here, Kitty, ye are safe." His voice was like sweet nectar for her soul.

They both gazed into each other's eyes for a long time. The concern in his eyes and his strong hands on her made her feel safe. She relaxed, taking in a deep breath.

When he thought she could handle her emotions better he moved his hands to her shoulders, massaging. The flight attendant came back, putting down ten little bottles with cups of ice, four sodas and some peanut packages quietly, not wanting to distract either of them.

Cat was not hyperventilating anymore so Hendrick looked away to make her a drink. His large hand looked even larger as he handed her a mixed drink, "Drink up, love. We have a long flight." His voice was as sweet as he could make it.

"Will you keep-," Cat looked away, embarrassed to the point of tears. When one drop traveled down her face, she gave up asking him. She hated that he made her feel safe. Finally, she gave a fake smile and took the cold drink from him.

Hendrick lightly brushed his fingers against her cheeks, "Aye lass, I'll keep touching you." Hendrick knew what being overcome by a horrible emotion was like and in that moment a person just needs an anchor. He could be hers.

Cat gave him a real smile and did as he said, taking a big gulp of the bitter, dark drink. Ironically, she enjoyed the way the cold liquid burned going down. *I'm going to need a lot more of these.*

The rest of the flight went well. Whenever she felt her terror coming back she grabbed Hendrick's arm, which he didn't seem to mind. She was practically in his lap anyway. Most important, her sickly smell turned into more of a sweet and sour scent of intoxication, which the Unnaturals didn't seem to mind as much.

Other than that, Cat didn't remember a lot of the flight. She consumed little bottle after little bottle. If there were any other significant events, the rest was a blur.

Now that she was off the plane and sober, all she wanted to do was take a shower to get rid of the hangover yeasty odor that seemed to be oozing out of her skin. *I'm going home on a train when this is all finished. There is no way I will get back on a plane.*

On the drive to Hendrick's friend's house, Cat called Izzy to let him know what was going on. He had volunteered at the precinct before, so he knew how to get into the CIU database. If she needed him to.

Not a lot of people use computers anymore but there were a few at the precinct. Izzy sold his kidney for a laptop. He was the only other person she knew with one and asking David to break the rules twice in one day was not right. Being in Montana, Cat wasn't in her jurisdiction.

Izzy would have to do. She wasn't even sure she'd need him yet. Better to be prepared, then not.

Cat called her mom to let her know she was leaving town for a while and asked her to take care of Xena. Being so far away from Cat, the distance could cause Xena pain. Like intense, painful cramps and her mom was the best amulet maker she knew. So, she could whip something up to help Xena. She didn't belong at Cat's side at a time like this. She wasn't sure what danger awaited them.

Cat straightened her shoulders as Hendrick drove the rent-a-car into his friend Yvonne's bumpy driveway. A small blonde woman that she assumed was Yvonne stood outside waving. For some reason, Cat didn't like her. She was too pretty.

"Hello Yvonne, it's been a long time. I'm sorry it had to be under these circumstances," Hendrick said after getting out of the car and giving her a close body hug, "This lass is Cathleen. She's an investigator that's going to help us."

Yvonne gave her a bright smile. Then shook Cat's outstretched hand enthusiastically, "Call me Cat." At the touch of their palms, the brick walls of Cat's hatred crumbled. Cat could smell her lavender scent, which left her feeling calm.

She had on a light purple dress that went well with her brown eyes. They both said, "Nice to meet you," in unison. Cat didn't even hear her say her name.

Cat followed Hendrick into the house which was much more prominent from the inside. The moment her feet stepped inside a warm, happy feeling napped at her being, like a kitten drinking milk from its mom.

The walls were a beautiful sun-kissed yellow; the furniture was a glossy white with brown and green throw pillows. The same brown and green decorated the rest of the house, making Cat feel comfortable.

The only thing unsettling was her dining area. The room was huge with the same color scheme as the rest of the house, but the dining table was incredibly large. Its vibrant brown surface was wide and long, fitting at least fifty people.

Hendrick walked into the kitchen through the swinging door, so Cat moved to follow, her stomach rumbling in approval. Yvonne gently put her hand on Cat's shoulder, "Wait a few minutes, they are going to fight over the food. It might get physical depending on how hungry the men are. They only do it among themselves. Otherwise, they are house trained," Yvonne laughed at her joke. The sound was a sweet chortle. At the same time, she grabbed Cat's hand, pulling her to the bathroom.

"Is that a normal thing around here?" Cat asked and smiled to show Yvonne her joke was amusing.

Yvonne nodded and kept walking.

She let Yvonne lead the way. *That's odd, I think she is taking me to the bathroom.* She needed to take a shower anyway. There was no harm in Yvonne being nice. That was, until she turned around and reached for the bottom of Cat's shirt, ready to pull the thing over her head.

Ummm no.

"I think I can take my clothes off," Cat said smacking her hand away.

"Oh," she brought her hand to her mouth like Cat burned her, "I'm sorry. I didn't mean to upset you, I guess I'm just used to helping people. I run a halfway house for people in need," she waved a hand towards the ceiling as she spoke.

She walked away from Cat like a dog with its tail between its legs. While washing her hands, she looked into the mirror at Cat releasing a big disappointed sighed. "There are towels in here," Yvonne pointed to a shelf under the sink.

Cat looked to the already filled tub, and her curiosity got the better of her, "You bathe them?"

"Oh, I thought Hendrick told you what I am." She waved her wet hands towards Cat. "I'm a relaxer. Hendrick told me what happened on the plane, so I got fully charged for your arrival," she sounded offended.

Relaxers are Unnaturals that get their powers from the sun which explains that perfect golden skin. How their skills work always fascinated Cat, they take heat from the sun and transfer the soothing warmth into a person. The warmth manifests as calming thoughts or a replacement of negative emotions.

When they become of age, they find jobs like a masseuse or a medicine man.

Cat looked at Yvonne's hopeful gaze and crumbled again. Having a relaxer was part of her bucket list anyway. "Fine, get me naked," they both giggled and blushed a little. She tilted her head down to let Yvonne take her black shirt off.

As she stood there in her lacy gray bra Cat had an urge to fill the silence, "How are you going to do this? I can already feel the magic working," she paused her babbling when Yvonne smiled. Yet, the urge to fill the silence came back, "This is my first time. I love that you have this kind of

business; I've always wanted to do this. How long have-"
Yvonne stopped her with a hand on her mouth.

"Good Lord, calm down." She took an exaggerated
deep breath, "Feel the warmth running through your body
sweetie. Because it's your first time, your body will fight the
effect."

She did relax until she had only her underwear left to
take off. Her face was beet red and the room was thick with the
fresh potatoes scent of embarrassment she emanated.

***

"Don't worry, you can do the rest. I'll help you wash
your hair and back." Yvonne put her hand in the cooling water
and instinctively it bubbled to life.

"Cool. I wish I could do that," Cat said almost
dropping her arm from her exposed nakedness.

Yvonne turned around, so Cat could get completely
naked and jump in the bath. Cat had her arms raised, putting
her hair up, when Yvonne accidentally glanced in the mirror
and caught a glimpse of the symbol on the inside of Cat's arm.
Directly across from it were bold, beautiful, familiar marks.

Oh, great sun Gods, is that a Dragonvire symbol?

Without thinking, she turned and faced Cat, lifting her
arm forcibly before she could step into the bathtub. "What is
this?" Yvonne asked.

"Aaah! Stopp!" Cat screamed, flabbergasted, and tried
to smack her hands away.

***

"Wait. You can see it?" Cat asked, forgetting about being uncomfortable. "No one except my parents have ever been able to see the tattoo."

The big swirling shapes were something she was born with. One had fire in the middle and the other had a stone. On her pale skin the markings looked more like a tattoo than a birthmark, so she called it a tattoo.

Yvonne looked at her with her head tilted to the side and her skin crinkled around her eyes. "Yes, of course. What does it mean? I know what this side means, but what's the swirly rock in the middle?"

The two women were so immersed in the intricate markings that when the bathroom door crashed open making tons of wood chips fly everywhere, they let out a wretched scream. They leaned into each other to shield their eyes.

Gaining her composure quicker, Yvonne jumped in front of Cat's exposed naked body, shielding her from showing off her goods.

Cat's hand reached for a gun she knew she didn't have. *This is the second time, dammit. You need to get it together.*

She never took her gun from her work bag. It was too far away to be useful now.

Cat relaxed slightly when she recognized the scent of one of the men. A masculine peppermint and campfire scent. *Hendrick.*

"Where are they?" Hendrick asked, sword in hand and blue eyes looking around. He looked like he was ready to kill anything in his path. Cat looked at both men in surprise. Their shirts were ripped, and both were sporting cuts and bruises. *I guess they were hungry.*

"What the hell are you talking about? I was giving Cat a bath." Yvonne tried to explain, but she was getting so mad her skin turned red.

"Why did you scream, then?" Hendrick's friend said, putting away his sword.

Both women looked confused for a second, "Maybe when you charged me."

"Possible," Yvonne said blankly. Her mind was leaving fight or flight mode gradually. Quicker than Cat knew was possible for a relaxer, she grabbed a hanging towel to drape over Cat.

"I need to show Hendrick. Cover up." Her eyes pointed at Cat's exposed breasts.

In a frantic movement to grab the towel, Cat's embarrassment spiked and shot a fresh course of adrenaline through her. *I'm freaking naked!*

"I need this arm up, sweetheart," Yvonne said with an apologetic look in her eyes. She knew Cat had issues with nudity and she hated to do this to her, but they needed to see. "Look." She pointed at the symbols on Cat's arm and body.

"Holy Goddess you are gorgeous. I'm Jake. Nice to meet-" Hendrick's friend stopped when Hendrick slapped him in the back of the head. "Ow, what?" he finished. It made Cat even more uncomfortable. So, she took a couple of steps back.

There were too many eyes on her. The towel was like thin paper against their stares. A few faces in the hallway looked away to be polite. Everyone in the house stood in front of her.

If she weren't so intrigued by finally knowing what her tattoo meant, she would have pushed everyone out of the broken door kicking and screaming.

"Chill, Jake, don't make this worse than it has to be for her," Yvonne defended Cat. The gesture warmed Cat's heart. She had never had someone protect her before. Other than her mom. Everyone always thought she could handle things for herself. Most of the time they were right, but it still felt good to know someone cared enough to step in and defend her against their own people.

Cat wanted to bring the focus back to her tattoo, "Can you see it?"

"Of course, we see it, we aren't blind," Jake said letting a small hint of a Scottish accent show.

"Why do you bear the mark of a Dragonvire?" Hendrick interjected.

If the Goddess hadn't told her what these guys were, she'd be scared. She'd seen people get killed for being accused of things like that.

"I don't know. I was born with it." She licked her dry lips. "I've never known what the symbols meant."

"How do you not know?" Hendrick asked, his face inches away from her tattoo.

"My parents said this one is the sign of my people. I never knew exactly what it meant because they didn't know either," she replied, stepping back a few feet.

"Why didn't you get it looked at?" Yvonne asked her.

Cat was getting nervous, Hendrick wouldn't give her space. He followed after her with every step she took backward, "I tried, and then they would disappear. When I tried to find out myself, other people didn't see them." She took a deep breath before admitting the final thing.

A stinging pain slithered its way into Cat's mind. *Ow, stop, blocker.*

"There's something else. I was going to tell you this anyway. I can tell you have a blocker in the house. I can feel them probing my thoughts. Fittingly, I'll spill the beans; I know what you are."

An eruption of how, run, and kill her sounded from a few people out in the hallway. Cat didn't pay much attention to them. The death stare coming from Hendrick was her priority. The way he kept walking until he pressed her against the wall made Cat's heart hammer in her chest.

Hendrick put a hand up, silencing everyone. "Continue Kitty but be careful what you say next. I'm sure you understand why," his voice was liquid poison.

Cat did understand. If she said one wrong word, he'd kill her. He would have no choice, and she knew that, if she were a threat to his people's lives there would be no mercy. With a sour taste in her mouth she continued, "The Goddess told me to help you. She sent me on this mission to find your brother."

Someone yelled, "Lies" from the hallway.

"It started out as a rescue mission, but something changed." She stopped again, not sure if she wanted to continue with Hendrick so close to her.

His eyebrows went up, she had no choice. "Your blood is royal and whoever has him found out," she whispered, hearing squeaks and squawks behind him. Hendrick was going to say something, but she interrupted.

"No, let me finish. Because of the power of your family's blood, they are going to sell your brother to someone powerful. This individual is unknown, but they want to take over everything."

"When you say everything, you mean-" Yvonne said stepping into view next to Hendrick who was still pressing Cat against the wall with his massive body.

"From what I saw, everything means the world," Cat said with wide eyes. "Using your brother's blood, they created something that looks similar to zombies. But different. Rage leads them, and they don't eat you, they just chomp on your flesh."

"Zombies don't exist," Jake's icy voice chimed in.

"Well, there was a spell to erase their memories. That caused a mind raging anger to take over. The process hurt like hell, so I could understand why. It was like my brain was on fire. Anyway, they attacked each other, chomping on each other's flesh. That's why I say they are similar to zombies," Cat explained what she saw, her eyes pleading for them to believe her.

"Wait, what I don't understand is why you keep saying things like you were there?" said another person Cat didn't recognize. His short blonde hair looked like Yvonne's, though.

"That's because I was there. The Goddess wanted me to see and understand the true nature of what is going to happen. So, she sent me into the future. From what I saw, it's an evil bronzing spell that turns the world into a light brown horror flick," Cat said, her eyes getting glossy. *Why the hell should their approval matter, I can do this on my own.* She wasn't sure why, but she wanted them to trust her.

"I heard something like that existed when I was a child," an older woman said as she stepped into the bathroom. "It's an old spell. And it literally does change everything. The goal was to make everything the same, so there wouldn't be any more Unnaturals. Everybody would be a Natural."

Hendrick turned enough to look at the woman speaking. She was elderly, but beautifully elegant. Her kind blue eyes and long, flowing silver hair had Cat wanting to run into her arms for safety. But she thought twice when she looked deeper into those eyes. They were full of power and the way they shined against her dark skin made her eyes look mystical. Subsequently, Cat decided against it. *For all I know she's as angry as the rest.*

"Are ye sure Nan?" Hendrick asked, his voice gentle.

"Yes, and like the lass said, it takes an obscene amount of power. Something only our bloodline could give," Hendrick's Nan said as her hand gripped the teal necklace around her neck.

"Holly hell, we need to get Chris back before they use his blood. Let's get to the warehouse; we should have had seventy-two hours before the Hunters disposed of him. Now, who knows how much time is left," Jake said storming out of the room, punching his fist in his palm.

"Wait, what warehouse? And why that time frame?" Cat's shoulders relaxed against the wall. She was only slightly aware of her nakedness now. Hendrick was shielding her body enough to where she wasn't mind-numbing bashful.

Hendrick looked down at her, "Izzy called me when he couldn't get a hold of you. My people brought me up to date with what has happened. Jake and Ethan, did some investigating before we got here," Hendrick said. "They had Yvonne reenact everything and she was able to remember most of the license plate number from the van. And as for the time, that's how long it takes to fully drain us."

Wow, what do they do with them for three days? "Okay, let's go," Cat unintentionally pushed her body against Hendrick's firm one. The feeling of his muscles against her soft breast had the room filling with her sweet arousal scent. *Seriously, body?*

His eyes darkened, "You can take a shower, Kitty. Two other friends of mine are on their way," Hendrick smirked when her voice squeaked.

"She needs a bath," Yvonne chimed in.

"No time, Yvonne. We need to leave quickly," Hendrick smiled down at Cat when she thanked him.

"I'm going to wait in the kitchen." Without looking, he pointed down, quietly telling her to cover up.

Another squawk escaped her, and that potato smell masked any other emotions. Her whole body burned as if it was on fire. How could she have let fabric slip down her body? *What is wrong with me?*

Cat bit her lips nervously. "I have a question," she said, stumbling on her words, "Why do you believe me? Don't get me wrong, I'm grateful, but you don't seem like a trusting person."

***

Hendrick lifted his shirt, uncovering a mark the same as Cat's." The other mark is of the Sapphire Charms. They were our sister protectors. No one could get to the Gods with both of our kind protecting them. So, if the Gods could trust us, who am I to not trust?" He walked away quickly, not willing to talk anymore. There were a few things he needed to take care of to ensure Cat's safety.

Seventeen

HENDRICK LEFT CAT in the bathroom with Yvonne. He knew his team was already in the kitchen eating all his blasted food. That was where they always were.

He told Cat they weren't here, so she could take a shower and be ready for this mission. If she went now, her smell could attract the wrong attention. The poor lass had to drink her liver away to calm her nerves.

He had never had someone trust him like she did on the plane. The least he could do was repay her trust and let her explain things. A few years ago, he would have killed her without listening to her explanation. *If they look like a trader, they probably are,* was his motto.

To be a better leader, he needed to bring something else to the table other than protection. The way they had been living was not practical. He needed to change things somehow and being more trusting of people was a start. Who knows, maybe she could help him.

Most Dragonvires do not survive getting abducted, she could be the ticket to saving his brother. If the Goddess believed in the two of them working together, so should he.

He sighed when his palm touched the kitchen door. The way he led his people gave them the right to argue and berate him. He wasn't a fan of it though.

When Hendrick pushed open the swinging door to the kitchen, the peppery scent of roasted-to-perfection pork wafted toward him. He took a deep breath, filling his nostrils with the delicious smell. His stomach rumbled. *They better not have eaten all the meat.*

As soon as the swinging door tapped closed, everyone turned to him. Nobody missed a beat. They bombarded him with copious amounts of questions until their voices fused into one massive din of noise.

The light blue walls and dark cherry cabinets made him feel like he was walking into the ocean. He was off balance with all of them talking at once as if a riptide was trying to knock him off his feet and rush him away to parts unknown.

Hendrick made out a question that seemed to lurk on the edge of the roar of those voices, "Why the hell is she still alive?" He recognized his old friend's accent even before he saw Ethan sitting on the side of the table closest to the kitchen door.

"Yeah, she's a Sapphire. They could kill her and use her soul amulet to make that reality come true," Ethan's cousin Keanu said. His jaw was tight, and his eyes narrowed at Hendrick accusingly.

Hendrick scowled at Keanu the way a dad would to a rebellious teenager. Keanu had trouble taking orders from people. If not for Ethan whipping him into shape, Hendrick would never have trusted him.

The past couple of years Keanu had proven his loyalty and friendship by being there for everyone when they needed him. But right now, he looked like the hell maker he once was sitting in the chair agreeing with everybody's anger. He was like salt to the water washing over Hendrick, and the damn thing made his eyes sting.

"It might not even be about Chris," Jake chimed in. He didn't seem as angry as the rest. His eyes were gentle and considerate.

"She's too much of a liability, I agree, but think for a second my brothers. She might be as big an asset to us. It's not every day you find someone that speaks with the Gods." Marcus' kind and humble voice made every person think for a second. The storm of sounds quieted.

Marcus was the youngest of the bunch, so he was not haunted by the Dragonvire's past like the rest of the team. He

had never had to endure the horrifying screams of his family dying, so he trusted people more easily.

Hendrick was grateful because that brief silence that followed Marcus' comment gave Hendrick enough time to rekindle his thoughts.

He smiled when Yvonne walked into the kitchen. She must have given Cat a small calming session. "He's right." She flung her long blonde hair over her shoulder and cocked her hip like an older sister about to knock some sense into her younger siblings. "I can feel her aura, it's not evil. She wants to help."

"I felt something dark in her Yvonne," Maria's disappointed Italian voice chimed in, making the uproar wave grown massive.

"The darkness is like a hovering shadow, not a consuming one. She is good." Yvonne stood over everyone sitting down, her calming nature pushing out into their minds.

"I say bullshit. She's lying about everything. The Blaigeard wants our blood magic." Ethan stood up and his bulging arms slammed into the table. Beads of sweat broke out on Ethan's brow, and the veins in his arms pulsed with anger. He wanted her dead.

"That's enough!" Hendrick shouted, his voice echoing off the walls. Just like when he wanted his voice to calm women, the deep allure can turn into a demanding one. He watched as heads dropped and butts sat back down in their chairs. "Cat is going with us. I am certain she will help us find Chris."

"Hendrick, no disrespect my king, but are you sure you are the person to make that decision?" Maria asked. Besides Yvonne, she was the only other person in the room that wasn't a Dragonvire. She was the reason all of them could be together without being detected.

Only blockers can mask the heat of their power. Hendrick never visited his family anymore without a blocker nearby. Unfortunately, they were hard to find, which meant he didn't get a lot of family time.

"What do ye mean?" Hendrick narrowed his eyes at her. The outer rim of his orbs turned orange.

"Well, it's the month of your parent's death which always gets you a little hero crazy. We are all the same way, but you blame yours-"

"I understand that's how I've been in the past, but this is about my brother." He gave her a stern look, "Anything else? Now is the time to spill it."

Maria hesitated, the look on her face said she hoped she wasn't about to go too far with her next words, "I saw the way you looked at her, Hendrick. It's the same way you looked at Clarissa." Maria stopped and lowered her head when he put up his hand. He wasn't going to hit her. He was silencing her.

Clarissa was his previous girlfriend. He had trusted her. She got her tiny claws into him and he was blind to her flaws. The she-devil ended up drugging him to get to his blood on their one-year celebration. Once she found out what he was, she wanted to get rich by using his blood to turn things to gold.

Little did she know, the only one that could ask his blood power to do that was Hendrick himself. He never did, though. He never would. Not for all the unicorns and red lions in the world, because the price was too high. Whenever Dragonvires created gold, they had to use a piece of their soul. Consequentially, they aged more rapidly.

The Blaigeard had ended up at the end of his sword when she tried to backstab him again.

"I know you are concerned, worried even that Cat is like Clarissa. But she is not like that. Cat is our sister protector, and it would be foolish to deny her help." He put down his hands trying to convince them without using his royalty. They were his family. "She has as much to lose if people find out what she is. Izzy even said no one knows she is an Unnatural, so she has twice as much to lose. We will just have to make sure they do not get to her. Okay?" Hendrick was asking them to trust him.

He inspected his group of friends, shifting on his feet, at their culpable stares devoured him. Every eye held distrust, each jaw was clenched, nostrils flared. He looked intently at them, absently lifting his chest, waiting. He was their Alpha, but they had the right to say no.

The torturous silence was killing him. The little droplets breaking out all over decorated his skin. He couldn't remember a time when his heart ached with anticipation as much as at this moment.

Someone needs to get up and punch me or something. Physical combat was easy to deal with; the emotional stuff, not so much.

***

"Okay boss, I'm down," Marcus said, getting up to put a hand on Maria's shoulder. Marcus believed in Hendrick and would do anything for him. He was usually a good judge of character. There was something about Cat that was right to Marcus.

***

"Me too," Maria folded her arms tight to her chest. Maria trusted Hendrick with her life. She owed him everything and would do anything for him. Nevertheless, she wasn't going to let another woman hurt Hendrick.

Yvonne was next, "I'm always with you brother." She bowed her head with grace. The happiness was rolling off her in waves. Yvonne was always on his side no matter what.

***

"Me too," Jake said, "besides, she's a hottie, and we need more of that around." The girls rolled their eyes and scoffed at him. Jake was a playboy, but he was loyal. He continued, "My place is by your side, Hendrick."

Hendrick didn't want to show his emotions, so he hid behind keen eyes as if considering everyone's words. Deep inside he was dancing for joy. He never made all the right choices, but he always had his people in mind. His vision blurred, *My people still believe in me.*

Hendrick watched Ethan with strained eyes, as if he was staring at the suns' harsh gaze, not his oldest friend. No matter what, Hendrick refused to persuade Ethan in any way. If their friendship didn't hold merit for Ethan to trust him

anymore, Hendrick would take the metaphorical sword to the chest and respect his decision.

He watched, Ethan sizing him up. Hendrick could see his intelligent, introspective orbs not looking at him, but searing past his flesh into his being. They were diving into his soul, weighing its worth.

When Dragonvires cohabitate for extended periods of time they can connect with one another's spirit. Hendrick's dad used to say it was a way to make sure evil wasn't in their dragon's den, and Ethan was using that ability on him.

Hendrick lifted his chin higher, like the key to his soul was through his neck. He didn't know if Ethan knew what he was doing, but if he did, Hendrick had no qualms about letting him in.

***

Ethan's hand twitched, so he closed his hand before it was noticeable. He was torn inside. He wanted to trust Hendrick's word. Yet, he remembered all too well the kiss of betrayal a new person could give to his people. To trust a new person was the hardest thing Hendrick could ask of him.

As their souls intertwined, the sense of warm love and fierce devotion fluttered around Ethan. Everything was okay in the depths of Hendrick. Ethan was worried Cat had put a curse on Hendrick or fogged his mind somehow. There was nothing like that inside of Hendrick, though.

So, Ethan tilted his head, not quite understanding why he was doing this, but trusting he knew what he was doing. He nodded slightly and said with uncharacteristic softness, "Aye, I'm with you."

Everyone noticed a change in Hendrick's stance; he looked like a weight had been lifted off his back. The nonchalant look he gave betrayed by the light in his eyes. At this moment Hendrick was happy, and not a lot could do that these days.

To make sure of the decision, Hendrick explored the room, meeting each person's eyes. In turn, they nodded their approval without hesitation. Even the people not going with them bowed their heads.

***

Hendrick's mood lifted. In fact, it went from anxious to ecstatic so quickly as if he might float away at any second. "Okay, we leave in fifteen minutes. Be ready," Hendrick ordered. His people still had faith in him, and that's all he could ask for in his friends. Now, it was time to eat!

His brother needed him to be strong. *I'm coming Chris hold on.*

Eighteen

MARIA SLAMMED THE swinging kitchen door open. She was still frustrated with the group's discussion. If she was honest with herself, it had a lot to do with jealousy. She would never admit that though.

Marcus bumped his shoulder on hers, "Stop being a sour puss. Hendrick knows what he's doing."

She sighed, "I know, Buba. But I don't trust her."

Ethan called Marcus's name, so he hurriedly said, "Just don't be stupid." He lowered his voice, "If you do, just don't get caught." Marcus smiled and ran towards Ethan.

Maria bit her lip conflicted. When she saw Cat was still in the bathroom she made up her mind. Maria was going to take matters into her own hands.

She walked into the bathroom and slid under the blanket Yvonne must have put up to give Cat some privacy. The steam made Maria feel like she had walked into a sauna. Perfect, Cat was still in the shower. *I'll just zip in and zap her.*

Maria peeked into the shower to check on Cat. Cat was turned away from Maria, letting the water cover her face. Maria's green monster came out at the look of her flawless skin and full bottom. If Maria had beautiful curves and skin like hers maybe she wouldn't be single.

Maria thought how unfair her loveliness was; strong, confident posture, lean muscles in a voluminous cage, and gorgeous green eyes that could knock a man out if they looked too long into those mesmerizing depths. She had extra weight on her, but when Maria thought about how hard she had tried to gain weight and hadn't been able to, the rotten fruit smell of jealousy decorated the air around her.

If the skank was going with her people, she was going to be damn certain there wouldn't be any surprises later from her. She thought about waiting for Cat to come out of the bathroom where Yvonne had left her, but she couldn't risk anyone walking by. If they saw what she was about to do, they might keep her from going with them to find Chris.

I can't let that happen; I need to find him.

Most people do not know the power blockers possess. Blockers like Maria have more than just defensive abilities; they also have offensive powers.

Without thinking too long about it, she pulled the shower curtain back and jumped in. As soon as her shoes hit the water, a flying fist met her jaw. Maria was a pretty good fighter, but this woman seemed to be crazy fast like the Dragonvires had been when she trained with them.

"What the hell are you doing in here?" Cat's voice whispered in a high pitch squeak as she pressed her forearm to Maria's neck. The soft flesh was wet, so she kept slipping around.

Maria knew she wouldn't be able to best Cat after feeling her strength. So, she used her power. Maria's petite arms reached for the back of Cat's neck. One lite touch and Cat went limp in her arms.

Maria tried to rotate both of them to prevent Cat from falling. Holding her up was a lot harder than Maria expected. Her arms were already shaking from Cat's weight.

Cat was too slippery. The warm water made Maria's grip falter on Cat's neck, which meant Cat kept fighting back. Usually, once Maria latched on, they turned into non-moving dolls. In their dormant state, Maria had complete control.

But Cat's eyes were not dormant, which meant she could gain control again. They shined bright with her power. Maria pushed her fingers harder on Cat's spinal cord. After a few seconds, Cat's eyes submitted to her power. Maria gave a big sigh of relief.

"Are you here to kill us?" she asked Cat's mind. The delicate caress of her power from Cat replied *no*. Like this, Cat couldn't lie to Maria. Her power pulled the truth out of her victims.

"Are you after the Dragonvire's blood?" Maria asked, the black tar of hate soaking her heart. Maria hated that Cat looked even prettier wet. Cat's power responded again. Its weak voice only received in Maria's mind. *No.*

"Then why are you here?" She felt guilty, which only made her angrier.

The Goddess contacted me to ask if I would help save the world from the blood curse. She said if I helped, there was a better chance it would not happen. Cat's blank face made Maria feel even worse.

Maria asked the only thing she could to make herself feel better. Something was off about Cat, and she wanted to know what. "Then why do I sense something off about you? Tell me what you are hiding."

Cat didn't respond. Instead, she pushed images of that horrible night at Maria. She couldn't explain what happened to her. So, she showed her.

Maria gasped at all the blood in her mind. Her heart dropped at the pure anger, fear, and sadness pouring out of Cat. "Good Blocker god, what the hell happened to you?" Maria wasn't getting the full story, just bits and pieces, and she felt horrible at what she was doing.

Something that was pure evil had touched Cat's life, and she had been fighting it ever since. Maria did see the way

she changed when she got tired of feeling like a victim. *Goodness, you poor woman.*

Everything she saw was like a wrecking ball to Maria's hatred. Her eyes leaked with sorrow by the time she was finished, "I'm going to give you a gift," Maria leaned in to kiss Cat's forehead where her third eye would be in order to link to Cat's emotions, "Auferat."

Maria took her hands-off Cat's neck, sucking at her forehead. If anyone came in they wouldn't see what she saw. The bright blue and red colors floating to her puckered lips. The sweet taste of emotions fluffed into her mouth. Like cotton candy it melted, absorbing into her taste buds.

Maria's body began to shake. *The weight of Cat's emotions must be too much for me.* "I'm so sorry for that. I didn't understand," Maria rubbed her palm over Cat's wet hair. "I can't get rid of all those emotions, but this will help you live happier," she watched as Cat's eyes blinked awake, dazed.

"It'll only last as long as I do though, so if you are like Dragonvires and live ridiculously long, they will come back.

Cat straightened in a slow peaceful manner like she was floating. Her lips stretched into a wide smile, "Oh, my sweet Goddess, I feel so free." Tears fell down Cat's face when the humongous weight lifted from her chest. She whimpered and coughed at the same time. Cat considered Maria's soft, caring eyes, "Thank you."

Maria smiled at her, "No one deserves to walk around with that much pain inside them. If I could do it for everyone, I would."

Removing emotions takes a lot out of a blocker. The impact was like a scar on her soul. One she would wear proudly. She felt Cat's kindness and beauty. Yvonne was right. Maria was happy she was wrong; it meant hope for them all.

"I'm sorry I did that to you, Cat. I needed to make sure you weren't going to get Hendrick killed."

"Well, next time, let's try to talk it out. If I didn't feel so good, I might be angry." Both women chuckled.

"You'll feel extremely peaceful for a while. All your emotions will be extreme, though, while your body gets used to the change." Maria stepped out of the shower and grabbed a towel, so she didn't leave tracks on Yvonne's brown carpet.

Cat looked down at herself. "A few weeks with you all, and I might be walking around naked. I forgot I was naked."

Maria closed the curtain, "That's an effective way to start an orgy."

"No thank you." Cat's disgusted voice made Maria smirk.

"Don't knock it."

"I'll knock whatever I want. The last time a man touched me he ended up possessed by a demon and burned in an ally. I'm not advancing my already pathetic love life to a homicidal love life."

"Ouch, that sucks. You might have a point. No wonder I couldn't get rid of all the crap in your life. It's too massive." With that, Maria left, not wanting Cat's hyper-emotions to turn sour.

Maria had done the best she could; now it was up to Cat to prove herself to everyone else. As long as she helped them find Chris, she was happy.

Nineteen

CAT WAS A SOBBING mess when Maria left the bathroom. The tears hidden by the water cascading out of the showerhead weren't sad or scared tears. They were happy tears. She didn't feel sad or scared anymore. Her body was lighter, as if Maria had lifted a huge boulder off her shoulders.

"Wow," Cat said through a huge smile. Her laughter became hysterical. *I've never felt this good before. I feel like I can do anything.*

"Hello sweetie, Maria said you needed me?" Yvonne opened the shower curtain enough to see her face when she heard Cat sobbing. "What's wrong?"

"Nothing. I'm so happy and feel like I can fly," Cat leaned against the shower wall. Her hand pressed against her chest. The excessive thumping against her chest was like her heart getting ready to explode.

"She didn't." Yvonne whispered to herself, covering her mouth with her hand, shocked that Maria would do this. "Hendrick is going to have her head when he finds out. Let me help you." Yvonne was going to wait for Cat to get out but watching her slide down the wall with her hand on her chest scared Yvonne.

She had heard of a blocker's touch accidentally killing people, so she wanted to calm Cat down before her heart exploded. She reached for Cat, getting wet in the process, grunting. She'd forgotten about the water.

"What are you doing? Are you out of juice or something? Why is she still hyperventilating?" Maria stormed into the bathroom in some new dry black clothes. "I can feel her heart expanding in the worse way. Calm her, dummy."

"Don't call me a dummy, and I was just about to," Yvonne turned scowling at Maria. She had been working with Maria for years now, and they always seemed to butt heads.

At a youthful age, Natural Hunters murdered Maria's parents because they were helping Dragonvires hide from them. The main Dragonvire was none other than Hendrick. Her mom had a safe plan set in place if things ever went wrong. So, when the goons burst into their house, Maria ran into the safe room. Maria's mom called Hendrick with her last breath.

In a few hours, Hendrick was there to get Maria and ever since, she had been like a sister to him. Now, Maria was overprotective of him, but Yvonne couldn't believe she would go so far as to hurt Cat.

Yvonne touched Cat's wet knee, pushing away some of the water drops to grip her knee. Her hands glowed yellow and heated up like the sun. The warmth wouldn't burn her skin, but it would burn away some of the overwhelming feelings she was experiencing.

Yvonne laughed as she tugged on Cat's emotions. The tickling sensation of the happiness that emanated from Cat didn't feel right to Yvonne. There was too much of an overpowering glee vibrating off Cat.

"Whoa." Yvonne groaned inwardly. "I don't know if I can handle all this emotion." Maria tried to help by putting a hand on Yvonne's shoulder. The blocking sensation on most of the overpowering happiness helped keep Yvonne focused.

If anyone came in at this point, they would have a sight to see. There was a mystical train of energy flowing through all three women. Golds, blues, and reds snaked up their arms, "What the hell did you do to her Maria?"

***

"I helped her out. I took most of her fear and hatred away. This is not my fault; she had so much bad emotion it's making her other feelings go berserk," Maria responded, still holding onto Yvonne's shoulders, and squeezing them tight.

"We need to fix this before Hendrick finds out. You know he'll have to punish you even if he doesn't want to. You went behind his back and disobeyed an order," Yvonne's voice was low and harsh. Maria knew she was right, but after feeling what was buried inside Cat, she couldn't be sorry for her actions. She had helped Cat, and to her, that's all that mattered.

After what felt like forever, Cat's breathing settled into a steady rhythm and her face darkened to a more normal glow. Maria let go of Yvonne and stumbled back, winded; she let Yvonne finish the calming by herself. Cat looked up through her wet, dark hair that stuck to her face. "What in all of Hades was that?"

Maria interjected before Yvonne could speak, "That was your mind not understanding the new you." She knelt to be on the same level. "You had so much nastiness and gunk clouding your emotions that when I took most of your fury and fear away, it overcompensated on your other emotions."

"Why did it feel like my heart was going to explode?" Cat asked, putting her hand on her heart again.

"Because it was," Maria said, giving her a pointed look.

"Well, we were able to fix it, that's all that matters," Yvonne's soothing voice centered her. She turned off the water finally, now that Cat could be without her constant touch. Cat looked at Yvonne, and her sweet loving smile helped clear her mind.

She reached out her hand to Cat, "How do you feel?"

"I feel a lot better, thank you." She paused and looked at Maria, "Thanks to both of you. I am feeling great." Cat's eyes opened wide when she looked around, remembering she was still naked in the shower.

"Alright, we will be in the kitchen making you something to eat if you need anything else," Maria pulled on Yvonne's arm.

"I was going to help her get dressed and-" Yvonne wasn't able to finish because Maria interrupted her.

"No, you are not. Can't you see the girl is tired of us seeing her naked? I haven't even seen her with clothes on for goodness sakes. I'm pretty sure she wants to be alone." Maria pulled Yvonne away again. This time she let Maria move her. Yvonne had a bad habit of thinking everyone wanted her help.

Maria saw Cat mouth, "Thank you." She nodded her head and let the warm, pleasant feeling of helping another person wash over her. She stayed with the Dragonvires not just out of loyalty, but to help people. Now she wanted to help Chris.

She couldn't imagine what they were doing to him. The thought made her vision blurry thinking about it. A few weeks before he was taken, Maria fell for Chris. No one knew because the group's blocker was supposed to be off-limits.

Just in case the relationship went wrong, Dragonvires could not afford to lose the only thing keeping them hidden from Hunters. So, when Hendrick's deep voice yelled, "We are leaving in two minutes," Maria was relieved. She needed to find Chris. Her heart couldn't take the blow of losing another person.

Twenty

CAT GRABBED HER phone from one of the many pockets in her black leather jacket. The tiny thing buzzed in her hand, *Rebecca again?* Between her and her mom, the stupid phone wouldn't shut up.

"You're going to want to leave that in the car," Yvonne commented next to her as they walked to the big black van parked in front of the house.

"I know, if I didn't think I'd get a lecture from these two I'd answer, but I need to stay focused," Cat said as she pressed the side button and turned off the phone. "I'll call them later. Getting chewed out in front of everyone does not sound like fun." Cat climbed into the vehicle smiling. Yvonne snickered and followed behind her.

Cat's eyes roamed around, the dark gray interior was dulled with age and had cut marks all around covered up by duct tape. However, the seats looked clean and cozy like they put in new ones. She went to the back, so she would feel comfortable.

Cat was not a fan of people sitting behind her. Images of hands wrapping around her neck or a knife getting pressed to her throat made her paranoid. She was able to relax with a wall behind her. Or in this case the back doors.

The moment Cat sat down, Jake and Marcus jumped on the spot next to her and wrestled each other for the seat. While two men up front mumbled about how Cat wasn't even that sexy, so they needed to knock it off. They thought she would take their fighting as a compliment, but she was embarrassed more than anything. She hated that potato smell.

Maria told her that her other emotions would intensify since the dark feelings were gone, and she hadn't been kidding. The way she was embarrassed right now she might as well have been naked again in front of everyone.

If Hendrick's Nan hadn't stepped in, Cat was sure she would have been in emotional overload again. This time the trip wouldn't be as pleasant.

Hendrick's Nan peeked her head through the open van door and said, "Jake and Marcus, move, Yvonne and Hendrick will be sitting next to Cat."

Yvonne smiled and eagerly joined them in the back. "I like to sit in the very back, so I'm not bombarded by everyone's aura, remember?" Yvonne wrapped her arm in Cats. Cat's squished posture relaxed in the seat. Yvonne was a nifty woman.

That relaxation would help her during the long two-hour trip in the van. Even though they were on their way to rescue Hendrick's brother, all this was like a road trip with friends. The feeling was blissful to Cat. She's never had so many friends.

When everyone was in their seats, Cat was grateful she'd had a shower now that she was inside the packed van. She couldn't believe how hot it was in here. She was glad Hendrick told Maria to dwindle their power heat capacity. The area around them cooled down.

Once that was over she was happy with the chosen seats. Ethan was driving, and Keanu was in the passenger seat. Both men had the same dry personality and chestnut brown eyes from what she'd noticed. Other than that, they were complete opposites.

Ethan was a tall, dark-skinned man built like Hendrick. His short dark hair and sharp features put Cat on edge. The fact that he stayed away from her like she had a contagious disease made it easier.

On the other hand, Keanu, with his red hair, short stature, and soft features was pleasant enough. He introduced himself, but that was as far as he went. She didn't think they were going to have a complete conversation anytime soon. He stayed close to Ethan most of the brief time she observed him.

Maria, Jake, and Marcus were in the seat in front of Cat. They were the jabberers of the bunch. And the ones who got all the games going. Games like I spy with my eye and alphabet with license plates which didn't work too well because cars were rare, but there were a lot of wagons, so that ended up changing to what type of wood is the wagon, and a game where they named diverse types of foods.

Cat thought it weird, how everyone seemed so calm.

Yet, she guessed, with all the running and fighting for their lives, they learned how to cope with all the crap and enjoy the little stuff. Cat smiled at each of them, wishing she could wrap them all up in a hug and keep them safe.

She already liked Maria for helping her but watching how full of life she was with Marcus made Cat like her even more. They were like children with each other.

It's hard to find joy in a world where friends are hunted down. *I'll have to get the secret from her later.*

Her short black hair and small frame looked odd next to Marcus, though. He towered over her. His blonde hair and kind eyes had even Cat coming out of her shell to play games with them.

The only one she was awkward around was Jake, and that's because all the winking he was throwing at her. The funny part was, he was an attractive man. Ear length black hair and a soft glowing smile on a muscular frame would be any girls dream man, but she didn't see him that way.

Cat looked around, loving the beautiful trees passing by, but she couldn't help herself from studying everyone. It was hard to decide who was the best-looking person in the group, although, Hendrick was more her type.

Everyone had the timeless beauty companies try to manufacture in bottles for a profit. They were all so different, and without the heat, in the car thanks to Maria, no one would guess the prize the van had inside.

After a couple of hours of games, Marcus showed off his abs. In the middle of his show Hendrick's soothing voice broke the conversation, "This is the turn, mate." Marcus's brown hair flung forward as his lean body was thrown back.

Ethan pulled the steering wheel to the left jerking all the passengers around. The dark gray road must have suffered a few battles during the war because the shadowy surface was covered with the brutal memory. The cracks and potholes were massive and scattered everywhere. Driving fast on the road would have shredded the tires.

Cat's heart hammered in her chest in anticipation. When she saw the huge sign hanging from a black, eerie, three-story building, her heart almost stopped beating entirely.

A Dollhouse factory.

Her throat went dry and her hands shook uncontrollably. She sucked in her emotional episode before everyone noticed. *Dang it Maria. Couldn't we have sucked the defective stuff out another day. I'm freaking out here.*

"Alright lass?" Hendrick said, almost inaudibly. She shook her head to make him shut up. If she spoke or he pushed the matter, she might break.

It had to be dolls. I can't stand those no blinking bastards. A chill ran through her body as she thought about sleepless nights because of those prying eyes staring at her. She used to cover her head at night to get a little rest.

At an early age, with the end of the war coming about, Cat and her parents had moved in with her grandparents. Unnaturals attacked their neighborhood, so they didn't have a choice.

At first, she loved living there. She still had milk and cookies before bed sometimes. But the happiness didn't last. Cat's grandma, before she passed, used to collect grade A designer dolls. When she could no longer walk around her bedroom, she stuffed them in Cat's room.

One by one, they got out of the van to make sure the area was clear. Cat didn't know why they thought no one could see them. The sun was bright, and the ground was painted white, so the sea of black clothes getting out of a black van was bound to get some attention. Hopefully, no one was home. *Then we can get our black clothes wearing butts out of here.*

"Scared, pussycat?" Hendrick taunted in Cat's ear as he helped her out of the van. Cat glared at him while flipping him the bird.

"Why, do I always get an urge to punch your face in when you talk? Yes, I'm fine." Cat wiped her leather pants and black shirt off like she was rolling around in the dirt. She

figured keeping her hands busy would prevent them from
shaking.

"Good, because you're my partner," Hendrick looked
at her with a smugness tenting his lips and eyes.

"I wanted Cat to be grouped with me," Jake said,
frowning like a wounded child. "I promise to make it worth
your while," he coughed in his hand when Hendrick raised an
eyebrow, "Later that is." He leaned in close to Cat and wiggled
his eyebrows.

Marcus approached. He walked with a limp that most
guys thought was cool. Considering both of them were
awkward in their movement she had to guess this was for her
benefit. Little did they know it had the opposite effect on her.

"No, she should be with me. I'm stronger than you,"
Marcus showed his bulging arms flexing his muscles.

"In your dreams. It's not how big you are; it's how you
use your strength," Jake retorted, waving him off. Cat wasn't
sure who jumped first, but they both ended up on the floor
smacking each other.

Hendrick grunted and walked over to them. In one
quick move, Hendrick banged their heads together and
separated them. "Stop embarrassing yourselves. This is about
Chris, not silly games. Now let's move on before you get
flogged, mates." He walked away, but his tone held a power
that couldn't be ignored.

Both Marcus and Jake's faces were bright red, especially
where their heads had slammed into each other. Hendrick
ignored their grumbling.

Everyone separated into small groups. Hendrick and Cat had the main floor with all the finished dolls. Ethan and Maria headed for the top level with the doll heads. The middle floor housed all the limbs, and that's where Jake and Yvonne had the pleasure of going. Marcus and Keanu got the basement with the defective dolls.

"I hate dolls," Cat mumbled to herself, ducking under their little bodies stretched out everywhere. *Where is a torch when I need one?*

Hendrick chuckled, "You never had a doll as a child, Cat?" Hendrick's large body moved with silence and grace around all the obstacles in the room, both he and Cat were trying to stay hidden just in case. Hendrick could not feel anyone, but people could be hiding their presences with an amulet.

"Yes, in fact, I had way too many. I hated their beady eyes staring at me. They would follow me around with them." A shiver ran up Cat's spine as she saw the dark black holes of their eyes watching her like they did when she was a child.

"All that is missing is a rocking chair," Hendrick turned to her and gave her a proud gaping mouth grin. When she just blinked at him, he sighed, "I forgot, you were not around before the war when television was so popular."

"Well, are you going to tell me?"

"The story of the rocking chair?" He gave her an astonished glance back, "Are ye sure?" Cat nodded impatiently. "There isn't much to tell. It was a horror movie about a

murderous doll. When he was in a rocking chair, the wood would move on its own. Definitely a creepy movie."

"Your storytelling sucks, but with this one I'm glad. I don't need nightmares about dolls rocking in my house," Cat pushed away a doll head sticking out from one of the many bends.

"Don't worry, you won't have to dream about their pleasant faces, I'll get a dozen for you and little chairs too," Hendrick gave a quiet, pleased chuckle.

"You better not," Cat said a little too loudly, making both their heads duck into their shoulders. Cat gritted her teeth together and shined a contorted upside down apologetic smile at Hendrick.

"Don't worry Kitty, I'll protect you from the big bad dolls," Hendrick said, grabbing her hand.

Cat jerked away from his hand. "Stop that!" She backed up into a large bucket of dolls that seemed to reach out and grab at her leather pants. "Aaah!" With an urgency, she moved closer to Hendrick.

She straightened her shoulders next to him, "If you want to hold my hand I guess I should let you this once," Cat hissed, wiping her hands. She hated showing weakness, but that's all she seemed to be doing around Hendrick. Cat's pride was a bitter mess. But her pride could shut up right now. She wouldn't have let go of his hand for anything.

"That's very kind of you, lass," Hendrick took her hand, and with his thumb, he made circles on her cool flesh. They kept moving. His smile got bigger as her grip tightened.

"Why do you have such a mix accen-" Cat tried to ask, but he interrupted.

"My mother was from England and my father was from Scotland. When I get uncomfortable or too comfortable, my blended accent comes out. I learned quickly, accents cause too much attention. But the habit is hard to break."

Creeaak.

"What was that?" Cat gripped Hendrick's arm. "Dammit. I hate this place, let's go get your brother and skedaddle."

"It's probably just an open window, lass. Let's try to keep our wits about us, okay," Hendrick kept her close to him. As much as he wanted her to stay calm, he needed to remind himself to stay calm as well. Something didn't feel right in here.

Tap, tap, tap.

The pitter-patter couldn't have been a rat unless these rats ran on two legs. Maybe his eyes were playing tricks on him as well because the shadows crept closer.

"What is it?" Cat whispered. She stopped moving when she saw his body language go defensive. Almost like a cats' fur spiking up, his shoulders did the same. Cat couldn't hear anything, but she went on high alert.

He didn't say anything, just put his finger to his mouth to silence her. He pointed straight ahead to keep them moving. Hendrick didn't want to scare Cat, so he didn't tell her anything, he led them forward. He was hoping that was the right choice.

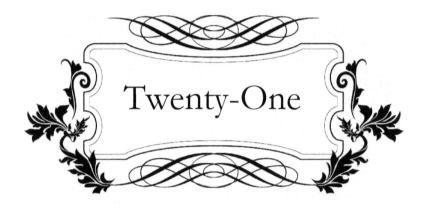

Twenty-One

HENDRICK'S STOMACH clenched at the sound again. *What the bloody hell is that?* His senses went on high alert. He couldn't quite hear what was going on in the distance, so he tapped into his vampire beast and let it ripple through him, polishing his skin and lengthening his teeth. He loved the feeling of his beast.

The sleek vibrations were different from his dragon beast; he was more wired with his vampire side. Like he could run a hundred miles because he wanted to.

The exotic and thrilling power coursing through his veins took over making him feel youthful. He needed to be careful his vampire beast didn't make him stupid though. The beast already made him more arrogant, so he'd have to watch that, but right now, he needed the accelerated hearing his vampire side provided.

The amped up speed that came along with the power he might need, as well. He could hear a caterpillar pushing its way out of its cocoon from a distance and be at its side before the thing made it halfway through. Hendrick smiled, thinking about all the things he loved about his vampire.

Shut up scoundrel and pay attention. He argued with his beast. Hendrick's head twitched to the right following a sound his sensitive hearing picked up. *What's that?*

He slowed his stride when a mystical texture in the air caught his attention. The humidity and air pressure dropped making the room hard to breathe in. *Why do I feel like I'm trapped in a box?* His eyes kept darting into every shadowy corner expecting a Hunter to pop out.

His vampire beast didn't like how claustrophobic the room had gotten. The ghostly feeling made his skin glisten with worry. Contrary to widespread belief that vampire's hangout in cemeteries or hide in the shadows at night waiting for a tasty morsel to fall in their lap, they are actually the life of parties and the ones showing off for all the girls.

The fact that it was so dead in here was the reason his vampire was so edgy. The feeling prickled at his body like static electricity making his hair stand at attention.

Cat noticed Hendrick's posture change, so she leaned in closer to him, "Does it feel like someone sucked all the cool air out of the room. Or is it just me?"

Hendrick wanted to keep the mood light until they didn't have to, so he smirked at her, "Going through the change so soon, puppet?" he pushed out his pheromones after. Hearing her heart hammer in her chest was distracting and this would ease her worry.

"Bite me," she retorted. Her remark only made Hendrick smile. He loved that she could keep up with his sarcastic personality, most women got offended.

"Only if you ask nicely," he taunted her, enjoying the way her heart skipped a beat. It had been a long time since he had the pleasure of biting into flesh. The sweet feel of his teeth piercing tissue made his senses change. Instead of keeping his eyes on the shadows, they were on Cat now.

Everything inside of him wanted to feed on her. He was like a junky wanting another fix as he salivated in anticipation.

In addition to the speed and increased hearing abilities, there were other perks as well. The pheromones he secreted to allure his prey were a huge perk in his job and a plus when he was hunting. He also could feel on an enticing level because of his skin changing. So, someone grazing their finger over his flesh was like lightning shooting through his veins. But that wasn't always a good thing, and it didn't make for the best warrior.

Unfortunately, his two beasts could not exist at once. He had to choose which one he wanted. Did he want amplified speed and hearing from his vampire? Or did he want intensified vision and strength from his dragon—who was a much better warrior? This was the question he asked every time he went into battle. Hendrick chose his vampire to be able to listen and to calm Cat.

He stretched out his hearing which came back with nothing. Abnormal for a warehouse, there should be bugs or rats roaming around. The only sound decorating the room was like little feet. Somehow different, though, like the sound was recorded and not actually happening. He bit the inside of his cheek in frustration. Something terrible was going to happen, he could sense an eerie presence of evil. The place was too quiet.

Regardless, if they wanted to challenge him now, he was ready. His shoulder twitched a few times telling him his beast was in full force and ready to attack.

He groaned at himself, loathing how his thoughts became hazy as blood-lust clouded them and his fingers twitched slightly. Every time he had too much of his beast's adrenaline pouring through him that happened.

Hendrick struggled to keep his vampire under control as they walked along the path. The free spirit inside of him wanted to run, be free and bite shit, not be quiet and alert.

Stay focused, I need to find Chris.

"I think I'll pass. I'd rather visit a gynecologist than do that," Cat said, not looking at him. She was still looking around, oblivious to his change.

Her words calmed his beast a little, "You've never been bitten by a Dragonvire have you?" He looked at her with wide,

astonished eyes. He remembered a time when people would travel great distances to be considered being bitten.

"Why do you look so surprised? Did you peg me for a Dragonvire whore or something? It's not like I know tons of them." Cat tilted her chin down and let her forehead lean toward Hendrick like she wanted his thoughts to jump into her brain.

Hendrick smiled. He had never seen her forehead crinkle so hard. "Nothing, lass."

Now, she was getting annoyed, "What?"

He looked at her to make sure she really wanted to know, he shrugged and continued, "Dragonvire venom is an aphrodisiac. If I bite you, it'll be more enjoyable than the gynecologist. I promise." The way he looked her up and down made the heat in both their bodies rise.

His eyes were burning holes into Cat's skin everywhere he looked. She understood what he was saying. *He wants to bite me.* Her eyes widened and her cheeks blushed cherry red. "Oh." She paused to think, "Oh." She let out a nervous squeaky laugh, then smiled, which made her face all the redder.

"Alright there, puppet?" he said, enjoying himself as he watched her blush up a storm. He didn't know why, but his face got hot too, like they had shared a secret between them.

Cat tried to hide her embarrassment, but that dark potato stink clouded around her anyway. Which only made things worse. *Betrayed by my own scent.*

She had worked with the worst kind of perverts and knew how to handle them, but with Hendrick, the things he did were different. She couldn't help herself. Every time she was near him her heart fluttered like the muscle had sprouted wings and wanted to be free from her chest to be in his arms.

Her embarrassment lifted, and a warm, pleasant smile stretched her lips. Her heart sounded like her cat Xena. The first time Xena laid eyes on Cat she flipped out pushing against her crate in hope Cat would touch her. If that wasn't a good omen, Cat didn't know what was. She could feel her calming touch now.

"What ye smiling for?" Hendrick asked. He could hear the way her heart calmed, and her body relaxed.

She looked into Hendrick's sensual gaze as she walked ahead of him, distracted by her sudden happiness. She wasn't paying attention to her surroundings and her booted foot tripped on something. Cat not so gracefully tumbled to the floor as if someone lassoed her neck and pulled her down.

***

Hendrick mentally slapped himself on the forehead knowing he'd let his vampire beast distract him after all. He reached for Cat as she tripped forward, grabbing her arms, and turning her around, "I got ye, lass."

I should have been paying attention, not distracting her at a time like this.

He noticed the thin, clear wire she snapped as it traveled up the wall. The sound of the loose wire waving around reminded Hendrick of an angry snake. *I hope my mistake doesn't cost me, my brother.*

Twenty-Two

WHEN CAT TRIPPED over the wire, she knew she had messed up. *Dammit it all to Hades' wicked flame, I am the stupid partner that trips over a booby trap.* If her old partners could see her now they'd piss in their pants from laughing so hard.

If that wasn't bad enough, here she was in a total damsel in distress pose in Hendrick's arms. "What did I just do?" Cat looked up at Hendrick's concerned expression and any feeling of hope that she didn't do a major screw up was gone. Who knew his face could make so many wrinkles?

He must think the worst of me. They both stood unmoving, afraid if they moved, things would get worse. Hendrick was trying to find the wire's end game. He spotted it before the cable released a cup full of blood. The big ball of red liquid dropped down, heading for a bucket of clear, steaming water.

Hendrick knew what that was, "No!" he screamed, making ripples of energy splash at Cat's skin like he had flicked water at her. "If the blood makes it into the water a curse will be activated." He ran for the steaming liquid. With his speed, he could probably make the distance despite his destination being halfway across the room and up on a bunch of wooden crates stacked in a pyramid.

Cat clung to Hendrick's body as he ran. Halfway there, she managed to jerk him back as a wall of flame spiraled to the ceiling. Cat threw him to the ground and landed on top of him. She heard the red liquid splash like the bucket was right next to her.

She rolled off Hendrick. A bucket of pink water was leaking pink fog. The way the mystical fog slid down the pyramid was beautiful. Cat shamefully enjoyed the beautiful silent dance the fluffy pink clouds were making. The lethal waves of fog were terrifying and mesmerizing at the same time.

"That's not good," Cat stood up, eyes blinking rapidly. Like she had just been staring at the sun. She was happy, though, she finally had her weapons with her in the time of need. "I'm not sure what the fog has in mind, but let's keep moving. We aren't going to find your brother lying on the floor." She groped for her sidearm to make sure the smooth metal was still there.

Hendrick followed, pulling out his sword first, which made Cat smile. She opened her leather jacket, so she could have access to her other weapons and whip her gun out if anything came out of the fog. "Right you are, lass," Hendrick admired the arsenal she held and the curves underneath.

The pink smoke overflowed, covering the floors, and traveling up the walls. "I don't like how this stuff is surrounding us," Cat said, moving along the open path. The muscles in her neck throbbing from the stress building up.

She was scared out of her mind with all these creepy dolls around, and the thick, horrible pink fog seeping up the walls. Now they had to wait to see what the curse had in store for them. All of it was enough to give her a heart attack.

Dammit all to Hades, Maria, you've made me a scaredy-cat!

Hendrick ignored her and pointed at a room in the back of the building. The three white walls forming a box room looked like an add-on, "I bet that's where he is."

"If he is here," Cat remarked. She had a feeling Hendrick wasn't going to accept his younger brother not being here. She could tell by the hope in his eyes. They reminded Cat of a lost puppy encountering a human. A piece of his heart would break if he wasn't here.

Her sympathy intensified like the rest of her roller-coaster emotion overload she has been having because of Maria. This was not fun. When she was scared, the fear was like acid to her blood, when she was mad, the anger was like a hot iron bar to her flesh, now this sympathy was like an ulcer bursting in her throat. She'd had enough of this. *Freaken Maria, how am I supposed to work like this?*

A movement caught Cat's attention snapping her out of her sympathy invasion. She swung around, gun in hand, arms straight as she aimed for anything that moved. "Are you okay lass?" Hendrick asked. His body was stiff and angled forward, protecting her back.

"Yeah, I thought I saw something move," her eyes were squinting into the dark shadows that seem to eat the light. Another movement from the opposite direction caught both their attention. "There it is again. You saw it, right?"

"Aye lass," he knew something was on the move. The footsteps didn't sound recorded, and there were a lot more feet. Cat turned back around, taking up the rear as they moved along.

They were more than halfway to the room when Hendrick stopped, making Cat bump into him. "Hey, what's up?" She looked over her shoulder.

Hendrick didn't respond; he froze in shock. Right in front of him was a little body. Its plastic frame had on a pink sundress, its skin was milky and the blonde curly hair that made her look like an angel. All except those red eyes; they were pure evil.

"Kitty, I can't believe what I am seeing but-" Cat interrupted him before he could finish.

"No, you won't believe what I'm seeing," Cat said, her voice shaky and high-pitched. Their backs pressed together, so he could feel her trembling. Without thinking twice, he flipped her over his arm, switching places with her.

His eyes shot out from his head at the sight of thousands of the same blonde dolls crawling out of the tubs. There were a few antique dolls with fluffy cotton bodies and rigid plastic limbs. Those dolls had a tough time standing up, so their limbs flopped around as the dolls tried to get to Cat and Hendrick.

"That's not possible," Hendrick whispered breathlessly, the sword in his hand wavering a bit.

"I hate to ruin the moment, but the fog isn't sticking to the walls anymore, it's coming back down," Cat said while shooting the doll in front of their path.

Take that, demon cunt.

She laughed when three more stepped toward her in a line. Their bodies didn't move right. They looked mechanical.

Bang!

She shot all three at once. "Let's move. We need to get to higher ground," Hendrick barked, stepping closer to Cat. Like a set of siamese twins, they moved together as a unit.

Hendrick's huge sword clanged against the heads of the dolls, making them pop off or shatter. The whistle from the speed of his moving sword reassured Cat. And her bullets soaring through the air gave her excited goosebumps. *We could pull this off.*

They reached the tower of carts in time. The pink fog pushed against the boxes trying to coat everything in its devouring path. "I might be able to stop this; can you keep them off me?" Hendrick shouted to be heard over the dolls chattering teeth sound.

She snapped her head to look at him, mouth gaped open. She watched his pleading eyes and sucked in her fear, "Yeah, I got this, just keep it short," Cat turned around. If the dolls had figured out how to climb up, she'd be screwed. She took a big breath of air noticing they were still having trouble and for some reason, the fog wasn't rising anymore.

Hendrick ran up the rest of the tower. Cat didn't know what he planned, she hoped it was good.

The damn dolls climbed over each other to get to Cat. Their mouths clicking as they opened and closed, "Alright, here we go."

Bang, bang, bang!

Her gun went off, taking multiple dolls down at once with each shot. Over and over she did this, using her skills to keep them at bay. But there were too many of them and those tiny sharp teeth were piercing into her skin.

The minutes felt like hours, she was knocking them off with her feet and shooting their little heads off. "Ow! The little shits are biting me." Their teeth must be sharp because they were penetrating through her leather boots. *Dammit, not the boots!*

After a few minutes, Cat heard Hendrick saying, "Just a little longer Kitty."

Cat looked at him as he sliced open his arm from the wrist to the elbow. Thick crimson blood gushed out, "What the hell are you doing?" Cat didn't watch him long, though, sharp teeth bit into her legs. "Aaah!" *I'm getting tired of being chewed on.*

Bang!

Her last magazine was almost empty.

"Well, I'm running out of weapons, and I can't feel my legs anymore. So, hurry." Her voice cracked.

Click.

Her bullets finally ran out. "Dang it," she could feel Hendrick's worried gaze on her.

Okay, time for the big guns.

In a typical situation showing her power was not an option, but this was an exception to her rules. She could die if she did nothing and let the dolls chew on her.

Besides, what did she care if Hendrick knew she could perform spells, he already knew she wasn't a Natural. That was more than most knew about her.

Because it is rare, and he could use it against you. An angry voice deep inside of her whispered. "Shut up, there's no way I'm dying to keep the secret," Cat muttered to herself. She would have to deal with the consequences later.

With her right hand, she pushed out her power. The sweet taste of lavender splashed in her mouth and the intense electricity coursing through her body begged to be released. "Volant," she flung tons of the little doll bodies into the air. She heard Hendrick behind her mumble something like blimey.

She kept using minor incantations to send any doll that came near her flying into the wall. But one after another, their little bodies kept coming for her. Their sharp nails grazed her skin as they somehow learned to jump.

With the left hand, her mystical voice recited, "Congelare," and a few dolls holding sharp things in their little hands froze in mid-attack.

Cat swayed as the room spun, *Whoa, that was a strong one.*

After a few minutes, Cat staggered around. "Oh no, crap!" Her body got heavy and her legs quivered under the stress. She wanted to collapse from her exhaustion.

Her vision blurred. *Uh-oh,* she pushed herself too hard. Everything moved in slow motion…

The stupid things were still coming.

She put a hand to her knee and said, "Ignis," one last time. *If I must die fighting, so be it.* Her body went limp. She was like a loser in a Mortal Combat game and at any moment a deep voice was going to announce, *Finish her.*

She tried to at least control her landing and go straight down. Her body wasn't having any of it, though. Her body was directing her right into the deadly pink fog.

Her soul was too tired from using her power to do anything but fall. She screamed in her head as she fell but nothing came out. The pink fog laughed at her as she dropped, opening its mouth to devour her like everything else.

Cat closed her eyes refusing to watch herself die. When her descent stopped, she opened her eyes. She was inches away from its stinging depth. *Holy hell.*

Something firm on her body pulled her away from the sea of pink. She looked up.

"I've got ye, love," Hendrick swooped her up in his arms and rested her head on his chest.

"You can fly," she smiled. Her voice sounded like a pathetic whisper as if she smoked fifty packs a day.

She opened her eyes again; they stunk and begged to be shut. Hendrick looked down at her. He was holding onto a thick brown rope that hung from the ceiling. "Maybe not," she said, and closed her eyes again.

"The dolls are dying, love. I mixed my blood in the potion and overturned the curse by casting my own. But, the fog is still rising. I have lost too much blood. I cannot hold us up with my power." He shook her in small gentle waves to focus her fluttering eyelids.

"Water," Cat tried to say, but her throat wouldn't let the word form loud enough for anyone to hear. Hendrick had to put his ear to Cat's mouth.

"Did you say water?"

She licked her lips with her last bit of energy, pushing through the pain to talk. Her movements were slow, and her eyes would barely stay open. She took a deep breath trying to spit out her words, "You need water to release the poison?" Cat could taste copper on her tongue and smooth liquid rising in her throat.

"Brilliant," he looked around for a few seconds. *Perfect.*

He slapped her cheek gently to get her awake, "Can you use your power to activate the sprinklers, Kitty?" He hated putting saving them all on her, but he didn't see any other way. She was the only one that could save them both.

"I can try." She lifted her weak shaky head. The water sprinklers were several feet away.

The pink fog sizzled Hendrick's boots. "Hurry lass," he pulled his legs up higher on the rope. The other sliced and bloody arm held Cat but his grip on her was weakening.

She whispered the spell, but nothing happened. "It's okay love. You rest I'll-"

"Shut up, so I can build up my strength." Cat stiffened

Cat could feel a power source, so she pulled on the orange glowing static. She opened her eyes after a few seconds, and she was grasping Hendrick's head. Her fingers were pushing their way through his soft hair.

"What are ye doing lass?"

"I don't know, but it feels right."

***

If things were different, he would have said something charismatic, but the fog was up to his ankles and sting through his leather pants. He weakened as if the fog was sucking the power out of him. The drowsiness was coding his brain. Soon he would lose control of his grip.

To distract himself, he focused on Cat's face. The beautiful flesh was compelling enough to pull him back to the matter at hand. When the vibration of her power prickled his skin he got concerned, "Kitty?"

She turned away, almost falling out of Hendrick's grip and pointed her finger at her target. Her soft dark hair was floating around her face, framing the shining teal eyes as she screamed the word, "Ignis!"

Twenty-Three

HENDRICK'S MUSCLES tensed at Cat's dead weight collapsing in his arms.

Whatever she had done, worked. Better than he expected. Instead of one sprinkler going off, they all went off at once, pouring water onto the pink fog.

He sighed as the fog began to disappear, "Thank the Gods."

Hendrick smiled as he looked at Cat; he squeezed her tighter despite his aching arm. "The bloody woman did it." He stepped onto one of the cubes carefully. The horror house could still be active.

Hendrick waited for the fog to disappear with shaky arms. His left arm was still burning from where he sliced the skin open to deactivate the curse. The counter curse was a long, arduous process that he needed time to finish.

He was glad Cat was with him, if any of his people were here with him they probably wouldn't have had survived. When Dragonvires lose blood, they lose their strength and power. So, he needed someone with abilities like her to have been successful.

He smiled down at her disheveled body. *Only she could have pulled this off.*

"Right love, let's finish this," Hendrick said, stepping down from the top cube while kicking off what was left of the dolls. As he made his way down, he put his bloody palm to Cat's lips to heal her.

Her skin and muscle in her legs was almost gone. A shiver went through Hendrick as he looked at her once flawless skin. Now, she was full of bites and boils from the fog.

It was amazing she lasted as long as she did. Hendrick felt guilty, so he was glad his blood would fix all those marks.

A soft female voice whispered as his foot touched the last step. *Wait, Dragonvire.*

Hendrick wasn't sure if he was imagining the soft command or if the voice was real. When the soft soothing voice continued, he listened. Listening didn't seem to help, though, because he didn't understand what she was saying. So, he repeated the word out loud.

"Mostrati," he said, unsure of his pronunciation. His face scrunched up trying to say the word right. The unfamiliar word left his mouth and he fell back covering his face as a huge silent explosion erupted right in front of him. He stumbled back.

Hendrick could feel the warmth from the flames. He didn't breathe until the blaze collapsed on itself. *What the bloody hell was that?*

A loud crash on his left had him grabbing for his sword from his back and flinging the weapon at the next threat. His nerves were shot. With the blood loss and something trying to kill him every five seconds stressed didn't even come close. He steadied the shakiness.

"Hey dude, it's Marcus and Jake." He stuck his empty hands out from behind the wall. "You almost got me."

"You can come out," Hendrick grumbled.

"Hendrick you'll never believe what happened," Jake said, darting out. Followed by a slower Marcus. Then, Maria and Ethan walked up behind him dragging an injured Keanu.

"I'm sure I can guess," they all stopped, looking around.

"Of all the tricks of Hades, there must be thousands of dolls scattered around," Maria whispered, as her lower lip trembled.

Jake cleared his throat, "Okay, maybe you do know what happened," Jake finished, backing up absently while trying to put some distance between him and the dolls.

Hendrick rushed over when he noticed Keanu, "What happened?" he asked clenching Cat a little tighter to his chest. He could feel his heart pounding against Cat's cheek.

"I'm not sure, Keanu hasn't fed with his vampire beast in a while. I think that's why he is not healing," Marcus stepped next to Jake, answering Hendrick's question. His eyes were wide, and he sounded like he was panting.

The ache in Hendrick's chest expanded. He tried to stay calm for his people. If the leader freaked out, everyone would. He could freak out later.

Maria chimed in when Hendrick looked her way, "This last week my neighborhood was attacked by vampires, so I've been taking vampire poison in my coffee. Just in case one of them got the bright idea to attack me. I can't help him. Sorry, sir." She bowed enough to show the top of her head.

***

"What is this nonsense? Why ye no ask for help lass?" Ethan barked at her, crossing his arms. Maria and Ethan weren't the best of friends, but Ethan protected his own. Maria was part of his family now. Knowing that she didn't ask for help made him angry.

"This is not the time, old friend," Hendrick put his hand on Ethan's shoulder, "Where's Yvonne?" Hendrick continued.

***

"I don't know. She went to find the source of the curse when I got trapped," Jake cleared his throat as he said the last words. "Those doll arms were no joke. They had razor sharp nails…" his voice trailed off. "We thought Yvonne was here, or Cat could help."

"Well, both thoughts were wrong. Ethan, go find Yvonne," Hendrick's tone was lethal. He didn't fight so hard to stop the curse just to lose Keanu and Yvonne. With that, Ethan put his thumb to Keanu's forehead which showed his love for his cousin and ran back upstairs.

"How is Cat?" Maria asked. She paused before continuing, "I'm sorry sir. I couldn't block the curse; it was too strong. I managed one floor, but that only helped Ethan and me." Hendrick put his finger to her lips to stop the nervous blabbering.

"It was not yer fault. I have a feeling this was done with Chris's blood. Ye are no match for royalty blood magic. I'm just glad you kept each other safe."

Cat surprised everyone. She shot up from Hendrick's arms, "Aaah! Aaah!" Her eyes were bloodshot as they looked everywhere and nowhere at the same time. Hendrick could see a hint of the teal power in their wildness. She reminded him of a scared, primitive cougar. She was ready to attack at any moment.

Hendrick could see the sparks of power trying to push through. "You are okay, Kitty. I got you, remember?" She jumped backward, stumbling around when he reached for her.

Cat ran her blood-caked hands through her dark hair. "Dolls. Disgusting dolls everywhere," she mumbled, and pulled at her hair. Her legs were too shaky to stand. She leaned against the wall and slid down the smooth surface curling her legs into her chest.

She looked feral. Hendrick's heart broke. She must have been dreaming about the attack. At least her legs were looking good. Her boots were gone, and her pants stopped at the knee, but at least her skin was better.

Hendrick walked to her with silent steps, "The dolls are dead. You gave me enough time to counteract the curse. Thank ye." He touched her knee, "Ye saved us all." When she pushed harder against the wall, Hendrick stepped back.

"Yeah, they bit my legs," she said pulling her legs into her chest. Her eyes and voice were still uncultivated and confused.

"I healed you," Hendrick said with his teacher's voice.

She fumbled around her legs, rubbing her hands up and down them. "Good," was all she said.

"You should thank him," Ethan appeared behind Hendrick with Yvonne at his side. She had similar bite marks and scratches as Cat, but she still knelt to help Keanu.

"Don't give him too much, if you are not okay," Hendrick stated not wanting her to give her life for his. Yvonne was that type of woman; she'd do something like that.

"Ethan gave me some blood, so I'm healing. I'll be alright."

"I don't need to thank him. He knows I'm grateful," Cat looked at him with venom in her eyes.

Ethan was going to say something else… His eyes darkened as he stared at her. The hatred not hidden well all over his face.

Hendrick put up his hand to stop him before he could say another word. Out of all his friends, Ethan was by far the most cold-hearted.

Considering his past, Hendrick understood. When the kingdom got attacked, he was the lead warrior. Ethan never forgave himself for letting a traitor into the territory.

To top it all off, he had to watch his mother and younger sister burn to death. Screams like that haunted even the bravest and strongest warriors and could scar them for life. But, he had no right making her feel low like that. She did help to save all them.

"Okay Lass, your job is done. You helped me out just like you told the Goddess. Ethan is going to take you back to the van." His tone was calm and gentle. He didn't even use his accent.

Cat snapped back at him, "What? Hell no, I almost died trying to get to that room. I'm not leaving until I see what's in that stupid room," Cat eyes burned in the light, but she looked at Hendrick, "I never quit a mission halfway through," she tilted her chin up.

Ethan grumbled a few things, but Cat ignored him and stood up, her face still heated in anger. Her emotions were not letting a little dislike go; the thing wanted something little to be something humongous. The peppery scent of her anger stung her eyes. *Stop that.*

Hendrick could smell her honey scent burst into life along with her anger. The scared feline-look she had a few moments ago dissipated as the vibration of her power increased.

Hendrick's body burst to life as well, he'd never admit this, but he was more confident with her at his side. The warmth in his chest increased until the heat shined through and reflected in his smile.

"Good," he managed to say.

"Don't smile at me like that, you're creeping me out," Cat brushed off her clothes. She tried to wipe off the dry blood, but that didn't work well, "You look like you are going to eat me."

Hendrick laughed, handing her one of the knives Ethan had, "I'll refrain from smiling."

Twenty-Four

EVEN THOUGH THE Goddess had tried a few times before to disobey the rules and interfere magically, circumstances had never allowed her to. She was not to interfere in the human's lives—even if the human was hers, and the fact that she had interfered meant trouble. The only thing she had going for her was that both Sapphires and Dragonvires were the God's old protectors.

Maybe I will get away with it?

The way The Three were glaring at her, she doubted it. She would be locked in her chambers for a week, for sure. So, she could not interfere again. The only way would be through the central globe, without actually going to their dimension of course. The smaller ones were only meant for visuals.

If only she could convince The Three. They were the leaders of the twelve gods and the strongest. She never liked their constant dictatorship, but they set the rules for everyone to follow. The Three also gave the rest of the nine Gods duties to guide special people.

Now, the Gods left everyone to their own devices, but sometimes they still helped by sending a bit of guidance to humans when they needed it. And every God had a select few they shared their abilities with.

Since the war, that number had dropped dramatically, though. Most humans could not be trusted with such power anymore. There was too much fighting and hatred. Giving them, such power would be like throwing gasoline on a lit flame.

She is one of the few Gods who still communicate with beings in the human dimension. As much as the gods had pulled away from the dimension, they still wanted to help. She tried to help physically with the nonsense going on over there, but that was rule number one here. The God's job is to guide, not fix the problems for them.

There were two Gods of war, two Gods of wisdom, three Gods of love, and five elemental Gods, including her. And all of them were a pain in her corporeal ass. She was the Goddess of wind, the one who messes up a woman's hair to feel connected to them. A free spirit who thinks, as gods, they

should help out more, but her word meant nothing here—not without the votes backing her up anyway.

She used her wind abilities to keep the flames and fog off Cat and Hendrick, for the most part. Until the others noticed her focusing too hard on what was happening around the globe. She was so careful to not use the magical connection with the other gods to fuel her energy. *They were too intelligent for her liking.*

The Goddess closed herself off to all of them, hating how everyone was perched in a circle watching the big events going on in the human's dimension like they always did. The Three said, *this time we spend here will bring us closer together,* she had another feeling about it and they were not good feelings. There was nothing worse than sitting around watching the humans' world go to Hades and not be able to do anything.

She could nudge the humans the right way to help keep them safe, but never to interfere. When she saw Cat needed help, nothing else mattered. If they didn't tie her up, she was going to help.

She wanted to tell Cat how to use her powers. The way to a Sapphire's most potent abilities is through their emotions. That is why their hair changes colors for their mood; it helps their skills come out.

Most have a tough time using their powers, especially if they cut their hair. Yet, short hair doesn't stop them altogether. Their heart controls most of their abilities, which is why Cat is so good at her job. Her heart is in it.

And the murderers who cut out Sapphire's heart to use its remarkable powers know that. As soon as the heart touches sunlight, the muscle turns into a powerful amulet. What they don't know is if they die happy or loved, the power is much higher. That power was only meant to be a backup plan if somehow all other defenses failed for the Gods.

The Goddess smiled as she remembered how the Sapphires were once honored. The Gods used to pamper them with loving caresses to keep them powerful back when the Sapphires and Dragonvires were a part of the great Kingdom. Sapphires used to transform into fluffy cats the size of panthers. There was even a rule, if a cat sat on anyone's lap, the person could not move until the cat got up and left.

The rule became so popular the even humans honored cats. Of course, those were normal size cats, but the gesture still warmed the Goddess's heart.

The Goddess laughed, making everyone's piercing glares deepen towards her. *That was my fault.* The Three were whispering among each other even quieter. *Oh, stop staring at me like I betrayed you all. I just assisted with a little magic and gave a foreshadowing.*

When she was a young goddess, the Gods were in control of the humans. All Gods took guilty pleasure in toying with their creations to watch it unfold. Like a crazy game of human chess. She even indulged in the game sometimes, but quickly learned to treat a human like a toy was not the right thing to do. So, the humans choosing to act on her rule without being forced made the gesture that much more special.

She closed her eyes, making them shine bright white to put energy into Cat before they made her leave. After the vibration in her core subsided and the task finished, she looked around cautiously. *Good, no one noticed that.* She was blessed they didn't notice, she was in enough trouble as it was.

Her poor sweet Cat was about to change forever. She is so brave, so lovely, and so traumatized by her past that the Goddess hoped she could handle everything that was coming her way next.

She didn't know exactly what her destiny had in store for her, but she had her on her side. And the Goddess would do everything in her power to keep her safe.

Twenty-Five

CAT'S JOY RATIATED off her until the scent fumigated all around her. Her lips stretched to the point her jaw hurt, as she smiled at her two long pale legs free of bite marks. And her eyes softened with love.

They're back to normal. I never thought I'd want to hug you, legs, as much as I do right now. Her eyes narrowed as they drifted lower, *I wish his blood would have worked on my boots, though.* Nothing was left, so she slipped the holey things off, knowing they wouldn't help much in the ratted state they were in.

She stood with ease, letting her bare feet push into the cold floor. Hendrick's big, comforting hand wrapped around her small one to help. When they both let go, she was ready to face whatever this horror house had in store for them next.

"I'm still going wit ye," Ethan puffed out his chest to look bigger. The fact that he was over six foot and built with muscles everywhere didn't matter to him.

Cat bit back a smile when his chest deflated as Hendrick replied, "No, my good man. I need someone with your strength to stay with the others just in case this goes wrong." There was no reason to risks everyone's lives. If he didn't make it, he wanted his people to rescue Chris.

Ethan and Marcus were going to argue with Hendrick, but he held up the big hand that was just holding Cat's hand to stop them. "Cat, Maria, and I are going forward. Marcus, you take the left and Jake, you to the right," he said with pride and authority in his tone, like a real leader.

Ethan punched the air and went to stand next to Yvonne.

That got Cat a few hatred glares. The way the orange around the edges of their eyes shined gave her chills. She didn't know a lot about Dragonvires, but she did know their dragon beast was overprotective and loyal. They apparently didn't like an outsider showing them up.

"You ready?" she asked Hendrick, getting anxious with everyone standing around staring at her.

"Wait," Maria said, coming up to Hendrick, "I don't like it. I can sense magic close to the room, but I can't reach it. It's like it is slipping out of my blocker grasp."

"Well, what would you like me to do? Not go in there? What if Chris is there?" He gave her a pointed look. She was his voice of reason most of the time. After everything they went through, he couldn't leave. Even if Chris was not in the room, someone or something important was.

She was silent for a few seconds, "Can I at least help you before we go?" He knew what she meant. She wanted to help ease his tension and stress. As a Dragonvire, he was vulnerable to such a high blood loss earlier. Hendrick couldn't risk being too jumpy or tense.

"Sure," he bit the inside of his cheek. That was a nervous tick Hendrick could never get rid of, although he tried. Getting help from people was a sign of weakness. It made him feel weak which was why he liked Cat so much. She pushed her way into things. Instead of the depowering he got from most people wanting to help him, Cat empowered him. She was his equal, not a servant trying to help him when he was lacking.

Maria stepped forward, bowing slightly when she noticed his body get stiff. She put her hand on the back of his head. A spike of electricity zinged through him as she pulled on his emotions.

His tense muscles released. At the same time, his fast beating heart slowed to a steady rhythm. With a sly look on his face, he turned to Cat, "You too?" He asked lifting an eyebrow at her.

"I think I've had enough of her in my head, thanks," Cat said crossing her arms over her chest.

"What do you mean, lass?" His body stiffened again. Maria straightened at the same time. The movement made them look like puppets on a string.

Maria interrupted Cat before she even started, "I wasn't going to let her come with us without knowing her intentions. I know you vouched for her, but you know what happened to my family. I refused to let it happen again."

Hendrick knew all too well what betrayal was, and it had hardened his heart as well. His eyes softened a bit, but she still shouldn't have done that. "When?" He asked, directing the question to Cat. His tone let Maria know to keep quiet.

"Umm, it doesn't matter. I forgave her," Cat replied coyly. His eyes shined orange at the rim, so she just sighed and told him. "In the shower."

He turned to Maria in a slow, stiff movement that seemed to make his eyes shine an even brighter orange. Hendrick reminded Cat of a wild animal at that moment. Maria was smart; she stepped back.

Maria hesitated to look at him, but once their eyes linked it was like an invisible force tethering them together. They were in a power staring contest. Whoever broke contact would lose.

Cat's eyes blinked sympathetically for Maria. Until Maria bowed her head in front of Hendrick, "I'm sorry, I was only doing what I thought was right for my people."

"I understand that." He stepped closer to Maria, "But when I give a direct order, you do not get to disobey me because you feel like it. There is no time for this; I will deal with you later." Hendrick turned around to join Cat. "You will stay with Ethan."

They both moved cautiously toward the room at the back, kicking dolls out of their way. Chills ran down Cat's spine when they walked by the tower of crates. She was going to have nightmares about that for years.

"Alright, I'll go first-" Hendrick didn't get to finish because Cat interjected.

"Not happening. We go together. I don't sense more than one person, that doesn't mean there isn't more. You are the king of Dragonvires, it could be an ambush. My goal is to prevent the chompers from happening, not make it happen sooner," she scolded him.

Hendrick knew she was right and arguing was pointless with her. A single nod was his answer. He didn't have the strength to argue, his focus was on his brother right now.

So, they moved together like a pair that had been partners for a while, moving in sync with one another. The rest of them scouted the outside. The last thing they needed was a magical ambush.

They made the journey more than halfway when things went south again. "Hendrick get out of there!" Maria yelled running forward, making the rest of the group do the same.

That's when the two hit a force field. The tan light expanded, reaching for Cat and Hendrick, trying to pull them into its depths, "Don't let it-" Cat tried to warn Hendrick as well, but it was too late.

They backed up, but that made it worse. The shield exploded in front of them. Hendrick turned to tackle Cat, putting his body over hers which meant his back got the full brunt of the explosion.

The flames kept firing forward, burning the flesh on Hendrick's back. "No!" Cat yelled. Her legs and arms were in sheer agony, making her vision go black from the pain. The smell of their burnt flesh hurt her nose as if someone had rubbed pepper sauce in her nostrils.

Goddess…

When the flames finally stopped, Hendrick was lying limp on top of her, and the force field was sucking the life out of them both. It's cold, wicked grip dove into their being, slowly drinking the life out of them.

Cat's vision cleared for a second and her head fell to the side. Yvonne and Maria were banging on the shield, yelling something Cat didn't understand. Cat knew what the force field was, so if there was a chance of Hendrick and her surviving this, Cat needed to tell them what she knew.

In two sharp breaths, Cat shouted, "Death shield." She hoped someone heard her. The pain stopped, and a cold, sticky darkness crept its way to her. Until all that was left was darkness around her.

Twenty-Six

NO MATTER HOW many times Yvonne saw death, she could never get used to it. As Cat went slack under Hendrick, Yvonne covered her mouth to stop herself from screaming. *Don't panic.*

Hendrick was down for the count. He sacrificed himself for Cat, and if they couldn't get to him soon, he would be dead. The explosion gave him critical wounds. Most of his back was gone, the thick flesh burnt away.

Maria stopped the death shield from draining both of their life forces dry.

Their only hope was to wake up Cat and have her heal him quicker, "Cat. Cat." Yvonne laid down to get on the same

level as her, "Come on sweetie, wake up," Yvonne said with a
bit of enthusiasm, hoping her cheerfulness would help wake
Cat up in a way that wouldn't panic her.

She pushed against the barrier again. The yellow shield
was a solid wall, but it looked more like Jello. *Stupid igloo of death.*

Everyone hated that they weren't strong enough to get
inside. They had been pounding their fists against the barrier
over and over, but that didn't seem to have an effect at all. It
still taunted everyone with its strength.

"Gods, please help," Yvonne said with mournful
pleads. Yvonne closed her eyes in defeat. *What the hell are we
going to do?*

***

She opened her eyes, ready to tell everyone it was time
to go. Someone had set this trap, and they would be coming
back, which meant they needed to leave. Cat's eyes fluttered,
"Cat, sweetie, can you hear me?" Yvonne cried out, losing her
composure.

Cat looked up from the ground when she heard a
muffled woman's voice. "Goddess?" Cat replied.

"No, it's Yvonne," she said, as Cat's eyes focused on
her pained face.

"Hello," Her voice was still small, and it was like her
lungs couldn't get enough air.

"You were right. You are in a death shield, but Maria
was able to keep it from killing both of you." Cat's eyes drifted
shut, "No, no, no, Cat look at me." Cat did look at Yvonne, but
she was so tired her eyes didn't focus.

"Hendrick needs you." That got Cat's attention, and her glossy eyes cleared. "The legend of Sapphires told of the great mystical smoke that was able to amplify powers. Do you have the ability to use the smoke?"

Yvonne's frantic voice wasn't registering entirely with Cat. But she knew what she was saying. She needed to push out her smoke to amplify someone's power. She gave Yvonne one nod; her body was so tired and weak it was all she could manage.

The problem was, Cat didn't know how to smoke. It just always happened. Yvonne remembered the tales about them being emotional creatures. Their hair and smoke would activate their emotions which got them killed when a Hunter was around.

***

Cat religiously cut her hair and Yvonne was betting that kept the hair color at bay, but what about her smoke. "Cat, look up. Hendrick is dying." Yvonne hoped this would work.

If Cat couldn't do this, she didn't know what they would do. She mentally crossed her fingers.

***

Cat looked up as Yvonne said that and her oxygen-deprived brain registered Hendrick lying on top of her. Her body woke up a little. The adrenaline shot through her body, "Hendrick?" Her voice was still weak, but her insides were stronger.

Hendrick was on top of her, his eyes were open but not seeing. *Oh, my Goddess is he…*

Like Yvonne hoped, Cat's smoke burst out of her like a wildfire burning inside her. Except the smoke didn't rise like normal. Instead, the gray cloud moved with intelligence, and it covered Hendrick's body.

The air around them became heated, filling Yvonne's eyes with water. Yvonne got up from the ground, "Oh thank the Gods," she said and could hear similar whispers from the others.

When Hendrick jerked awake, Yvonne released a breath she didn't know she was holding. They watched as the wound on his back knitted itself together.

"What the bloody hell?" Hendrick asked, looking around and showing everyone his fangs.

He looked magnificent with his disheveled hair and scorched clothes. Like a warrior ready to strike to save the queen.

"Not that I'm ungrateful, but what happened, pet?" he asked when no one answered the first time. He looked around in the thick smoke until he noticed Cat lying on the floor, crushed.

Yvonne's tears slid down the barrier, "Cat healed you," she said with a huge smile.

"That's why I feel supercharged," he said at her side now, lifting his head. In a swift movement, he pierced his teeth into his wrist.

"What are you doing, Hendrick?" Jake asked, his voice stressed and worried.

"What do you mean? I'm going to heal her, of course."

"You should wait until the smoke is out of your system, or at least wait until the smoke completely disappears. We don't know the effect your amplified blood will have on Cat," Jake tried to explain.

"He's right, sweetie," Yvonne interjected using a name that told Hendrick he was acting irrationally. He couldn't think straight; he had tons of adrenaline coursing through him that made him feel invincible. Like when his vampire beast was running things.

"Nonsense, it will only heal her faster," he said putting his bloody wrists to her mouth, "the lass needs it. Ye worry too much." If Hendrick was honest with himself, he knew they were right, but he couldn't bear it if she died because of him. The death shield must have pulled on her life source harder because she was the most likely to live.

Hendrick pulled his hand away from Cat's mouth. A gust of strong wind stirred Hendrick and Cat's hair. He looked at Cat, noticing that the wind came from under Cat. He stood up. The force of the second blow of wind smacked him against the shield. The inside of the shield sizzled against his exposed skin.

Whatever happened, it was enough to make the shield crumble at everyone's feet. Hendrick looked at Cat, and the smoke was decorating the cement ground.

All eyes were on Cat. Blinking, dumbfounded. The Sapphire was floating. The strange part was Cat's smoke drifted to her back where it clumped together, forming something. "Is

that what I think it is Hendrick?" Yvonne asked, standing next to him.

Hendrick didn't answer, the smoke answered for him. The gray fluff was forming into wings. If he could touch them, he knew they would be soft. The now wholly developed wings expanded, raising Cat up higher.

The way the wings wrapped around Cat's back made them look like extensions of her.

"What's happening?" Yvonne said, crumbling into Hendrick's arms. She didn't want to faint in front of everyone, but this was ridiculous. Cat was her adopted sister.

Yvonne's older sister and her family were a few thousand miles away and hadn't spoken to her since her chosen career path wasn't a lawyer. Yvonne opened her safe house instead. Her family moved away shortly after to be closer to Yvonne's older sister.

Yvonne had tried to rekindle their relationship but failed. So, this instant connection she had with Cat made her whole-body tremble with enthusiasm for the future. Yvonne had only had that immediate connection with one other person. Hendrick.

"Maria, can you do anything?" Hendrick asked. When she didn't answer, Hendrick looked around, "Marcus where is Maria?"

***

"She-" he stopped when she wasn't behind him anymore. "Maria?" Marcus shouted. "Shit, no," he said as he saw Maria's petite body walking towards the corner of the room. *Of all the Dragon Gods, what is she thinking?*

Both Marcus and Ethan yelled her name at once. Their bodies flew towards the room. Marcus got there first; he could hear his heart pounding in his ears.

Smack! Another shield slammed into place covering the small office room in the corner with Maria inside. It was about ten feet away from Cat's and Hendrick's shield, but Marcus could tell the shimmer globe was the same.

Marcus's body slammed into a shield trying to grab her. Maria was kneeling on the floor. "Maria! Maria!" Marcus screamed mindlessly, pounding on the tan shield, unaware of the boiling effect on his skin as he did so.

Marcus couldn't lose her, she was his world and his only connection to his family. She was his little sister's best friend and for all intents and purposes was his sister, too. He already lost the rest of his family; losing her would break him.

He looked over at Ethan and Hendrick punching holes in the walls, blood seeping from their fists. Marcus was so dumbfounded. Twice in one-night Dragonvire's blood had failed him.

That's impossible?

He saw it then, the panic in Maria's eyes. She wasn't alone.

Twenty-Seven

WHEN THE SMOKE slowly disappeared, absorbing into Cat's flesh before expanding into smoky wings, Maria couldn't wait anymore. She liked Cat, but Chris could be behind these walls.

She could feel a heartbeat in the room. If it was Chris, the mission would be over and everyone else would be safe. If it wasn't Chris, well she'd worry about that later. The odds of him being in there were high. She hesitated for a second, thinking about Marcus. She was being stupid right now, but her heart wanted to hold Chris in her arms again.

She heard Hendrick call her, but she already had the doorknob in her hand. Her blocker senses hadn't picked up anything foreign.

She couldn't stop now. Pushing the door open had her using all her muscles. *Why is this door so heavy?* Her heart slammed into her already heaving chest. She loathed how her chest was moving fast, taunting her.

She heard Marcus's worried voice and she quickened her movement, opening the door all the way. A dim light was on, so she could make out blank white walls like the rest of the warehouse. The room was so quiet, she was surprised how loud her heart sounded, the muscle sounded like a jackhammer to Maria.

She was a blocker, so her blood couldn't be used like a Dragonvires, so it was best that she went in first. That's what she told herself anyway. If this was a trap, Maria would be screwed, but she knew it was better for her to get caught than Hendrick.

Here's hoping for the best.

The room was an eerie dark. As if the room heard her thoughts, the lights flicked on. As Maria looked around she thought her eyes were playing tricks on her. Black dots danced in her vision. She bit her lip hard, trying to focus.

Ow.

Gasp, Chris's body shimmered in the middle of the room as if a spell tried to hide him. She was so excited nothing else mattered. She would normally siphon the power surrounding the room, but Chris was so near nothing else registered in her worried mind.

I knew there had to be a reason for all the defenses outside of the room. Logic was not her friend at the moment. All she knew was she needed to save Chris.

The sound of her feet thumping on the floor echoed on the walls. The sound drowned out someone calling her name again. Her pleading arms dove for him. Maria moved in slow motion. She barely registered the tears stinging her eyes, she was so distracted.

The moment her needy hands tried to graze Chris's skin the image disappeared. Maria went flying forward where he was supposed to be. She caught herself and stayed kneeling, trying to understand. *Where is my Chris?*

With one big black swirl in front of her face, whatever vision had clouded her mind cleared in a huge gust of wind.

"No!" Maria yelled, putting her hands on the floor and using her blocker magic. She slammed her fist on the floor hearing what sounded like a handful of dice getting thrown on a glass table as her bones shattered. Her efforts weren't working.

Ultimately, the force of her punch squeezed some sense back to her brain. *Get up and get to the door, idiot.* The voice in her head taunted.

She looked at the door already knowing that path would be blocked. Someone was using a powerful blocker spell to prevent her magic from working. Those types of mystical spells were the only thing that could keep her from sucking the magic in this room dry.

She could see Hendrick, Jake, Ethan, and Marcus banging on the shield trying to force their way in. The tan shimmery liquid floating in between them mocked both of them.

Instead of running to the door, she went on the defensive and took out her knife. It was better to be ready for an attack, than not.

The only way she was making it out alive was in a fight. *Great, I'm screwed.*

"Haha, haha," an ugly high-pitched voice behind her laughed. It was the worst witch laugh Maria had ever heard. She swung around but didn't see anything.

"What the hell?" Maria's voice sounded like it was on a microphone. The sound waves echoed around the room.

Maria blinked, and in an unexpected flash, a woman was at her side, laughing again. She moved away from the hyena, but the stupid woman was too fast. Small, dark white hands gripped Maria's arm.

On the woman's other hand was a metal stick. "Silly girl, I didn't think you were this stupid. It looks like I lost the bet," the woman made a small circle in the air with her wand. A bright green light launched at Maria. The brilliant accuracy of the blast knocked her backward.

Maria got up quickly on shaky legs and darted for the door, making her muscles work harder than normal. She tried

to slam her way through, but just as efficiently knocked herself unconscious.

As she laid there going in and out of consciousness, she heard a deep, soothing voice whisper in her mind. *My lovely blocker, you have made me so proud. Don't worry, you are coming home to the beauty of Aria.* His sensuous voice seemed to hold her in a caring embrace. *Now, get up and say goodbye, my child.*

Maria knew deep inside what had just happened. As a child, her mom told her stories about the God of blocker beings coming to speak to them when they were destined to die. But Maria refused to admit that to herself. Her mom could have been wrong, and the God was here for guidance.

So, she opened her eyes, mentally shaking her head to clear her mind. She stood up trying to move quickly, but her body was too weak. *The damn spell is probably an energy sucker.*

She limped to the door. The boys were now trying to cut into the walls to get to her, but the holes were covered in the tan gunk as well.

The woman had her green light ready. She was like a cat playing with her mouse. She waited until Maria got up to start launching green energy balls at her legs and arms.

Maria had enough of her nonsense. She reached the door and pulled with all her might, using her magic. Her heart lifted when she saw the shield weakening. That wouldn't take down the shield, but her efforts might be enough for one of the Dragonvires to break through.

"You whore!" The woman's high pitch voice yelled. Maria could tell her voice held a little fear in its depth.

Before Maria could make a good dent in the shield, the woman's green light grabbed her, lifting her in the air. Its death grip pulled at her being. She could hear herself making gurgling noises.

The realization came to her. *Fuck, this is it for me.* She took one last sharp breath staring into Marcus's blue eyes. They were full of tears and she hated that she had done that to him.

Her body was completely still until the woman's power ripped at her. The strong pulling sensation ripped something out of Maria. *Stooopppp!*

The horrible sensations of knives digging into her flesh and pulling away her life force was unbearable. She heard a scream, but she didn't know if the noise came from her or someone else. Nothing else existed to Maria except the pain.

With the last tug, icy immobilizing water washed that blinding pain away. For a long moment, everything was still fuzzy. Once her vision cleared, it looked different like she was looking at an outside view of everything. She didn't fight the feeling because the agonizing pain had stopped.

The peace didn't last long as she watched her body crumbled to the floor fear settled back in. Anguish squeezed her core. She was getting sucked into the woman's wand. Maria knew she would stay there until the woman was dead.

She was grateful, there was no more pain. The cold groping at her was a horrible feeling. Like she had the flu, she was cold and hot in the wrong places.

From the corner of her eyes, she could see Marcus fighting the shield with all his might, bloodying the jello surface.

He looked different to her. A bright white light shone around him as well as Ethan and Jake who were making huge holes all over the room.

She stopped struggling to focus on him. Marcus wasn't her real brother, but she saved his life as a kid, and they had been inseparable ever since. "I love you Bubba. Please be safe and live happily. I'm sorry," her voice wasn't the smooth Latin texture that it always was. The sound was a cold soothing whisper that reminded her of ghost calls.

Boom!

Yvonne smiled as she saw Hendrick break through the shield and bust through the wall. The small hole she'd made must have been enough for him to break through.

"Nooo!" voices yelled from everywhere. With a savage twist of a wrist, Maria had a massive pull in her core. The gaping hole in her stomach grew until there was nothing left, she got pulled into the woman's wand.

Everything went black for Maria, but a sweet, beautiful warm glow held her in a soothing hug deep inside. She smiled, saying a little prayer that her stupidity wouldn't cause her Dragonvires to pay the ultimate price.

An anaconda of darkness wrapped its mouth around Maria, squeezing her tight until there was nothing left.

Twenty-Eight

CAT AWOKE TO a gut-wrenching cry. Goosebumps the size of blisters scattered across her skin. Water leaked from her eyes from the raw emotions in the air.

If she wasn't so dizzy herself, laying there with her hand on her chest gulping for air, she would have helped. A loud crash shook the floor underneath Cat and a blaze of heat covered her like a heating blanket. *Why did it just get so hot?*

The scorching heat opened her lungs.

Not a second later, Yvonne was at her side trying to help her stand up. Cat's legs were too wobbly, so she held out a hand for Yvonne to stop. That made her grip on Cat, she held her in her arms and sobbed like she needed to water the ground with her tears. Cat looked up at her when a few splashed over her skin, the tears rolling down her face were as yellow as the sun. And at that moment Cat wished she was a relaxer to help Yvonne.

Cat focused to clear her headed enough to understand words, "Are you okay?" Yvonne brushed a hand over Cat's hair.

"Ras," Cat tried to say 'yes' but her throat hurt too bad to say the words correctly. She cleared her throat a few times and tried again, "What's wrong?" her voice sounded a bit clearer, but it was hoarse as if she smoked five packs of cigarettes a day.

***

Yvonne kept crying and didn't answer. Everything inside of Yvonne was breaking. Even her chest didn't feel right. The sadness twisted her torso into a massive knot. Maria wasn't the best of people, but she was family.

***

The only response for Cat was chaos and a horrible scream that sounded like Maria's singsong voice. Cat's instincts kicked in, she leaped up as if she was connected to a rope.

The fluid movement startled Cat, making her balance waver and soaring her forward. She smacked into the floor and her cheek broke the fall. "That hurt," she brushed the dirt off her cheek, "I must have pushed too hard off the ground." She got up slower this time, trying not to let her dizziness make her fall again. Her weak body had been through a lot today; there was no need to add on unnecessary blows.

Why do I feel like I'm in water? She moved her arms around. Her body was weightless.

Cat shook her head to clear the fuzziness. Her eyes drifted to the man yelling again, it was Marcus. He was yelling Maria's name this time, like it was the last thing he would ever do, "Maria!"

Another scream erupted. This one by a woman and it was even angrier. It wasn't Maria. The shouts were too cold and bitter to be hers. *It couldn't be.*

She turned away from Yvonne's wide eyes. Her mouth fell open and she sucked in a breath. Out of all the faces she expected to see, the one she was looking at wasn't one of them.

"Rebecca?"

Hendrick held her by her thick platinum blonde hair and her hands bound behind her back. Cat gulped at the look of pure hatred tainting her sculpted brown eyes. It was Rebecca, no one could mistake her skinny, no curves body. *What's going on?*

Hendrick looked like he wanted to snap her in half, which Cat had no doubt he could do. He looked massive next to Rebecca. "Cathleen, help me, they are going to kill me," Rebecca's eyes were imploring and scared. "They are Dragonvires." Her squeaky voice made Cat feel uncomfortable, similar to vines wrapping around her and ripping her skin.

She struggled with a fierce anger that had her breathless by the time she finished. Hendrick looked at her like she was a temperamental child. When Cat didn't move to help her, she stopped and tilted her head. As soon as it was clear to her Cat wasn't going to help, that ugly look came back.

Rebecca snarled, "You are a good for nothing whore! You're with them, aren't you?" She hocked a loogy and spat the content at Cat from across the room. "Wait! Lusion was supposed to make you his slave. Where is he?"

Cat was still silent, too stunned to do anything. But Hendrick wasn't. "You mean the demon bloke? I killed him a while back, as easy as squashing an ant."

Marcus spoke next, his voice so throaty the heated voice sounded like a growl, "How do you know her Cat?"

"Rebecca lives in my building, but she is my friend. What happened? I don't understand." Cat was confused. *What the hell is going on?* She looked around, seeing the walls of the small room destroyed. If she hadn't seen the place before, it would have looked like an accident from the war.

"I was never your friend. I waited for years for you to access the curse to free Lusion, but you wouldn't open your Goddamn legs for anything, stupid woman!" Hendrick pulled Rebecca's hair tighter in warning. Cat heard an agonizing pop from Rebecca's back that sounded like a bat hitting a baseball, "I hate you!"

Cat lost her composure as the realization hit her hard. "Is that why you pushed so much for me to date?" Cat shook her head and looked up at the ceiling fighting off tears, "I confided in you, and I thought of you as a sister. You knew Lusion would kill one of the men you chose; you killed Bruce."

All the anger Cat had been bottling up from Bruce's death spilled out in a tsunami of loathing. No one deserved to die that way. Pictures of his dead body flashed in her mind.

The images made something inside of her darken and her thoughts turn deadly.

Cat didn't know she even moved. It wasn't until she could feel Rebecca's breath on her face that her actions registered, "I'm going to kill you myself."

Her hands reached for Rebecca's throat. She sensed the throbbing in her neck, and something inside of her changed. The adrenaline pumping through her made her hands twitch. The tingling sensation made all her senses sharpen.

She could hear Rebecca breathing and a liquid coursing through her body. Her eyes drifted to her neck that's where a steady flow traveled, and she wanted it.

No matter the price, the witch was going down.

Twenty-Nine

*P*OP. A STRANGE stretching sensation like pop-rocks exploding in Cat's mouth had her whimpering. She contorted her face in pain. *What the heck?*

After a few seconds, she relaxed as the pain subsided. When she opened her eyes and saw everyone's horrified expressions, she stopped breathing. The way they all had scared wide eyes, and a gaping mouth made the hair on her arms stand at attention.

Her eyes grew wide when she was going to say something, and before anything came out, everyone around Cat sucked in a breath. The tension in her brows increased as the air in the room was sucked out with that one unified intake. She worried when no one blew the air back out. They held it in standing like statues staring at her. Cat turned around. There was no new threat behind her.

Nothing was there, no three-headed monster to startle them. She looked to everyone else for an answer, but no one would look at her, "What?" Cat asked, her nose flared in irritation. No one would look at her except Hendrick. He was staring at her teeth in stunned silence.

Cat had enough of this stupidity. She turned her attention back to Rebecca, absently scratching her teeth. *If I'm lucky I'll have food stuck in my teeth.*

Deep inside she already knew what she would find. Although, when her cold fingers touched those new, extended canines, the fact was, it was still a shock and the long things pissed her off. Cat forgot how to breathe too. *By the Gods, how did I become a vampire?*

As if admitting the change triggered something inside of her, a weak pull to her middle burned her insides, but it only intensified as she ignored the sensation. There was only one way to describe her tummy rumbling; she was hungry.

The burn in her throat pleaded to get quenched. Nothing else mattered except her hunger. A hunger like she had never had before took over.

The excruciating pain blazed like a flame and coated her stomach. She knew what would quench her thirst, her hunger. The all-consuming urge didn't make sense to her, but she dove for the dark, throbbing line on Rebecca's neck that called to her.

She bit down hard and pulled at the warm and delicious thick liquid. One word kept repeating in her mind, *MORE*. She sucked hard until Hendrick managed to pull Cat's clenched teeth away from Rebecca's neck leaving jagged marks on Rebecca's flesh that pleased Cat more than she wanted to acknowledge.

The strength he had to use to pull her away surprised him. Most new vampires were weak and sloppy. She seemed different like she has been a vampire for years.

But that newly found feeding frenzy only happens once, so there was no doubt Cat was a new vampire. He knew all too well what that was like, and what yearning was like. He pushed Rebecca away from Cat gesturing for Yvonne to help Cat with her craving. She would be able to keep her hunger at bay for a few minutes.

Cat jumped at the touch of Yvonne's tiny hands. The vibration traveling from Yvonne had Cat filling better. The sweet sensation of cold soothed Cat's hunger enough so she could think.

Cat stood straight up slowly, making her movement predatory. She couldn't believe how much hatred she had inside for Rebecca.

In the back of her subconscious the dead person registered in Cat's mind. *Oh Goddess, no, it's Maria! What the hell happened! How can so much bad happen in so little time?* The fire in her turned into a nuclear bomb. Someone she thought she could trust had killed Bruce, set her up to be a demon slave, and now she had killed Maria.

The realization made even her soul turd black, and the anger built up into a tar. A bitter, nasty feeling coated her insides, making Cat feel dirty. If her mom could see her now, the hatefulness would repulse her, murderous Cat.

Cat's eyes blinked rapidly. Seeing an image of her mom's sad face was like having a bucket of ice water dumped on her. Her mom's large green eyes, dark hair, and muscular frame weren't meant to be sad. It would kill Cat to have her mom disappointed in her.

Hendrick put his hand on Cat's shoulder, pulling her away from her thoughts, "Not yet love, she could know where Chris is," he said in a caring, but stern voice. The voice reminded her of her partner David when she had just done something stupid, like punch her superior. That soothed her temper.

Cat's new senses let her pick up on everything in the room, even if she didn't want to sense any of her surroundings. Hendrick's wide eyes, Marcus's hateful stare at Rebecca, Jake holding him back, Maria's corpse in the small room, Yvonne away from the group to her left and secretly crying, and even further left, Keanu moaning in pain. But the one she noticed the most was Ethan's stare. He spoke of murder.

Not that she could blame him. In his eyes, ever since she had been in the Dragonvire world nothing but bad has followed them. He hadn't met her until Chris was kidnapped, or been told about the chomper curse, her triggering the curse in the warehouse, distracting everyone while Maria went to her death, and now her best friend was the enemy.

It didn't matter that all of it was a coincidence; she could tell Ethan thought she was the problem. And all she wanted to do was help.

That hunger inside of her spiked again. The wicked feeling that wanted Ethan to touch her, so she could rip his head off and drink from it. *Whoa, where did that come from?* Cat asked herself, the thought was enough to startle her back from her hunger again.

***

The tension in the air was suffocating for everyone. Ethan was holding Marcus back, so when Ethan left him to get closer to Cat just in case she attacked again, Marcus was free. Being faster than Ethan he was only a few steps away from his revenge for Maria's death. He would run for his chance at killing Rebecca as soon as he saw an opportunity. There was nothing more important to Marcus than Maria. Chris could wait until they found another clue.

***

Rebecca was glad she learned how to make an allusion wand, now. Lusion's assessor, as much of a jerk that he was, he was right. It came in handy. She slyly pulled out the wand she had been concealing for her escape.

All she needed to do was call forth the borrowed demon power to get out of here, and she'll get the fortune the demon's promised her. *I can't wait to buy a television and microwave. I'll finally be living the dream.*

The green sour magic built up inside of her until the magical force settled in her fist. The energy was like a large bug closed in her grasp. It wanted out.

Hendrick's grip tightened on Rebecca and looked down at the floor where he thought the wand was… Nothing.

"She's got the demon wand," he yelled right before she punched him across the room. Ethan ran for Rebecca, but she used the rest of the mystical force to punch him as well.

She took a deep breath, letting herself build up more power. She was only a lower level witch, so the power Lucian gave her was hard to use. *I have the strength for one more big incantation, then I need to get out of here. I took out their Blocker like planned. I'm not dying for them.*

***

What happened next occurred so fast a Natural wouldn't have been able to keep up. Marcus took his chance. Rebecca was distracted by punching Ethan's face in. Marcus got an angry grip on Rebecca's neck and said harshly, "Now, you die." He was so full of hate; he didn't see her grip tightening on the wand.

"Not by you, foolish boy," she said, raising her wand to his head, "Mortem," Rebecca's ugly, squeaky voice shouted.

Everyone's heart dropped at Rebecca's one horrid word because they all knew 'mortem' meant death. An invisible force slammed into Marcus, and he clasped his heart, crumbling to the ground. Everything in the room froze as his body fell to the floor, lifeless.

***

"No!" Yvonne screeched in horror. Her sobs were loud and pained now. She didn't care if the entire world knew she was crying. "No, no, no," she whimpered until a fervent heat struck holes in her heart and she collapsed on the floor, unconscious.

***

Cat couldn't believe what was happening. She tried to help, but her body chose that moment to be overwrought by the idiotic emotions. All the emotions Maria had taken from her slammed back into her.

She stood there looking at Marcus's dead body unable to move, as a wave of emotions froze her in place.

She could sense Hendrick to her right and vaguely registered Keanu crawling over and dragging Yvonne away. *What the hell is wrong with me? How did I let it get this bad?* She had never had a mission go this wrong before.

***

Ethan and Hendrick were at Marcus' side in the blink of an eye. Hendrick already had his knife out cutting his palm, ready to use his blood magic to help Marcus. But as soon as they touched him, they could tell he was an empty shell. *Nooo!*

Hendrick didn't care anymore if she was the key to finding Chris. Rebecca needed to die. They would have to find another way. He looked back at Rebecca as she said an incantation with her wand.

She was calling a portal to her.

"Son of Hades," Hendrick said as a green force began spinning behind Rebecca. Hendrick only had a second to think before he saw Cat leaping for Rebecca. She grabbed her upper leg as the bright light absorbed them.

Hendrick dove for Cat.

He reached for her legs and missed. Luck was on his side as his firm grasp latched onto her ankle instead. The swirling depths took Hendrick with them. Yet, no one else could follow for backup. They were on their own.

Thirty

*U***GH, BLOODY HELL.** Hendrick's arms ached as he pushed his way through the slimy goo of the portal walls. He hated jumping into someone else's portal, the trip was painful and took a lot of strength to get through.

If he wasn't careful, he could get stuck. And to Hendrick, that would be the worst death possible. He would drown in all this goo, and he wouldn't be able to do anything but let himself rot here until maybe someone stumbled upon his body. Which was unlikely.

He would use portals more often if they weren't such darn expensive amulets to get. There were only two ways to call a portal, with an amulet, or with a demon wand. And there was no way he was using a demon wand.

The few times he'd created a portal the trip went by quickly. Out in a flash of light was the way he liked to travel, but he was using someone else's portal now so the process of getting through was substantially longer. And he couldn't hold on to Cat's ankle, so he had to fight his way out.

If fighting through the sticky, squishy layers wasn't bad enough, he also had to accomplish this blind. The light could burn his eyeballs. It didn't matter who or what a person was, that would suck.

Hendrick's fingers grazed against the exit making another shot of adrenaline spike through him, "Damn lass is already a pain," he grumbled as he smacked jelly obstacles out of his way.

A ping of guilt had him moving quicker; it was his fault she was reacting with her anger. He couldn't believe he had turned her into a vampire. She couldn't become a full vampire, though, because he wasn't a full vampire. Yet, she was fucking close enough.

All signs pointed towards a new vampire, except her new strength. That was a major surprise and made him worry. No Dragonvire had ever made someone into a vampire before. Their blood didn't work that way, or at least it hadn't.

The end of the portal needed to be torn open. Thankfully, his dagger made it through with him, so he thrust it into the portal wall. The sound reminded him of pushing a sharp knife through thick skin.

Once he got a hole big enough for his hands to fit, he ripped the portal opened and shoved himself through the narrow opening. It was arduous work. This was probably the only time he wished he didn't have so much muscle because that meant the hole had to be bigger.

He laughed to himself. Mother nature was giving birth to him. Somewhere in the portal, he must have taken a wrong turn because now the entrance was up in the sky. But he didn't realize it until it was too late. As soon as Hendrick pushed out, he was falling to the ground. A portal dimension is a tricky place, it has a mind of its own, and the gooey depths loved to change for people.

"Bloody Hades!" Hendrick pushed on his inner being, but his dragon beast wouldn't form. Going through the portal-drained him. He couldn't shift without feeding. "Come on now. Can a man get a break?" He kept falling. His muscles were not helping his descent. The extra weight meant he was going down faster.

His eyes roamed, looking for another way. *Here goes nothing.* His already stressed arms reached for the tree on his right. The branches scraped and whipped at his arms, but he couldn't grab hold of the trunk. *At least it is slowing my descent.*

He looked down at the ground groaning, "I'm still going too fast." If he fell at this rate, he'd still break bones. Every branch that cracked in his grip he used to pull his way deeper into the tree. Lashes of pain broke out as the tree whipped at him with a vengeance. If he didn't know better, he'd think the tree was attacking him on purpose.

Before he could come up with another strategy, he was clear of the tree and falling toward the ground. He managed to slow enough so the hard-packed dirt he landed on only bruised his back instead of killing him. "That was close," he was so breathless, but nothing could keep him from smiling at that moment. "Ye beauty, I could kiss you," he shamelessly rubbed the ground as if it was the sexiest woman he had ever seen.

Silently, he swore to himself never to go into someone else's portal again. Life was too precious to throw it away. He looked at the sky thanking the Gods for not taking away his life.

After a few long breaths, he got his bearings and looked around, hoping the lasses were there. But what he saw made his heart play drums with his lungs. The adrenaline that left his body during the fall poured back into his veins.

Everything was a dreadful tan, "Shit, the lass wasn't mistaken," Hendrick closed his eyes to make sure it wasn't his sight playing tricks on him. *Didn't think so.* The curse was real and for some reason, the Rebecca wench used her wand to teleport here.

If he turned into a chomper because of her, he was chewing on her first. "Alright," he needed to focus his hearing and sense of smell to find Cat. Finding her would be the hard part, with her new beast he may not recognize her smell. He has been running on a low battery all night.

Yvonne's mocking voice chimed in his head from earlier, telling him she told him so. *Next time, I will listen and pack*

blood bags and steaks in the car. However, even if he did bring that stuff, it was doubtful he would have gone to the car to fuel up.

Hendrick was not able to use his vampire's superior hearing, but he had always had great smelling senses. If Cat killed Rebecca now, she would be stuck with the vampire beast. Their only hope was that the virus she contracted from his vampire beast was the same as a typical vampire, which meant the cure was possible if she didn't kill anyone.

All they would have to do was find a powerful witch or demon to reboot Cat's life. The vampire virus was like any virus and could be cured as long as the magic didn't intertwine with her soul.

He took a big sniff looking for her. He smelt bark, and a sour smell he assumed was the curse. He tried again, and the hint of honey and mint wafted to his nose.

Got you.

"Aaah! I told you everything I know," Rebecca's squeaky voice screeched from a distance. Hendrick took off toward the screaming and her scent, cursing at himself for not being able to tap into any of his beasts to move quicker. He had worn himself out at the worst possible time.

I can't fail her. He pushed through a large bush to see Cat jump on Rebecca.

"No!" Hendrick franticly ran to her. He was half way there when Cat's mouth clamped on Rebecca's neck.

As he got closer, he reached for Cat, but she tore away with a chunk of Rebecca's neck before he could stop her. He looked dumbfounded at Rebecca laying on the ground. Her blonde hair covering her face. He knew from the moldy smell coming off her, she was dead.

"Cat…" She was on her knees. Her hands covered her blood-soaked face.

He clenched his fist, mad at himself for not being able to protect her. *I'm sorry love. I'm too late. The grave got you.*

Thirty-One

CAT KNEW SHE shouldn't have killed Rebecca, but the new beast inside her demanded the blood coursing through her. The fact that she was a horrible person that deserved it, was a plus.

She lifted her nose to the air as she sucked in the peppermint and chocolate smell. She noticed his scent had changed back in the warehouse, but she had other things to think about then. Her subconscious had locked it in her memory banks. That lovely smell was Hendrick.

When she looked at him, his scent changed slightly to a muskier masculine mix. The smell was like hot chocolate in the woods. His scent made her mouth water. She wanted to bury her face in the glorious smell.

When he took a step toward her though, she growled. She didn't want him seeing her like this, looking like a monster with ripped and bloody clothes.

After what she had just done, she believed she was, too. A wave of emotion rolled over her. *I'm the thing I've hunted for years.* A tear rolled down her face and she shied away from his stare. All she wanted to do was bury herself in the pit of her being.

Hendrick's voice made her stop, "Don't do that Cat." He stepped closer, "Don't give in to the darkness. If you hide from those feelings now, you'll never be able to get them back. Please love, look at me," he gasped, running towards her when he saw her eyes darken and turn into empty black holes.

Vampires used to tell her, *it's not me, it's the vampire beast,* and she thought they were weak or lying. Now, she got what they were saying. She could feel Cat in her core, but the vampire beast was consuming every part of her as if she was in quicksand.

His hands caressed her blood-soaked face. "No, Cat, look at me. Maria was murdered, so your emotions are heightened." *And your vampire side is taking advantage of it.* He didn't say the last part out loud. There was no reason to scare her even more.

She was already letting the vampire beast kill who she was. Her deep black holes stared at him, not quite registering him even though she was trying. "Aye lass, that's it. Tell me

something good in your life." She needed to remember an enjoyable time in her life to push the vampire out. When a vampire beast takes over, they feed on fear and anger. So, the joy would help ease the vampire to the side bench. She had to show the beast who was the alpha.

He saw her look up, a telltale sign that she understood him and was thinking of a time. A beautiful curl stretched her lips upward, and her eyes lightened, but it didn't last long. With a small shake of her head, her eyes blackened again, and her teeth sharpened.

"Whoa, where did you go?" he asked brushing a long strand of hair behind her ear. "What's holding you back, lass?"

Her body slowly produced a thick smoke like fresh green boughs had been added to a campfire. The gray and purple cloud grazed her skin. *That's different, it must be left over from her Sapphire abilities. All of that would be gone soon, now that she had killed someone.*

"No," Cat said in a harsh voice unfamiliar to Hendrick.

"Kitty, tell me what Maria helped you with. Whatever it is, let it out. It's not worth losing yourself over." Hendrick pulled her into his arms. "Tell me."

They sat in silence for a few minutes before she answered him, "I'm damaged." Her voice squeaked, so she clamped her hands over her mouth.

"Why would ye say that lass? I've never met a more amazing person than ye." Hendrick's heart ached for her. The memory was eating her alive.

"You don't know what he did to me. I'm damaged goods, dammit." She spat at him, using her vampire hormones to make him hold her tighter. He was never fond of the pheromones vampires give off. They could make a person go mad with lust. If they could bottle it, fairy drugs would go out of style.

Hendrick kept holding her until she blurted out, "No man will ever want me after what that bastard did to me." Her whimpers became a full-on uncontrollable cry, "Lance raped me… He raped me! He cut me over and over to rub my blood on himself. He drugged me and tortured me for hours. I still wake up screaming at night." Hendrick squeezed her even tighter against him. *By the Gods.*

Cat was close to hysteria. If she went too far, there was no bringing her back. She already had one foot in the grave.

He could hear her breathing. It was more like a wild animal getting ready for the hunt than a person. Where was Yvonne when he needed her. His voice wouldn't work for this kind of emotion.

"No lass, that loser does not get to ruin yer life twice. I know for a fact that ye are mistaken. That monster didn't break you. Ye didn't let him then, so, don't let him now." He was stroking her hair.

He closed his eyes praying he was saying the right things. The emotional stuff was never his forte. With his luck he was making it worse. The physical stuff was more his thing. If Cat wanted to get punched in the face, he would be the perfect man for the job.

"You don't get it; he might as well have killed me that day. Anytime someone gets near me, I run away or push them away. I can't date, I can't have friends, and you see how both those turned out when I tried. My date dies, and my friend was working against me the whole time." She snorted, and a drop of snot dripped from her nose.

"I feel dead inside. Now, I'm a monster." She ran her fingers along the sharp edges of her teeth and wiped her nose. Cat narrowed her eyes at Hendrick. She hit his chest. It didn't hurt. She was tapping at him, her fist hit softer and softer until she wept in his arms.

He held her tight until he couldn't take her weeping anymore, "Lass, look at me." She did. He could feel that she wanted to hide in herself to get away. A protectiveness boiled inside of him at the look of pain on Cat's face.

He didn't know what he was doing until his lips pushed against Cat's. The feeling of electricity coursing through his veins made his body burn with desire.

When she reciprocated the kiss, he deepened his hold and touch. He needed her closer.

Hendrick couldn't remember a time he wanted something as much as he wanted this right now, with Cat, "By the Gods, love, your mouth is magical," he said in between kisses.

His hands roamed her body, caressing the soft cushion of her luscious lumps. They went lower and lower, to squeeze her ample bottom.

She pushed him away laughing, "Not going to happen, Romeo," Cat said, clear-headed, like kissing him had cleared away the fog of emotions.

Hendrick watched as her vampire beast latched onto her skin, she was the alpha. The beast would become a part of her, not take over her body. Her skin changed as well. The warm flesh became cooler and lighter until it was a milky porcelain perfection. The dark circles under her eyes disappeared. Even her frizzy hair became silky.

When those dark eyes turned back to her lovely green lily pads, his smile intensified. She was even more beautiful.

Her happiness faltered, and she grabbed his arm, "We're not done yet."

Cat pointed at Rebecca's body. "She said there is a cabin a few miles away with the transfer person. With no other than that scumbag Lance. He is waiting for his new girl to arrive."

Oh, now I know why she was freaking out. Hendrick was going to say something, but she put a hand to his mouth. "The merchandise has already left, which I'm assuming is your brother, but she said they keep documents of everything."

She smiled with a gaping mouth, "He's expecting a new person to assist him today. He is expecting someone new to the organization." She pointed at herself. "I'm perfect."

"No, no. You are not doing that Kitty, especially after what you just told me. This guy knows the demon is dead if he put it in you."

"Yes, but not before handing me off to one of his fellow accomplices. I already look like I've been through hell. He'll think I was sent to help keep him entertained. Believe me. I know this asshole," Cat said crossing her arms, not liking the feeling of embarrassment warming up her neck.

"And she also said she was sent by him to kill Maria or weaken her. Because Maria was your biggest weapon to stay hidden. They are after all of you. This could be the key to finding your brother, Hendrick." She sounded a little too eager, and Hendrick knew it. Yet who could blame her for wanting to nail the guy?

"Well, you are a vampire now. So, you have the strength and the speed. But we should make a good plan of defense. You can get the documents and lure him to his death, but I will do all the main fighting and interrogation." He brushed his hands through his hair. Hendrick didn't like her doing this alone, yet he knew if he didn't attack with her, she would do it on her own.

Cat went along with his crazy orders letting him feel like that was how it was going to happen. Deep down she knew if there was an opportunity, she would kill him.

She changed the subject instead of arguing, "Could I get any weirder? And now my smoke is purple and blue," her face lit up like an apple. She was not a fan of being weird.

"What do you mean?" Hendrick asked, and scrunch his face. He looked at her like she had three heads.

"When fighting Rebecca, I shot smoke out to blind her. That's how I could get the wand from her. If I hadn't, she probably would have killed me." Cat's voice sounded distant.

"You used your Sapphire abilities?" Hendrick asked, shocked. His eyes bulged out of their sockets.

"Yeah," was all Cat said. She was waiting for him to say something horrible. Not sure what, but she knew it wasn't good.

To make herself feel better she filled the silence, "I'm dead…" Her eyes drifted down, "Will I have to sleep in a grave? At least you'll know which grave I'm in, it'll be smoking."

Hendrick couldn't answer any of her question and it pissed him off. He never heard of anything like this happening.

In the norm, vampires lose all their previous abilities when they turn. He had never heard of a vampire keeping their magic. And casting magic with only a word is a powerful gift.

Dragonvire's can cast spells, they could use their blood for curses, but they couldn't make magic appear.

He bit his lip and smiled at Cat. The hopeful glance she gave him warmed his heart. *She doesn't know how special she is.* He hugged her one more time, "Lass you are full of surprises."

Thirty-Two

CAT SIGHED AT herself for being here. The Gods seriously needed to get a new seer, so she could have been warned about this. *Remember, you must save the people from the chompers curse.* Cat kept chanting that in her head.

"It's been so long, sweet thing. I can't believe fate brought you back to me. Have you missed me?" Lance's chiming voice purred in her ears. She used to love his voice. Now, it made her want to throw up.

"You know I have. How could I not?" Cat hoped if she stroked his ego it would make him ignore her fear and anger scent. Hopefully, his ego wasn't too big that his head exploded.

As she thought about his head turning into slop her smile became wicked. *Now, that's something to smile about.*

She and Hendrick had a plan. Cat would flirt with the jerk, distract him to get the file, then lead him outside to Hendrick for questioning. Cat was glad Lance wasn't the head honcho with tons of guards. He was just another pathetic lackey. That thought made her smile even more.

Cat would love to do the questioning, but Hendrick wouldn't have it. He knew she would up the torture and eventually kill him without getting answers. And he wasn't wrong. All she had wanted to do for years was see Lance at the end of her blade. But he had been off the radar for years now. Not even David could find him.

"That's true. I do have a way with the ladies." Cat was surprised he didn't have a mirror in his hands while he said that. The way he licked his fingers and rubbed his eyebrows made Cat stifle a laugh.

I'm going to love killing you, prick.

"What do you think?" Lance looked at her expectantly. Those ugly bushy eyebrows rose up when she looked at him, puzzled.

"I'm sorry what? I was thinking of us together in my room." Cat's face heated, and her stomach dropped. She needed to focus.

A smirk of pride plastered across his face, "Aw, yes, that was a beautiful night. I knew you liked to be helpless and taken advantage of by me. It radiated off you. Does my little toy still like it?"

He bit his lip as his eyes roamed her ripped clothes. They exposed her breasts and were covered in blood. Her disheveled body must have turned him on because his deep brown eyes dilated.

Cat couldn't say anything; she nodded her head rapidly, yes. When it looked like he was suspicious, she bit her lower lip playfully.

"Good. And I see by your appearance you have a little more experience in what I like," he got up from the white couch across from the wooden chair she had chosen.

The way he crept to her made Cat get a cold ache in her chest like death himself gripped her heart. *Do not touch me, scumbag.*

She tried to make her uncomfortable gestures into excited gestures by pushing out her breast and sliding low on the chair. If she was lucky, he'd buy her efforts.

When a woman really wants a guy their sexual parts naturally drift towards the man unconsciously, danced around in her head. He used to tell her that while his finger traced her cleavage.

The anger scent got stronger. *Calm down Cat. Think of Hendrick and how it felt to be touched by him.*

"And I was expecting Rebecca, but you are a better surprise." His tone was mischievous.

Cat smiled, pretending it did sound like a clever idea.

His greasy hand grazed her shoulder, "My toy has been playing with others, hasn't she? It looks like someone healed you with a demon wand." His eyebrows rose as he walked behind her, grabbing her breast. If it was any other man, she'd appreciate the light circles being traced around her nipple. But not this man.

She held her breath, trying to calm down. "Look at all this blood you gave him, and I only got a little," he pinched her neck. "Bad toy. I'll be needing more."

By the flames of Hades, I am going to rip your manhood off and shove it down your throat. She pulled away from his advances. "I'm hungry. May I have something to eat? Remember how sloppy I get without food. I'd like to be my best for you," Cat lied her big butt off, crossing her fingers her lie would work. If he kept touching her, she'd say the hell with the mission.

"Of course, my toy, I need you strong for what I'm about to do to you." He walked to the kitchen. The swinging doors flung back and forward, taunting Cat. She couldn't move until they stopped.

"Do you want to know a secret, beautiful toy?" Lance yelled from the kitchen. Cat could hear the fridge slamming. The noise made her heart jump.

"Of course," she said as she walked to the desk near the fireplace in the middle of the room. She was glad he had plush white carpet, so her bare feet were soundless.

"Remember the jar of blood I took from you? I used it to stroke myself for years after that night. I knew you would eventually come around." His cheery voice made her throw up in her mouth a little.

She swallowed it, "I am flattered."

"You should be. I've told all my other toys about you, and they all hate your guts," he came out of the kitchen carrying two sandwiches and some chips.

Cat froze. When he saw her at the desk his eyes got darker, "What are you doing?" His voice stabbed her lungs. She couldn't breathe.

"I thought you could bend me over this gorgeous desk," she gulped. Hopefully, he couldn't hear her heart pounding so fast. The *lub-dub* sound was all Cat could hear.

Her nervous scent rose in the air making Cat try to distract him from the smell. She stuck her butt out and with a sexy lure, she rocked side to side.

His eyes softened, and his pupils dilated, "What an innovative idea, toy. But the cutting will be done in the other room, that's a five-thousand-dollar desk." He walked behind her again, making her bend over as he placed the food on the desk.

"Wine!" Cat squeaked pulling away from him. She took a deep breath, "May I have some wine to loosen me up, as well?" When he frowned, she continued, "It'll help my blood flow."

"Yeah, that is true." Lance turned around to go back into the kitchen. He mumbled something that Cat ignored. She couldn't do this anymore. She was at the edge of her tolerance. If he touched her again, he'd be getting his throat slashed with the letter opener on that stupid desk.

She looked at all the papers and sucked in her breath.

Dammit, they're demon papers. She could only read them with demon magic, a black curse, or fire.

She grabbed all the blank white and gray papers putting them in a folder and shoved them in her pants. They could figure out what they said later. She needed to get out of here.

She ran to the cabin door frantically, with a grunt, she swung the heavy wood open. The humid heat smacked her in the face as she stepped outside. The claustrophobic temperature clung to her like walking into a sauna. *Ugh, this is nasty.*

She looked around. The only color was in a small circle around his house. The rest was that nasty tan. She hoped there were no other residents around here because they would be chompers by now.

Cat jumped at the sound of something slamming in the kitchen, so she did the only thing she could.

Run.

Thirty-Three

LANCE CAME OUT of the kitchen with his bare manhood dangling, dripping red wine liquid all over the floor as he walked into the room. He'd already had a few glasses tonight and a couple more in the kitchen, so he was ready to play with his toy.

"I brought you a gift, my toy. Come play." His words drifted into the abyss, no one was there. The cabin was empty.

What the hell?

His face squeezed together in anger as he looked in every corner of the room. "Cathleen?" His voice cracked like a whip and the word vibrated in the empty room. His light brown furniture hid a few places, so he walked over to inspect them. *Maybe, she is playing a game of her own?*

He walked to the couch, maybe she was hiding there. The side and front of the sofa were empty making his heart beat faster. The sound of laughter echoed in his mind. His eyes darted around with purpose now.

He noticed the door slightly ajar and with an immediate urgency he swung around to his desk. The fact that it was empty meant his toy was gone. He growled and ground his teeth together. The desk looked cleaner than before like she wanted to taunt him by emphasizing how empty the surface was.

He cursed himself for letting her get the best of him. The bottle of wine crashed to the floor in a heap of glass and liquid. His rage increased as the red liquid splashed against his feet.

"Aha!" A boiling hot rage exploded inside of him, more heated than any erupting volcano.

An ear bleeding roar he let out shook the cottage. "No one makes me look like a fool," he said with a growl in his throat as his new demonic beast surged to the surface. His beast was slamming into place; there was no time to go outside.

The beast wanted her life.

Lance had kept his deal with the demon a secret from everyone, so no one knew of his strength yet. He didn't plan on the demon dying that he sold his soul to, but the way his power grew, no one was complaining.

The demon fused itself with his woodland beast making him exponentially more powerful. Deep inside, the evil monster was old as night and victoriously wicked like the actual demon. He loved it but controlling the beast's temper was something he still struggled with.

A groan escaped him as he grew taller and wider. It sounded more like an animal than a man. He hit the roof, his feet smashed through the carpet and the wood foundation of the cabin.

"I just got that fixed!" he screamed at the top of his lungs. At the same time, his arms extended outward, bulging his muscles.

Next was the part Lance hated, his skin turned lime green, and his pores opened letting a sludge poor through. The demon must have been snot man because that was new.

He was almost finished transforming.

The last part took the longest and hurt the most. His new demon beast subconsciously coded his mind, making him think and act differently. The way the evil tar slithered through him, gripping his brain was the worst feeling ever. He was meaner, and oh so much deadlier.

Lance would kill his own family if they were no longer needed. If he was honest with himself, being the beast was the only time he was free. As if he was a chain smoker and his beast was a puff of nicotine after a long grueling day. He craved his beast. Even as a child something always was off inside of him.

Now that his eyes had been opened to the high power, being in his usual, tan shell was a cage for him. *Never put a wolf in a kennel, it gets hungry,* was what his father used to say. Lance understood what he meant, now.

He was an entirely different person in the beast form. So much so, he named his creature Beastor. And that was his true name. The day he could show his true self to people and become their master was all he wanted.

He was willing to wait in the shadows of other leaders. Until he could kill them and take their place.

He knew the transformation was complete when his vision changed. All the shapes in the room were more pronounced and everything became clearer. His malevolent scowl darted from side to side. His walls were dented with age and his furniture had a coat of dirt on it that he couldn't see with his regular eyes. *I'm going to kill my cleaning lady. Worthless slob.*

The only thing he wasn't a fan of was the color change his demon eyes gave. All the vibrant colors were darkened and grayed slightly. Not enough to make him completely color blind, though. His red eyes were shining bright, for sure.

Aaarr!

The animal inside him was ready to play. He sniffed the air, loving the scent of the blood and fear she left behind. *Good toy be afraid, I can find you faster that way.*

He slammed the door making the hole twice as big. That's another thing he'd have to fix because of her, which made him angrier. He brushed off wood chips from his slimy skin.

He dreaded having to pass the magic blocker amulets around his house. Going into the tan curse was like having tons mosquitoes bite into his skin.

She was going to pay.

"She'll pay in flesh," he said with a hiss. A wicked smile wrinkled his face as he showed off his jagged teeth.

He used his four new, long limbs to push against the ground following the smell of rotten apple Cat was trailing behind her. Fear is the easiest emotion to track. He was going faster and faster until his movement blurred. The hiss of the wind in his ears and the forest vibrating through him made him even stronger.

A shiver of anticipation went down his spine. *Here puss, puss.*

Thirty-Four

CAT HATED RUNNING. The shock-waves pounding on her knees, and the twigs scraping her bare feet made her clench her jaw. She wished she could levitate to him.

In case Lance had sensors or magical detectors, Hendrick was miles away. So, she had a long run still ahead of her.

At least she wasn't sinking to her knees in mud with chompers biting at her heels, like in the Goddess's vision. She was grateful for that.

Despite everything, she was alive and hyped up.

The night rubbed against her flesh and called to her. She felt amazing. The large trees, bright moon, and soft dirt made her soul hum with glee.

She held her breath as she ran. Now that she was a vampire her body didn't need as much oxygen. She would have to test her new abilities later.

Except for her burning muscles. Even changing into a vampire couldn't stop her round thighs from blazing from the stress. She seriously needed to run more often. So, running wouldn't be as stressful for her body.

An expected roar thundered behind Cat a few miles away. The sound-waves were so strong the rocks under her feet shot up, tripping her, which made her steady pace falter. She tightened her muscles, showing a little fear, and survival adrenaline spiked through her.

She pushed her feet against the ground faster. Tapping further into her new beast made her vision laser sharp. The comforting green shine lit a path for her.

Not that she needed the extra light. The tan curse wouldn't let the darkness turn things black. Everything was an eerie bronze; not even the shadows could change the core color.

She could hear Lance gaining on her; the way he snarled and snorted made him easy to hear. *Might as well blare a car horn stupid.*

Something didn't make sense though. Lance was a wilderness Beast, so his abilities shouldn't have exceeded hers. Not now that she had her own beast. She had studied wilder's skills and flaws. They get their power from the trees. Like a tree, if they get damaged in the roots, they die.

So, aim for the feet when fighting them. The shot won't kill them, but their energy source is damaged. Effectively, making them easier to take down.

They couldn't outrun a vampire, though. Even with the forest giving him strength. *His new speed must have something to do with the demon. Maybe Lance got more than just hierarchy power from the demon.* She contemplated that for a few seconds.

Her eyes widened as realization hit her in the gut. "Dammit!" Cat said as she tucked her elbows into her body and made her aching legs move faster.

She could not give up now, there was too much at stake. Her surroundings blurred, making her smile. *Maybe she'd survive after all.*

Crunch, dead leaves on the ground sounded like a grenade going off. He was closer than she thought. *Okay, maybe I spoke too soon.*

She said a small prayer that she would make it to Hendrick in time. If she was right about his boost in power, the situation had gotten a lot worse.

She didn't get to think of the consequences of Lance having new powers. In less than a second, a brutal force slammed into her. She grunted, her luck had run out. Lance's large body crashed into Cat's smaller frame. She tried to use their momentum to her advantage, but the blast of his monstrous body against hers was too fast.

Even with his strong hold on her, she didn't go down easily. With all her might, she kept him from pinning her to the ground.

Their bodies rolled around in the dirt, cutting into one another with their long, extended claws. When the documents fell out of her pants, he grabbed a handful of them and growled at her. He threw the papers down, leaping for her.

His disgusting odor seeped into her skin, making her skin slimy. His nasty smell soaked into the cut Lance was making on her sides.

Cat knew she was in trouble when he gripped her shoulders and pinned her down. A wicked grin stretched across his eyes as he let go of her, using his magic to keep her in place.

"Mmm, this looks familiar." He closed his eyes, "I sliced your smooth skin with my dagger?" He swiped a finger on Cat's face and scooped the seeping blood. Cat couldn't stop him; he had her pinned.

Lance wiped the blood on his chest causing ripples of goosebumps to form over his body. Cat watched how they traveled from his neck then lower.

She wanted to cut off his skin, so he could never experience that again.

"Do you know what the funny part is? I knew you would open your legs for me without the drugs, but I wanted to smell and taste your fear."

Her eyes widened.

He was too strong. The sickening fear was like black oil drowning her. It threatened to take over her. "No, no, no, no!"

His long claws cut at her again, but he wasn't cutting her to cause her harm. The assault was to rip off the rest of her tattered clothes.

Lance grabbed the documents from her and threw them to the side. Only stopping for a second, then attacking her clothes again.

Cat knew what he was doing. If she was naked, he could attach himself to her. Once his erection was inside of her, she'd be trapped.

That kind of demon attachment was different than a magical link, if a demon got the chance to inject someone physically, it was fatal.

He would latch his manhood inside, and it would not leave until he wanted it to. Demons do it for psychological torture. The more they struggle, the tighter his member got inside of them until the victim was utterly helpless and eventually dead. So, if the someone wanted to live through that, they would have to submit to the demon.

Knowing that was what he intended, Cat moved her legs and arms like a crazy person. She hoped he would either think she was letting fear run her and loosen his magical grip on her shoulder. Or, the movement would distract him enough to where Cat could find a way out.

When he loosened his grip on her shoulders, Cat hesitated only a second. She never thought her flaying around would work. She looked him straight in the eyes and slammed her knee into his groin and her elbow into his face.

Cat scrambled away.

Lance held himself with one hand and pulled her back by her ankle with the other. The terror in her eyes and the sound of her thumping heart Cat could have forgiven herself for, but the bitter cry that exited her mouth made her angry. He wasn't allowed to see her this way again.

She blamed it on his new, intense scratches. They were like lava on her skin. She could smell them boil. She could feel herself passing out. He kept saying, "I'm Beastor, I get what I want," as he tore through her flesh like butter.

She must have passed out because when she opened her eyes she was naked and Beastor was guiding himself toward her opening. "NO!" Cat screamed. This time she didn't hesitate, she elbowed him again.

She let her beast take over, flinging herself up and over his back. She dug her nails into his shoulder which made him cry out. The sound made her beast jitter with glee. Before she knew what, she was doing, her fangs sank into his neck.

That was a breaking point for Cat. She was not going to let this dirtbag win again. *Kill, kill, kill* chanted over and over in her head. Her body rose off the ground, but she didn't pay too much attention to it. All she knew was the bastard couldn't get loose from her grip.

She opened her eyes; their bodies were floating over the ground. As if connected to a rope, Cat let go of Beastor. Without her to hold him up anymore Beastor smashed to the ground. With all Cat's might, she dove for him and pushed her nails into his spine.

She could sense his demon magic surfacing again, so she only had one chance to escape. She needed to run. She needed Hendrick's blood to kill him. There was no way she could defeat him without weapons or magic.

When she was happy with the gashes in his back and on his neck, she booked it. Just in time, too, because Beastor put up a lightning shield. Anything inside the circle would be electrocuted. She hated demons.

Pictures of his body on her and his blade in hand had her call out for help, "Hendrick! Hendrick!" Damn her pride. Her life mattered more.

Cat ran to Hendrick who was waiting by some dark tan smooth trees. "Hendrick heads up!" she yelled, so he would be prepared for battle. His eyes brows bunched together like he didn't recognize her. He has been out in the curse for too long.

Beastor hadn't caught up with her yet which meant she had a few seconds to snap Hendrick out of it.

Just as she reached him, he shook his head, "Aye, love?" His voice was the sweet caramel smoothness that she loved about him. "Ye naked and cut up, what in Hades is going on?" he pulled off his shirt and helped it over her head in a blur of movements.

Cat was so flustered she didn't even care if she was naked, "Beastor is coming." She rambled, "Green, slimy, demon and has long, sharp nails. They almost cut my eyes out." She panted trying to fill her lungs with enough air to talk, "He's coming are you ready? The tan curse didn't-"

Hendrick's eyes widened as he cut his palm shoving the blood in her face cutting her off. She took one drink and pushed his hand away. Her cuts were healing because of her vampire beast, but not quick enough to his liking.

"I'm fine, kitty." He rubbed his palm on his pants as his skin knitted back together, "Who the blasted is Beastor?" Hendrick asked holding her arms to steady her when she wavered on her feet.

She paused for a second. Before she could answer, a familiar deep voice replied, "I'm Beastor." His black eyes shone in the moonlight as his green, disgusting body walked out of the shadows.

Thirty-Five

C AT COULD FEEL the vein in her forehead throb as Beastor stepped out of the shadows. His movements were slow and precise. Every step he took made Cat's heart pound faster.

"It looks like someone crapped you out lad," Hendrick lifted his chin to the demon. If there was one thing Cat was learning about Hendrick, he could win a provoking award.

A deep warning growl came from Beastor, like a feral dog ready to attack, "You are going to be a part of my crap after I eat you alive."

Cat tried not to show any emotion, but he was the one person her stoic dead expression didn't work on. She knew a flicker of fear escaped because his smile grew mischievous.

She cursed under her breath, knowing that smile was going to haunt her nightmares. The razor-sharp teeth and long stretched mouth was the equivalent of evil. His black gaping eyes were even worse.

***

Beastor got tired of waiting, he launched himself at Hendrick using his magic to push him back before swirling in the air. His big foot slammed into Hendrick's jaw. The man was more of a threat, so he was going to take him down first.

***

Hendrick moved so fast Cat could barely see his movements. He jumped to the side slashing his fist on Beastor's jaw and using his dagger to rip into his chest. Hendrick didn't have time to slice his palm with his blade, so it wasn't a killing blow.

The two tangled together on the ground, both trying to gain the upper hand. Cat watched, wanting to join in the fight, but their movements were a messy blur. If she jumped in, she could get Hendrick hurt, or herself. Hendrick already looked like he was slowing down. With his blood loss and tan curse, he was like a Natural.

Cat put up her hand. "Volant," busted from her lips until her body was trembling from energy loss. Beastor jerked to the side, but there wasn't the substantial impact she was expecting. Cat shook her hand and tried again.

Nothing…

What the hell?

Her beast wasn't helping her much. Either her abilities weren't strong enough in comparison to them, or she didn't know how to tap into her other gifts yet.

When she saw Beastor grab Hendrick's head and get ready to snap it, she couldn't stand by anymore. She leaped on a tree trunk and jumped on Beastor's back. "Of all the Hades sluts, get off me." His voice rose to a volume that hurt Cat's ears.

She bit his neck again, hating the tar taste of his blood flooding her mouth. This time she was different, like seeing Hendrick so close to death clicked something inside of her. Her muscles expanded and her power vibrating in her body became thunderous.

"Get off me bitch."

Instead of letting go of Hendrick's head like she hoped, he gripped onto it tighter, his power holding him down and his hands wrapped around his skull. She glanced down at Hendrick and noticed his skin looked a pale-yellow tan. *He's been out here for too long; the curse has gotten to him.*

Cat bit fiercely at Beastor's open neck to stop him from hurting Hendrick. But the beast wasn't going to let go. He shot green light into Hendrick's head.

The intense flash of light partially blinded Cat, so she pulled her mouth away from his neck to shield her eyes. When she opened them again, Hendrick's limp body was crashing to the ground. "No!" Cat's heart broke at the sight of Hendrick laying on the ground. With the tan curse seeping into him and the blood loss, she feared he wouldn't wake up.

Beastor grabbed a chunk of Cat's hair with his long arms and flung her forward as if she was a sack of potatoes.

She went with the motion, rolling forward until her feet hit the ground and she was in a kneeling position. Without looking back, she jumped on a large tan tree and bounced off its rough surface. She looked back at Beastor, smiling. She didn't know why, but something changed inside of her. As if someone wrapped her in a silk blanket and stuck her finger in an outlet.

The look of confusion on Lance's face made her feel even more powerful.

He tilted his head to the side and lifted his shoulder, "Okay, toy, you got my attention. Let's dance." That was the only warning before he attacked.

His movement seemed slower to her. She slammed her fist into his eye, swinging around to follow it with a kick to the face. His anger was getting the best of him. All that fury made his hits sloppy and easy to block.

"You're pathetic, Lance. Even as a massive beast you are nothing," Cat drilled into him. Using his human name to rub his face in her dominance.

She pushed her fist up nailing him under the jaw. The blue magic that slammed out of her was different, almost wild. When his body went soaring backward, Cat was star struck.

She stood there, mouth open. Her deep, slow breaths were the only sound she heard. That wild magic pushing against her skin was like little insect bites.

Cat walked to the body lying on the ground. Before she could reach him, those bites intensified, which had her stumbling around in pain.

Whoa, why do I feel so dizzy? Her vision blurred at the edges. Something was draining her. That strong intense power she just had flowing through her was gone now.

"That's impossible. How did you do it, you whore?" Lance, the tan shell, got up stark naked. "No one has the ability to pull a beast back to his human form." He ran to Cat, ready to kill her. She had made him shift back into his Lance form with her punch.

The stare he gave her snatched her out of her shock, and she tried to ignore her need to faint.

She knew he no longer wanted to play with her by the way his eyes pierced through her, and the crease on his forehead looked like devil horns forming. If looks could burn, she would be in flames.

She tucked and rolled to the left, diving for Hendrick. She grabbed the dagger he had dropped on the ground at the same time. Lance followed like an old-fashioned mummy with his arms extended and his movements slow. He even moaned in irritation.

"Sorry," she told Hendrick as she sliced his hand and lathered the blade in blood.

"You will not ruin this for me, cunt. I will be the alpha!" Lance shouted, kicking her in the side. She toppled over and held her injury.

He kept kicking her with the vengeance of a demon, pure evil. He smacked the blade out of her hand. "You nasty slut, I will kill you from the inside out," he said. His words sounded crazed; they didn't make sense. And he kept grumbling weird things.

He lifted her shirt up, leaning into her. "No!" she reached for the dagger. Cursing her new gifts, *where the hell did they go?* She was even weaker than before.

Come on something work! She might get psychological hemorrhoids from all the mental pushing she was doing. She needed to activate something inside of her. Except everything felt dormant.

She felt Lance's flesh on hers, but she couldn't reach the blade, he had his knees pressed into her thighs keeping her in place. *Come on, come on. No, no.* Her fingers brushed against the blades jagged edges, but she couldn't get a grip.

Her survival instincts kicked in, making her eyes water; high screeches ripped from her throat. She turned to focus on Lance instead. He was laughing at her, prolonging his brutal assault. She screamed and flung her arms at him.

A cement of a fist slammed into Cat's face making black roses bloom in her vision. Lance smiled down at her as she stopped fighting and laid there unconscious.

He knew the ultimate result would leave him victorious. Now, he would have his toy and make her pay for all the things she had put him through tonight.

"Now let's see if you are as good as I remember."

Thirty-Six

FOR THE SECOND time tonight, the Goddess broke the rules and interfered. This time though, she was in Cat's world. Her body kept disappearing in the wind as if it wanted to take her back home.

She looked around with caution. There was a reason why gods did not travel over here. Certain demons were immune to the Gods powers which meant she needed to be careful.

Both Cat and Lance were frozen in time. She knelt beside Cat. Her fingers shimmered in and out of form to push into Cat's prefrontal cortex. That was the only way to locate her emotion control center.

She gently poked around trying to activate the controls. When nothing happened, the Goddess pressed harder and quicker. She needed to do this fast, before the other gods noticed.

In her defense, she wasn't interfering, per say, just influencing the outcome.

She groaned. Yeah, she doubted The Three would see it that way.

Last time this monster attacked Cat, she wasn't aware of his actions until after Cat left her vision. The Gods had held her down to keep her from interfering.

"You will join Hades soon. I'll make sure he welcomes you personally," the Goddess glared at him. She wanted to throw him off her and send him to the fiery pits of Hades. If she did, however, she'd end up joining him there.

So, she looked back down at Cat. *She drained herself tapping into my power.* Sapphires were the only beings who could use the gods magic, but they drain themselves in the process.

She smiled down at Cat, her eyes dilating and face softening like a proud mother. Cat had used the Goddess' abilities to push the demon back inside of Lance.

As Gods, they had the ability to take an Unnatural's beast away and, as if the beast was gum stuck in their hair, cut it out.

She didn't have time to explain to her what linking with a Goddess really meant. Cat had the ability to access the Goddess's magic, but like tonight, the wild magic would drain her quickly.

She clapped softly in a repetitive movement when she saw blue and purple smoke lift into the air.

She turned to Lance with a disgusted look in her eyes. She could feel her face crinkle; an angry God was an ugly God. Gods were never meant to feel anger, so when they did, it showed on their face. Making them look their old age—which was why Hades was so hideous. The more time she spent with Cat, the more she felt human.

Maybe they wouldn't care? She lifted her hand to Lance. Before she could do anything, the ground shook under the Goddess's feet. She stumbled with grace, knowing who was warning her. "Alright," The wind blew her backward enough to make her stagger. "I got it." She looked at the sky. No one was there, but she knew they were watching her.

Being one of the youngest celestial beings, they always liked to keep a close eye on her. She didn't entirely agree with some of the rules. This was one of those times.

She ignored their whispers to return home. She knelt to touch Cat's face. Her heart warmed at what a fierce warrior her progeny had turned out to be. "My sweet Cat, that is all I can do. The rest is up to you." She caressed Cat's cheek noticing they were looking better already.

The Goddess glanced at the sky as another way to help Cat came to her. *They will have my head if I give her an wish charm.* She shrugged.

She made a circle with her hands and expanded her fingers making a bright gold orb form. The ground rumbled again, but she ignored the massive vibrations and pushed the orb into Cat's chest.

As soon as the gold ball disappeared, a large lightning bolt struck the Goddess's hand. "Ow!" She pulled her hand to her chest. "That was unnecessary." She would have that mark on her immortal skin forever, but if it meant she got to see Cat again the scar was worth it.

If you do anything else to change the outcome, I will lock you in hell with your brother Hades. A deep angry voice made her stomach drop.

With that, she closed her arms to her chest telling the eyes watching her upstairs she had finished. She elegantly bowed, and her right arm drifted down to her knees. As she straightened and pointed up, her body rose in the air.

The wind she commanded enveloped her. Her heart ached with regret. She wasn't sure she could live with herself if this didn't go Cat's way.

As the Goddess's feet landed back in her dimension, she cursed her maker for not giving her the power of seeing into the future. She turned on her globe floating in the middle of the room to watch what happened next, helpless to do anything but pray.

Please, let the council be with you.

Thirty-Seven

LANCE YELPED AT the sight of smoke coming from under Cat. *What they hell! Is she on fire?* When the smoke came from her mouth, Lance stopped and stared at her for a few seconds, stunned. She was unconscious, so he rolled her over to make sure. There was no fire under her, but he did get a pleasant view of her backside.

It made him focus back on the duty at hand. *Right, teach his toy a lesson.* The weirdness could wait. He had waited too long to have her underneath him again.

He rolled her back over, covering her body with his. He looked down at her with a resentful backbiting glare filled with hatred. Even the shadows clung to the creases of his face, enhancing his evil appearance. Nothing could stop him now.

He saw her smile. A soft, glowing smile that did do nothing to feed his psychotic nature. It pissed him off. She was supposed to be in misery. Last time she was so afraid and had so much loathing for him he got off just looking at her.

"That's it," he slapped her on her cheek, not hard enough to bruise. She didn't wake up, so he tried again. This time the smack echoed in the distance. "Wake up!" He smiled at the red mark on her face.

That's a good look for you, toy.

He jumped when her eyes popped open. She didn't look around or stir in confusion like he expected. Cat struck him hard in the face blackening his eye. He grabbed her wrist snapping her hand all the way back.

In the distance, he heard the sound echo, it sounded like someone stepping on glass. The sound was like liquor to the flame inside of him. *That's it. That's what I want.* She yelled and pulled her arm to her chest. Her reaction only made his smile grow wider.

He laughed at her cradling her arm. He saw Cat's jaw tighten and nostrils flare. Her reaction made his eyebrows go up. *Why is she not crying or pleading for me to leave her alone?*

She did something he never expected; she attacked. With her good hand Cat reached for his left eye. As her finger connected with the squishy ball, she pushed at its soft surface until she heard a pop. Dark tan liquid poured out of Lance's eye. "Aaahh!" he yelled.

He lifted off her with both hands covering his eye trying to stop the bleeding. Cat managed to wiggle her way out from under him. "By Hades, you are the worst toy ever." Lance's rage boiled over; he'd had enough of her. He would have to find another toy.

He grabbed her kicking legs and put them on either side of him. He dove for her neck, clenching his hands against her soft skin. Her eyes went wide, and her mouth gaped open. That look made a rush of excitement course through him. He leaned into her neck, essentially pushing all his weight into the choke.

He watched her crisscross her arms over his straight arms, trying to use her elbows to push his arms away. He laughed at her idiocy, "Do you think you can push me away? I'm much stronger than you, little girl."

***

Cat didn't give up, though, even when her face turned blue. She hiked her hips up as high as they would go and in that crisscross position, she pulled her elbows to her chest. She only had one chance to loosen his grip. In one quick push, she brought her body down and crunched up with her upper body, effectively making his elbows bend.

Yeah!

She squirmed underneath him, rolling to one side, then the other to put her feet on his hips. She still wasn't at her full strength, so this was not as effective as she hoped. Her feet flopped to his side where she didn't want them.

***

He screamed in frustration and took control of her again, "I hate you with a passion, cunt!" He looked at his hand, noticing for the first time that his blood was tan. "You've made me stay out here too long. The curse is affecting me," Lance swung his dull fingernails at her throat.

He looked at his hand, remembering it wasn't his green shifted form. "Damn you to hell," he said, and hit her in the nose.

Cat covered her face. He still saw the blood drip out. The sight of the dark red liquid made a crazed rage erupt inside of him. He grabbed her hands, jerking her arms out of their sockets.

She tried to ignore the pain and fight him. But he snapped her other wrist and put both her hands under each of his knees before she could do anything useful.

This time when his fist collided with her face, there was nothing she could do to stop him. She moved it side to side and struggled, but that made his eyes go wide and excited.

He kept hitting her until he was pleased with his artwork decorating her face.

Now, say goodbye whore. He bent to her neck ripping a piece of her flesh off with his teeth and pulled away. He pulled her hands out from under him to watch her struggle.

Cat's green eyes went wide with panic, and she grabbed her throat trying to stop the bleeding. Lance looked down at her as he chewed her flesh like he was eating chicken.

"Die slut. Tell Lusion thanks for me," Lance's said standing up. He needed to get back to the cabin before the tan curse went into full effect. His smile faltered as a low aching pain burned in his chest like a bad case of heartburn. "Whoa." He heaved as slobber ran down his chin. When he wiped it away, his palm came back with thick tan liquid.

"How 'bout ye tell him yourself lad," a man said behind him.

He looked down, "No." A blast of agonizing, red-hot pain fired his neurons. Tears wet his face as he watched the jagged blade piercing through his chest, being sucked back into a gaping hole that ran clear through his heart.

The man's warm breath against his skin was the last thing Lance felt before the bitter truth of never-ending darkness coiled around his soul, dragging him away to where Hades himself waited to show him the true meaning of being a toy.

Thirty-Eight

HENDRICK WISHED HE could have given her the kill, but there was no time. He could feel the curse's icy cold grip on the back of his neck as it pushed him into an unforgiving rage. Any minute now, he would be gone. His beasts were nothing but a whisper inside of him. He needed to get Cat up and get the hell out of here before it was too late.

"Come on Cat, breathe!" Hendrick put both hands on her chest and pushed down. He did this over and over never letting his elbows bend.

Ye can do it, let me see those beautiful eyes.

Hendrick woke up to seeing Lance or Beastor, whatever the bloody man wanted to be called ripping Cats throat out. After he killed the Blaigeard, he basically drowned Cat in his blood. But she still wasn't responding. *What can I do?*

His eyes twitched in every direction as he thought. There must be something from his childhood stories that can help. *Sapphires are your sister protectors, with them both factions are stronger, their smoke amplifies your power.*

"Shit, I can't remember a thing." He ran his hands through his hair and hit his head to help him think.

I can't do this again. The scared little boy that he never let come to the service pushed its way out. He tugged at his heart as the paralyzing chill flooded his body.

He watched as the tan color crept up his fingers like a disease eating his body. All of it overwhelmed him to the point of tears.

They fell like his body sprung a leak, and they tormented him. Their salty shower stood for weakness, failure, and everything he didn't want to be.

His pity party didn't last long; he pushed through the emotional wave drowning him, "No, not this time." He equaled out his weight on his knees again and started a new set of compressions. He heard her bones pop underneath his touch. *I'm sorry.* He was, but he would not let Cat die the way his mother did.

A werewolf ripped out his mom's throat, and he had sat next to her, crying, for what felt like forever. He hadn't been able to do anything about her dying. As the king, he was never taught trivial things like CPR. He had servants who did such things.

But this isn't my mom, damn it. I will not lose two people in that manner. If I can keep her blood flowing until her neck heals, she should be alright.

After his thirtieth push against her chest, he grabbed her face and tilted up her chin. He lowered his face to hers, and as he pinched her nose closed, he breathed two huge breaths into her mouth. He nodded to himself when her chest rose.

"That's my girl." Fresh determination pumped into him. If the air could get through her neck that meant the gaping hole in her throat was closing.

"Fight this lass. That Blaigeard does not win."

He beat down on her chest pushing the blood through her body, "Come back to me, my love." His hands trembled as he bent down to breathe for her again.

Lub…Dub…Lub…Dub…

Her heart was beating, "Yes!" He reached his hands out to the sky screaming all his emotions out. *I did it, mum, I did it.* He looked over his shoulder expecting a hand to be resting there. But there was nothing but air. The pressure of a hand was there though, regardless if he could see it or not.

Mum? A tear rolled down his cheek as the pressure released. *Please don't go.* The little boy deep inside of him was back, and he wanted his mother.

There was a tug at his heart and a wave of happiness washed over him from someone else. The beautiful sensation was his mother's way of saying, *goodbye my son, I will always love you, and I am very proud of you.*

He used to get so embarrassed when she said it in front of others. If she would repeat those words, just once, he'd let her tell the world, and nothing could make him get embarrassed again.

Hendrick put a hand on his shoulder where she once was, "Goodbye." He smiled the most uplifting joyous smile he had ever let stretch his face.

"You can't get rid of me that easily," Cat said to Hendrick. She thought he was saying goodbye to her. Her eyes fluttered open. They were still a little swollen, making holding them open difficult.

He grabbed her hand and squeezed it ever so slightly, "Right ye are, lass." Hendrick gazed into her eyes. "Ye better be careful though, I think ye down to ye seventh life now."

"I'll take that into consideration." She rolled over on her knees trying to get up. As soon as her weight was on her wrist, her elbows buckled, "Ow."

Hendrick was at her side, helping her stand, "Ye know it's okay to ask for help."

"So how do you propose we get out of here?" She looked at Hendrick. Those green depths pleaded for an answer and it hurt his pride a little to disappoint her.

She stepped over Lance's corpse and spit on it.

"I have no idea, but whatever we do we need to do it fast," he lifted his arm to Cat, showing her what the curse was doing to him. His arm was tan all around, and the color was still rising.

***

"Damn, can we get a break?" Cat grabbed his arm to inspect its tan surface. "How much time do you think we have?"

Until you are a mindless angry chomper who will want to chew on me. She didn't say the last part, he knew what it meant to go fully tan.

"Maybe twenty minutes. I can feel myself getting confused for no reason." Hendrick pushed them forward. They needed to get out of there somehow.

"How far do you think the curse reaches, can we outrun it or go to the cabin?" Cat was grateful Hendrick was holding on to her. She still was so weak. If it weren't for the adrenaline, she probably wouldn't be able to stand.

"Nay, las. I don't think I can." His face was long and tan. She hadn't even seen the curse rise. The virus snapped into place. He was looking at the ground like the hard-rocky surface was the comfiest bed he had ever seen.

"Well, let's go get the documents first. Then, we can leave." Cat's face tightened into a smile, but it was fake. She needed to get him back to the cabin.

Crunch, crunch. Good thing they weren't trying to be sneaky anymore because their steps were loud and clumsy. "Here they are," white empty paper was scattered all over the ground. Her equilibrium was off, so she stumbled while she picked them up.

The tan curse was inside of her…

"What am I doing here? Why are there papers everywhere?" She saw Hendrick pushing against a tree like it was a door. "I don't like it here," Hendrick whispered.

Oh no. Goddess, how can I get out of this? I'm too weak to drag him around, and I'm not sure I could beat him if he attacks me. That gaping blackhole of sadness and doubt was sucking everything out of her.

The wind picked up, blowing dry leaves up in the air. They danced around her face.

Make a wish… a small whisper of a voice drifted in her mind. The wind carried the leaves high, most of them hitting Cat's face. She huffed and stormed over to Hendrick with the papers rolled up in her hand. He was now sitting on the ground. His shaky fist hit the leaves that drifted in front of him.

She threw herself into his arms, wanting to feel his firm, reassuring touch on her one last time. She could feel the curse edging its way into her mind too, but she couldn't leave him here.

He put his arms around her and patted her awkwardly on the back like a stranger comforting a person out of obligation. He didn't know who she was anymore. The thought only made her close her eyes and cry harder, "Home. I want to be home."

Wumpth.

A huge gust of wind smacked into their bodies toppling them over. "What the…" Her back thumped on something firm and soft. Not the rocky dirt.

She laid there breathing hard as she let the cold metaphorical waves wash over her. Her mind cleared as if the waves washed them away.

Meow.

A sweet purr followed as a large thing with soft fur jumped on Cat's chest. *You are strong and beautiful.*

Cat's eyes shot open. Her heart sped up its pace making her feel anxious. "Xena?" She looked down, her black cat was rubbing her face on her chest.

Cat whipped around. A brown loveseat was tucked in the corner. It was hers… She pushed out a raspy breath as she smiled. Everything was hers.

Her vision blurred, "I'm home," Cat crawled to her loveseat to hug a pillow. In one arm was Xena and in the other, was the throw pillow. "The Goddess is good, I never thought I'd see you again."

Hendrick cleared his throat from behind her, "So, what am I, chopped liver? Done with me are ye?" Hendrick was sitting against the wall, resting his head on it, with his knees up and his arms comfortably resting there.

Cat smiled at him as she rested her head on the cushion of the couch. With her eyes closed, she sighed through her nose, "Not quite yet."

Epilogue

CAT UNDERSTOOD NOW that no matter how hard a person works on sewing their life back together, it only takes one tug of a loose thread and everything unravels. But once the fabric is gone, and there is nothing left but a tangled mess of threads, what happens next?

Do they pick up the pieces and try to sew the threads back together? Or throw the threads away and make something new?

Her life was a tangled mess. She was now a mysterious vampire and Sapphire mixed being--which shouldn't exist. And she had been trying to stay away from everyone because whenever someone was near, she wanted to jump on their necks. Thankfully, Hendrick had blood bags in stock. So, Cat was doing okay restraining herself. But every time a person got near her, she still wanted to sink her teeth into their sweet flesh. Hendrick said it would get easier once the vampire beast got settled into her skin. Right now, all it knew was feeding; it was her job to teach the creature to behave.

Everyone made it back to Yvonne's safe house and that's where they had been for half a day, mourning the loss of the two fallen warriors.

Everyone took Maria's and Marcus's death hard. Cat could cut the air with the sorrow seeping off everyone who knew them. Yvonne had been working on them all nonstop.

Because Maria was the Dragonvires only adult blocker, they couldn't have a proper funeral. The heat in the air was already bad enough with the seven Dragonvires in the house.

Only the closest relatives or friends were invited and that was due to Yvette, Maria's kid cousin. Yvette could naturally block a little of the magic, but not enough to keep the Hunters away. So, all of them were on edge, waiting for an attack.

Hendrick walked up to her and sat down. "Cat, I am leaving. Maria's cousin has one transport amulet. He has agreed to give it to you," he paused, chewing the inside of his cheek when she glared at him. "I came back in respect of my fallen people, but my brother is still out there and needs me. Both Maria and Marcus would have wanted me to continue looking for him."

Cat pushed against the cushion on the couch, her jaw clenching and pulsing, "I'm going with you," her fist clenched into tight balls as she refused to back down. She would not quit the mission.

"Nay lass, you did your part, and I understand why the Gods brought you to me now. Thank you, but-" Cat slapped him on the cheek and cut him off.

"But nothing. I'm as much invested in this now as you. I wish you would stop these stupid speeches. There's no way you are leaving me. It is all the Unnaturals being affected by this, Hendrick., not only your brother's life being at stake." She poked him when he grumbled something. "Do I have to tackle you to the ground again?"

Yvonne, eavesdropping from the hallway, laughed, and said, "Please do."

Hendrick picked up one of the many throw pillows on the couch and threw the fluffy gold circle in her direction. "Hey, don't throw things at her," Cat slapped him on his shoulder and pushed him away from her.

At the same time, Yvonne charged him. Her arms were going wild, "Not unless you are ready for war." She grabbed one of the bigger pillows.

Hendrick looked confused until he got hit upside the head with a square pillow. "How dare you hit royalty." Hendrick put a hand to his chest and lifted his chin. His lips were bunched together to keep from laughing.

"Oh, I am so sorry kind, sir, my mistake," Yvonne jumped on Hendrick, smacking her body into his. Hitting him with little strokes to the head.

Before Cat knew it, she was under attack as well. Jake jumped on her, flinging a pillow at her head. "Haha, it's time for a nuclear bomb attack," Jake pushed out a rotten fart for the three to share. Before any of them retaliated, he dashed off.

"Good Goddess, you stink, Jake. When I said treat me like your sister, I didn't mean fart on me." Cat covered her nose and dove into Hendrick's chest. As much as she wanted to pulverize Jake for doing that, the smile on his face warmed her heart.

Yvonne worked an hour on Jake before he would even crack a smile. So, she wouldn't dampen his good mood for anything.

Hendrick covered his nose, "Betrayed by one of my own," he fanned the air around them. Once the smell lessened, Hendrick reached for Yvonne's tickle spots, pushing his fingers into them. She was like his sister, so annoying her was a duty. Yvonne hopped off the couch like the cushions had caught fire.

"Don't do that. You know I hate it!" She moved her arm like it possessed a gun pointing at him. Her movements reminded Cat of a mother disciplining her kid.

"And I love being hit with pillows?" He crossed his arms.

"That's different. Now, I'm going to finish dinner. If you want any, Cat is going with us." Yvonne didn't wait for Hendrick to answer, she left the room swinging her hips in a victory.

"I like her," Cat slowly looked at Hendrick and she smiled at his beaten face. The way his line of sight drifted down, she knew she had won.

"Are ye sure, lass?" Hendrick grabbed her hand, rubbing circles into it with his thumb. The electricity between them vibrated up his arm. "Last time was awful; we were lucky we survived. Ye was turned into a vampire for bloody hell." His eyes softened as guilt coated his insides.

Because of me. He couldn't say the last part out loud, so he let his words drift into silence.

Cat squeezed his hand, smiling at him. She looked at him in the eyes without blinking to reassure him. "Yes, I'm sure." She shoved him with her shoulder, "Besides, I already faced my biggest fear. Nothing could be as bad as that."

Both their faces dropped then, turning into the same saddened scorn that everybody else had on their faces.

Could it?

Until Next Time

About the Author

In addition to her writing career, Tosha Miller is a behavioral technician. She's pretty sure all her clients are of the human variety. Or at least, she thinks they are. To learn more, visit her website.

Also, visit her on any other social media she has for her readers, including YouTube Channel, Twitter, Tumblr, Instagram, and Facebook.

Just search for Tosha Y Miller and she'll be there.

Never miss a book, sign up for her mailing list at www.toshaymiller.com

Acknowledgments

Finishing the first book in the Unnatural series is such a blessing. I am so excited about the future of this book series. I hope everyone else is, as well.

My first thank you goes to my boyfriend Todd Cardoza for supporting me. Even though my laptop was permanently glued to my lap, you never complained and still let me pick movies for us to watch.

I also want to thank all my beta readers, Danielle Jensen, Dami Miller, and Tiffany Murphey for all your arduous work. Also, a big thanks to my new friends on Fiverr, Christine Miller, Sarah Abiz-Strugala, Amy Vanhorn, and Marco Frediani for all your amazingly helpful work. You all helped make The Smokiest Grave possible.

A special thanks to my editor, Cindy Draughon, for helping me on this bumpy journey. With your help, I had the courage to finish and publish my bookbaby.

Also, I want to thank Kayci from Kreative covers and Les on germancreative for my fantastic book cover.

You are all awesome, thank you so much. I couldn't have done it without all of you. This world is just beginning, and I hope everyone enjoys the brain candy I provided. Stay Amazing!

Glossary

1) **Blaigeard** – Bastard, cunt
2) **Doaber** – Penis
3) **Volant** – Flying
4) **Ignis** – Fire
5) **Congelare** – Freeze
6) **Auferat** – Away
7) **Aye** – Yes
8) **Nay** – No
9) **Hades** – Hell, devil
10) **Fired up** – Being happy and joyous
11) **Unnaturals** – Magical people, Segregated and hunted people
12) **Naturals** – Humans
13) **Hunters** – Humans that have been trained to kill supernaturals
14) **Science keepers** – A group of human government that took everyone's technology

Note For The Readers

Even the strongest of beings are not invincible. The Sapphires and Dragonvires together make an effective team, but against a magic sucking blood curse their chances are slim. Stay with them on their crazy journey to rescue Chris, save the world from being taken over by chompers, and stopping the evil mastermind that's trying to destroy their world.

CPSIA information can be obtained
at www.ICGtesting.com
Printed in the USA
LVHW09s1732041018
592410LV00003B/697/P